ENDORSEMENTS FOR
THE NEPHILIM VIRUS
BY JOHN T. PRATHER

This book would make a great movie! It's a cohesive, fun ride through some of my most beloved topics—science, the supernatural, and the apocalypse.

Megan Fox
Actress – *Transformers, Teenage Mutant Ninja Turtles,
Jennifer's Body, This Is 40*

Get ready to wake up and find yourself in a nightmare of epic proportions. Each page is an adrenaline-infused adventure that will leave you breathless as each paragraph is another jolt moving you toward the heart-pounding conclusion.

Blending biblical history with modern high-tech thrills, John Prather emerges as a master storyteller with a tale that you won't be able to read fast enough. *The Nephilim Virus* is infectious and the only cure is to read this amazing story.

Jeff Dixon
Bestselling author – *Dixon on Disney* series

This story isn't for the faint of heart. It's a blood-pumping thriller sure to make your heart rate spike. *The Nephilim Virus* has villains that will make your palms sweat and a plot so real you'll be looking over your shoulder for Nephilim while asking your doctor to test you for the virus. This is an amazing book!

Kenny Schwartz
Emmy-nominated film and television writer –*American
Housewife; Modern Family; American Dad!;
Two Guys, A Girl and a Pizza Place*

N^{THE}ephilim
VIRUS

JOHN T. PRATHER

The Nephilim Virus
Copyright © 2017 by John T. Prather
Published by Deep River Books
Sisters, Oregon
www.deepriverbooks.com

ISBN – 13: 9781632694553
Library of Congress: 2017947275
Printed in the USA
Cover design by Joe Bailen, Contajus Design

Dedication

For Mom:

Twenty years ago, I promised you the first one. I bet you thought I forgot. I'm sorry you had to wait so long. You taught me the ability to read is the ability to live a million lives and to learn a million things. Thank you.

And for Mindi:
There is nothing without you.

Book I
Anak

Part I
Nick

1

I woke up at exactly 4:37 p.m. from the longest nap of my life.

A half dozen people dressed in scrubs and lab coats rushed into my room to examine me. Some poked and prodded; others watched monitors or tubes. Someone stuck a needle in my arm. When I pulled away, a Velcro strap clamped my wrist to a metal bar. There was a similar strap on my other wrist and both my ankles.

They finished drawing blood and wiped a cotton ball across the punctured vein. It felt like sandpaper. I tried to focus on breathing so I wouldn't pass out. I tried not to panic, but the walls were so close I could reach out and touch them. Could, if I weren't strapped down.

My hands shook, and I realized they were balled tightly into fists. A worried-looking woman leaned over me. Her lips moved, but I couldn't make out what she was saying. She stood up and pointed, yelling something. My breath was shallow. The edges of my vision turned black. The fingers of darkness reached toward the center of my sight.

People hurried out of the room. I closed my eyes and concentrated on each breath. In and out. In and out. I felt oxygen rush into the vacuum of my lungs and then back out as my body relaxed. In and out. One breath at a time.

Slowly, my senses returned. When I opened my eyes, the darkness was gone; so were the people. Only the woman who had leaned over me remained. Pretty, petite, she moved with the grace of someone comfortable in her own skin. Her blonde hair fell just over the collar of her white lab coat.

My eyes darted around the large room. Empty beds lined one wall. I did a quick count. Ten. There were monitors attached to each one. My nose itched, but when I tried to raise my arm to scratch, the strap bit into my wrist. It made me angry. I licked my lips, but my tongue felt like dry leather. My mouth tasted moldy.

I looked back at the doctor. She smiled at me. I didn't smile back. She reached out and snagged a chair, walked it to my bedside, and sat down. She adjusted her black-rimmed glasses before she spoke. Her eyes were green.

"How do you feel?"

I wanted to scream that I was tied down, but I didn't. I didn't say anything.

"Can you speak?"

I nodded.

"What do you remember?"

I tried to remember something from before I fell asleep, but my brain still wasn't functioning to full capacity. It was like a computer trying to reboot.

"Who are you?" I asked. My mouth was dry and the words came out jumbled. I tried again. "Who are you?"

She looked down at a clipboard and marked something. "Interesting that you would ask who I am first and not why you are tied to a hospital bed."

"OK," I said. "Why am I tied to this bed? And who are you?"

"Do you know your own name?" She made another note.

"Yes."

"How about we share information? I'll tell you who I am after you tell me who you are."

"Nick."

"Do you have a last name, Nick?"

"Reece."

"OK, Nick Reece. My name is Dr. Faith Richards. I'm a hematologist." She flipped a couple pages on her clipboard.

I licked my dry lips. "How do you know that's my real name? I could have lied."

She smiled. "Me too."

I smiled back. "Now, can you tell me why I'm tied to this bed?" I barely croaked out my question. She picked up a Styrofoam cup and lifted my head, and I drank the lukewarm water. It felt good dribbling down my chin.

"What do you remember?"

My brain seemed to have rebooted. "Lots of things. What do you remember?"

"I remember asking you first."

This girl was quick. I liked her. "I remember a crash."

She nodded. "Good. And . . ."

"I remember asking you why I'm tied to this bed." Two could play this game.

"How about this? You answer my questions, and I'll tell you why you woke up strapped to a bed."

"Why should I have to answer first?"

"Because you're the one strapped to the bed," she said without missing a beat.

She had a point.

"I remember being in a plane crash. I was flying to LAX. We were about thirty minutes out, somewhere over the desert, when the plane started to shake. The pilot came on and told us we had hit some turbulence but that we'd be through it soon. I was in the bathroom, so I went back to my seat and buckled up. I remember buckling up and then . . ." I paused, trying to piece it all together in the right order. She waited patiently.

"And then I heard a loud noise. Similar to a gunshot, except louder. And the plane jerked and started to drop." I paused again, trying to recall. "And that's all I can remember."

"That's OK. How does your head feel now?"

"Fine." It wasn't a complete lie.

"Do you remember everything before the plane crash?"

I searched my memory. Everything seemed to check out. I nodded.

"That's good. That's very good," she said. "May I take your pulse?"

She leaned across me and placed her first two fingers on my neck. They felt warm and soft. She was taking my pulse by hand even though I was hooked to a heart monitor. I could see my heart rate on the screen—sixty-two beats per minute.

She left her fingers on my neck for an eternity. Beneath the lab coat she was wearing a plaid, button-up shirt that matched her eyes. I stared at her neckline. A small, silver cross swung from her perfect skin.

She glanced down and saw me looking. Another smile.

"That's a beautiful necklace."

She removed her fingers and made another note on the clipboard. "Thanks." She reached up and held it between her thumb and index finger.

"So, Doc. Am I going to make it?"

She started to say something but was interrupted by a guy in scrubs opening the door. "It looks like he's still clean."

She nodded.

"Do you need me to stay and help?"

"No, thank you, Devin. I'll be fine. I can handle it."

Devin looked unsure, but closed the door as he left.

"Can I get out of this bed now?"

"Yes, but I need to tell you a few things first."

My patience was wearing thin, and I could feel another attack of claustrophobia coming on. I took a deep breath and willed it away.

"Your memory is correct. You were in a plane crash in the desert outside of Los Angeles." She consulted her notes. "The plane was carrying 137 passengers and six crew members. Of those, only you and three other passengers survived. The rest of the passengers and all the crew died in the crash. The surviving passengers rescued were found comatose. You were brought to Mercy General Hospital, and that's where you are now."

"I've been in a coma?"

"Yes."

"For how long?"

"Three years."

"I've been in a coma for *three years?*" I yelled, bucking at the restraints.

"Calm down, Nick." She laid her hand on my arm.

I thrashed on the bed, yanking the straps. "No! Why am I tied down? Let me go."

"I will, as soon as you calm down. I need to tell you one more thing."

Devin appeared at the door again. "Are you OK, Dr. Richards? Do you need me to sedate him?"

"No, Devin. Thank you. We're fine. Thanks for checking."

Devin looked even more unsure this time, but he backed out and closed the door.

I glared at the door as he left. *Breathe in and out. In and out.* Dr. Richards—Faith—stroked my arm. I focused on how soft her skin felt. How warm her touch. Slowly, my breath slowed and I relaxed as much as anyone could while tied down to a hospital bed.

"There's one more thing you need to know," she said. "But I need you to promise me you will remain calm."

I nodded.

"Promise?"

"Yes."

"Good," she said. "The world is quite a bit different than what you remember. It will be a big shock."

"What do you mean, 'different'? A new version of the smartphone?"

She didn't smile. "Quite a bit different than that, I'm afraid."

"How much could have changed in the last three years?"

"Too much." Her hand moved toward the strap around my wrist. "I'm going to show you, but remember your promise to remain calm."

"OK."

She removed the restraints one by one. I slowly sat up and tried to massage the feeling back into my legs, but they felt foreign to me.

"Be careful," she said. "You haven't used your limbs for a long time. You won't be able to walk. It could take weeks for your body to remember how to work."

I nodded and slowly slid my legs over the edge of the bed. My feet touched the cool linoleum, but they were still wooden—limp. I tried to stand, but my legs gave out and I fell back onto the bed. Faith watched, interested. I tried again, but I still couldn't make my legs work. I fell again. I took a moment to catch my breath before I tried again. Same result.

"Like I said, it could take weeks or even months of rehab before you can walk again. I'll get a wheelchair." She started to turn away.

"No!" I responded by trying to stand again. This time I used the bed to pull myself up. I was able to stay on my feet for all of five seconds before I fell back. But it was five seconds longer than I had stood in a long time. Sweat moistened my forehead. The doctor said nothing. She also made no move to get that wheelchair. Instead, she seemed extremely interested in my effort to walk. She continued to take notes on her clipboard.

For the next half hour, the doc intently watched as I relentlessly tried to stand on legs that felt like they had never been used before. Every single time I wobbled and fell back on the bed, but every time I stood back up a little faster and stayed on my feet a little longer. Slowly, I felt strength and feeling returning. Eventually, I took a timid step. My knees buckled, and I collapsed in a pile on the floor.

Dr. Richards quickly helped me back to the bed and once more offered to get a wheelchair. I refused and resumed trying to walk, this time staying beside the bed so I could use it for support. Thirty minutes later, I was able to stumble my way across the room with substantial help from the doctor.

"This is unbelievable," she said.

I grunted and fell heavily onto the bed. "What is?"

"That you can move at all. After three years you should have severe muscular atrophy. Most people can't even hold a spoon for weeks, but you walked across the room. It's amazing."

"It doesn't feel that amazing."

"It is. This could be very good." She thought for a second. "Or very bad."

"How so?" I asked.

"That's what I'm going to show you."

Thirty minutes later we exited the room, but at least I wasn't confined to a wheelchair. I still had trouble walking, but the pretty doctor kept her arm around my waist. I leaned on her for help, maybe even a little more than I had to.

2

We shuffled our way to the roof of the hospital. Outside my room there had been a handful of men and women dressed in hospital garb. They stopped and stared as we slowly made our way to the elevator, but a look from Dr. Richards sent them back to their tasks. Devin obviously wanted to follow us, but he stayed put. One younger girl in pink scrubs also offered me a wheelchair, but I turned her down. I needed to get my body back in working order and a wheelchair wouldn't help. Plus leaning on the doc for balance made the effort worth it.

As we hobbled toward the edge of the roof, she cautioned me. "Be very quiet."

Odd. But the sun on my face felt so good I stayed silent. The day was still bright and warm. Spring, maybe? The light seemed to revive me a little more. On the corner of the roof I noticed a man with what looked like a rifle, or possibly just a long telescope. He was looking out from the hospital. I followed his gaze.

The hospital sat in the middle of a large open area. All the trees and bushes had been cleared from around the building for at least two hundred yards in all directions. At the outskirts of the bare ground, a tall, chain-link fence surrounded the property. It made the place look more like a compound than a hospital. Three more black-clad men stood at each corner of the building, all peering out at the fence. I looked at Dr. Richards, raising my brows in question, but she motioned me with a finger to her lips to be quiet. She handed me a pair of binoculars she had picked up on the way out.

I put the lenses to my eyes and scanned the property again. There wasn't a single person inside the fence around the hospital building. Not one. But it did look like there was a group of people on the outside. I readjusted the binoculars and looked again. Hundreds of people wandered around on the other side of the fence. They all moved slowly, like they were tired. But no one seemed to be trying to get inside the fence. I brought the glasses down and looked at the doctor. What was going on?

She motioned for us to go back inside and opened the heavy, metal door. When it closed behind us, she said, "There is one more thing I should show you. It will help you understand."

We hobbled back to the elevator.

"Why are all those people out there?"

"Do you have any family, Nick Reece?" She used my full name.

"You can call me Nick."

"Thank you, and you can feel free to call me Doctor." She smiled.

I chuckled. It felt good. "OK, Doc."

"I'm kidding. Call me Faith."

"Whatever you say, Doc." She laughed.

"Do you have any family, Nick?"

"No. Not that I know of. I was given up for adoption when I was a kid. No one took me so I bounced around in the system. As soon as I was legal age, they turned me out and I made a go of it on my own. Been that way ever since."

"Does that make you feel unwanted?"

"What are you, Doc, my shrink? I thought you were a hematologist."

She smiled as we stepped into the elevator. She scanned a security card from her pocket and pushed the button for the basement.

The elevator moved downward slowly. I took the opportunity to try again. "What's going on? Why are all those people out there on the other side of the fence?"

"They're . . . " She seemed to be searching for the right word. ". . . sick."

"Then why aren't they in here? This is a hospital, isn't it?"

"It used to be."

"Used to be? What does that mean? And what do you mean by sick?"

"It will be easier if I show you." As if on cue, the elevator stopped and the doors opened. We were in the basement.

3

We made our way into the room, and I only had to lean against the wall to catch my breath once. Faith led me to a glass lab that stood in the center. But when I got closer, I saw that it wasn't a lab at all; it was more like a glass cage. Steel bars ran along all four corners to reinforce the thick glass. There was someone inside.

"What is this place? Why do you have a person locked inside a glass box?" The words come out sharper and louder than I intended.

Faith straightened and let go of me. "You don't understand. We didn't have a choice. So shut up until you know what you're talking about!"

I shut up.

"Just watch."

I did. The man inside appeared to be in his mid-twenties. He could have been good looking at some point in his life, but now he didn't look right. His skin was too pale. His green eyes had a vacant, glazed-over look. He wandered back and forth very slowly and aimlessly inside the cage, similar to how the people outside the fence had moved.

"He can't see or hear us. The glass is one-way and it's sound-proof. The oxygen is pumped in from the outside, so he can't smell us either."

I wondered why she was telling me about the box instead of the human being inside.

She walked over to a microphone built into the glass. I could see a speaker built into the wall on the other side. She clicked the button. "Hello, Steven, how . . . ?" Her voice broke, and she released the button.

Inside the box, Steven came alive. It was as if he turned into another person. His eyes went from pale green and lifeless to a burning orange color. He threw himself at the speaker and clawed at it with his fingers, trying to tear it from the wall. His fingers started bleeding, but the blood didn't slow him. He continued clawing with all his might. Scratching. Digging. Trying to bite the glass like a rabid animal.

Faith pressed another button and the space inside the box slowly filled with fog. Steven kept biting and clawing at the speaker until the haze enveloped him. Still, his bloody fingers parted the fog and dug at the speaker.

Finally, he stopped.

"You see?" Faith's voice broke the silence. Tears streamed down her face.

I said nothing. I still had no idea what was going on.

She took a breath and wiped her eyes with the back of her hands. "All of those people you saw outside the fence are also sick."

"Why aren't they in here? With him?"

"We can't let them inside the hospital with us. They don't understand that we—that I—want to help them."

"What's wrong with them?"

"They're infected. They've been exposed to a blood-borne virus."

"You mean like . . ." I didn't want to say it. "Like zombies?"

"No." She sighed. "Zombies are fictional characters in horror movies. They are undead. These people are very much alive. They eat, they breathe. They're just sick. The disease makes them even more alive. It makes them superhuman."

"How so?"

"How much do you know about blood?"

"Not much."

"Then I'll keep it simple. The virus binds to their red blood cells, much like the O2 molecule does. The circulatory system goes to every part of the body; the blood feeds every organ. The virus gives them almost superhuman muscular strength and speed. The only area that seems to be adversely affected is the brain. Infected people show a severe decline in intelligence and mental acuity. We're still not sure why that is, but we think blood flow to the brain has been stunted. It's the only reason we have since we've been unable to communicate with an infected person." She looked back at Steven. "He can't understand that I want to help him."

I said nothing as I tried to process the information.

"The five senses are heightened slightly, with the possible exception of taste. We still don't know how their taste is affected."

"What do they eat?"

"Except each other, they'll eat anything living. Including us."

"Us?"

"They're especially drawn to the sound of humans, any human-like noise. And smell—they can smell uninfected blood. They are drawn to it. It drives them crazy, like sharks in the ocean."

That explained the box. "That's insane."

"It's a lot to take in all at once. Do you need to sit?"

I shook my head. "Continue."

"They also have a recovery rate much higher than the normal human. The average adult human has about five liters of blood in his body. That blood is made up of roughly 54 percent plasma, which is mostly water; 45 percent red blood cells; and only about 1 percent white blood cells, which are a major part of the body's immune system. The white blood cells are how our bodies fight disease and injuries."

I was trying to follow along. "So, the virus in the infected people kills the white blood cells, and their bodies can't fight the disease?"

"You would think so, but no. Actually, it's the opposite. Infected people have *more* white blood cells. About 55 percent of their blood is made up of white blood cells."

"Over half?"

"Yes. They have virtually no blood plasma. This would kill a normal human because the blood would be too thick for the heart to pump it through the body, but somehow the virus in the red blood cells makes the heart strong enough to handle the pressure."

"Then how can they be killed?"

"We don't know."

"What do you mean you don't know? Can they die?" I asked.

"Not that anyone has recorded."

"Wait. They can't be killed?"

"No."

I was speechless.

"They have more blood than a normal human. We think this helps account for their increased strength and speed. Like I said, the average adult has close to five liters. We think the infected have somewhere between eight and ten liters. Each red blood cell can carry up to four oxygen molecules to the muscles to help them perform and then recover. As soon as your body can't deliver any more oxygen, you tire out. But if your body had twice as many red blood cells—"

"You'd be twice as fast and strong," I finished for her.

"And you would recover twice as fast."

I thought about it. "Is that why you said it could be very bad that I'm up and moving so quickly after my coma? Are you worried I'm going to turn into that?" I pointed to the glass cage.

"He's not a '*that*.' His name is Steven!"

I had touched a nerve.

She took a breath. "Your blood shows no infection, but it is very unusual that you recovered so quickly. Most people would be in rehab for months, and some never recover the movement you have only hours after you woke up."

I didn't want to think about what that might mean.

"Is there a cure?"

She turned back toward the box. "Not yet."

4

We stood silently for a while. This all sounded implausible . . . impossible. Unless I had seen Steven with my own eyes, I never would have believed her. Never in a million years. Yet here I was, standing in front of a glass box with an infected human inside. A human who could no longer speak or think clearly and had just tried to tear a speaker out of the wall because he heard a voice coming from it.

The fog in the box started to clear. I could just make out the shape of Steven lying on the ground. His bloody fingers had already healed. His eyes were closed, and the steady rise and fall of his chest gave him a peaceful look. It was hard to believe he was the same orange-eyed rabid animal from a few minutes ago.

"How long will he sleep?"

"Not much longer. We have to pump massive amounts of anesthesia in there to put him to sleep, enough to kill a regular human several times over. But it still only lasts a few minutes on him. It takes a higher dosage each time, and each time he wakes up a little bit faster. His body is building up immunity."

"How many of them are there? How many people have been infected?"

She wiped away a tear at the edge of her eye and straightened her glasses before turning back toward me. "Are you sure you're ready for that answer?"

"How many could it be?"

"A lot."

"How many?"

"Two hundred million."

The number was staggering. "In the world?"

"In the United States."

"Impossible."

"I wish. Why do you think we're in here?"

"But that's two-thirds of the population."

"Yes. And more every day."

"Is anyone immune?"

"Not so far. Not that we know of."

"What about the rest of the world? How many people are infected? Is there anywhere untouched by the virus?"

"It's hard to tell. As far as we know, there is nowhere that hasn't been exposed to the virus. Most estimates say the rest of the world's percentage is at least as high as ours, and it's possible that in some countries the entire population is infected. But that's really just a guess."

My legs felt weak. "I think I need some air."

We made our way back to the roof, and Faith once again motioned for silence as we made our way outside. It was unnecessary. There was no way I'd make a sound after what I'd just seen.

I sat down on a lawn chair and watched as the sun dipped below the horizon. The men in black on the corners of the roof remained in their positions. Faith left me alone, but soon came back carrying two plates of food. I couldn't remember the last time I had eaten. The food was basic hospital fare, but it tasted great to me.

It started to grow cool in my hospital gown as I finished the mushy peas, but I didn't mind. Goose bumps rose on my arms, but I refused to go back inside. Shivering in the cold reminded me I was alive. And I planned on staying that way.

5

I woke up at 9:37 a.m. on the second day of my life. My new life. I dressed in the scrubs someone had left at the foot of the bed. I left the room they had given me to sleep in—this one had only one bed and thankfully no restraints—and found Faith in the cafeteria. She was sitting with three men in black security garb. I felt surprisingly strong today. My body was recovering quickly after lying in bed for three years.

I grabbed some scrambled eggs and toast that sat under a warming light on the cafeteria line and took an apple from a small basket before sitting down next to the doctor—Faith. Ever since our trip to the basement, I had thought of her as Faith. I got the feeling I had stepped into the middle of an uncomfortable conversation. Faith introduced me.

"Gentlemen, this is Nick Reece, the guy who woke up from the coma yesterday. Nick, this is Commander Al Harris. Everyone here calls him Commander." She pointed at a square-jawed guy with black hair who looked like an older version of GI Joe.

"This is Darius VanDyke, but everyone calls him Van." She motioned toward a black guy. Around my age. Friendly face.

"And this is Bo Bryce." Bo looked like a football player. Blond, solid build, arm tattoo.

"How'd you sleep?" she asked.

"Like a baby."

Faith filled me in as I bit into the apple. "We need to make a supply run into town today. We were just discussing logistics."

I swallowed my bite. "I'd like to go."

Faith and the Commander shared a look.

"I thought you might," she said. I could see Bo shaking his head out of the corner of my eye.

"It's always very dangerous," the Commander said. "Dr. Richards told us she introduced you to Steven, so you know how serious the situation is out there."

"Yes." I set my apple on the plate and ignored the rest of my food.

"How are you feeling, Nick?" Faith asked. "You've been in a coma for three years and your body hasn't been used at all during that time. Your muscles have been atrophying for a while. And like the Commander said, it's very dangerous out there."

"I'm feeling great." A half lie. "Never better. My body is like a car, built to be in motion. I need to see what's out there."

"We don't need you getting all of us killed just because you want to see the sights." This from Bo. The Commander shot him a look.

I ignored him. The Commander and Faith were calling the shots, so I only needed to convince them.

I turned to the Commander. "I won't endanger anyone. I'll follow your lead and listen to everything you say. I won't be a problem. I can help." Then to Faith: "I swear I'm feeling fine. You are one incredible doctor. I feel strong, and my body is already back to a 100 percent. Like I was never in a coma."

The Commander looked me up and down, evaluating. I took another bite of the apple and tried to look confident.

"Your call, Doc," the Commander said.

We all looked at her. "I'll give him a physical capacity test, and if he passes then he can go."

"OK," the leader of the group said. "If you pass with the doctor, meet us on the loading dock at ten till noon. Wear black."

I hoped one of these guys was my size because I had no clothes.

The three men stood to go.

"Shouldn't we wait until it's dark out?" I asked.

"See?" Bo said.

"No," the Commander said. "They see well in the dark. No reason to give them any more advantage. See you at 11:50. Don't be late."

They left.

6

Faith finished my examination at a quarter till noon, after scribbling endless notes on her clipboard. I wondered why she didn't use a computer to keep track of everything.

"So, Doc, how does everything look?"

"Good. Remarkably good. From the results, it's hard to believe you were in a coma less than twenty-four hours ago. Your GCS rating was three for multiple years; that's the worst score you can get. After four months at that level, the rate for even partial recovery is below 15 percent. But you showed very little dysarthria and have less muscle atrophy than you should after a three-year coma. Totally remarkable. Your body has recovered very quickly."

"I told you, I'm resilient." I gave her my best smile. Her knees didn't seem to go weak.

"Apparently so. It's a good sign."

"Of what?"

"I'm not sure yet," she said.

"Are you going to show me the way to the loading dock?"

"It'll be better if you go down alone. I'll tell you how to get there. But be careful, Nick."

"You worried about me, Doc?" I grinned, wanting to see her smile again.

The corners of her mouth twitched up. "Yes, I worry about all my patients."

"Speaking of patients, where are all your other patients? There were ten beds in my room—all empty. This doesn't seem like much of a hospital."

She looked at her watch. "You better get down there. They won't wait on you."

After she gave me directions, I headed down to the loading dock on the service elevator. For curiosity's sake, I punched a couple random buttons and peeked out on the floors. Nothing seemed unusual. Certainly nothing on the level of the thing in the basement. It struck me that hospitals were like little cities and had everything a group of people might need to survive a holocaust. Including medications and plenty of beds.

When I arrived at the loading dock, Bo observed me with the same disdain as he had at breakfast. "Passed your physical with Dr. Richards, *Kemosabe*?"

I smiled more than was appropriate. "Flying colors. Best shape of any man she's seen in a while."

"Cut it out," the Commander said. "Here, wipe yourself down with this." He tossed me a bottle of motor oil and a rag.

I gave him a questioning look but obeyed.

"It helps mask our scent," Van said.

"How well does it work?"

"Well enough, unless the Nak is within a foot or two."

"If one gets that close, it'll be too late for you anyway," Bo said.

"Nak?" I asked.

"The Anakim. The infected. We call 'em Naks," Van said.

I poured more oil on the rag and wiped my arms. "Why motor oil?"

"You're as dumb as a Nak, aren't you, Kemosabe? They don't attack machines. Motor oil makes you smell like a machine. Try to keep up, huh? And don't get us killed."

I bit my tongue. Every group had one just like Bo.

The four of us piled into a blacked-out SUV. Van driving. Me and Bo in the back. Right at noon the Commander keyed a walkie. "We're ready down here."

"Roger," the voice crackled. "Start the countdown now."

The Commander punched his watch and waited. A scream rang out from somewhere outside the building. None of the men moved. It turned into a painful wail. We still didn't move. It was a female voice. I wanted to hop out and help, but there was nothing I could do. It was painful to listen to. I waited while her scream echoed in my head.

The delivery door slowly rolled open. The Commander clicked his watch again and said, "Go."

7

We pulled through a maintenance exit in the outer fence and peeled out the opposite way the scream was coming from. The automatic gate closed behind us.

I couldn't take it any longer. "Aren't we going to help her?"

"Who?" the Commander asked.

"The woman screaming."

Bo laughed.

"There is no woman," Van said. "It's a speaker hidden in the woods. We use it to draw the Naks away from the gate so we can leave unmolested."

"Oh." I felt stupid. Time to stop talking and start watching and learning.

"Some Neph is gonna get you quick," Bo said.

I didn't ask what a Neph was.

We drove north for a while, and the world outside the window looked about the same as I remembered it, with one exception. It was quiet. Too quiet. There were no people anywhere. We stayed on a two-lane highway for about fifteen uneventful minutes.

We pulled off the highway into an industrial park and did a slow drive around several buildings. Not a soul to be seen. We stopped next to the loading door of a large warehouse, our truck tucked between two semis. Bo jumped out and punched a code into the keypad beside the loading bay. The door rolled open just enough for Van to pull inside. I exited the truck only after the Commander nodded his OK.

The warehouse was stacked floor to ceiling as far as I could see with pallet after pallet of canned food. It must have been a busy distribution hub at one point. Now there wasn't a worker to be seen.

The Commander surveyed the area. "Find Hector," he said. "Reece, you're with me."

Van and Bo nodded and headed off in separate directions. "You know how to drive a forklift?" the Commander asked.

"No," I said.

"Then I'll drive, you load." We found a forklift and he loaded a pallet into the back of the SUV. The Commander had me remove a box to make room. Once we were finished, he led me to a smaller room, maybe an office, where we gathered a few other items—batteries, a box of fruit, a bag marked "clothes," and a crate of paper. We loaded these into the truck and waited. Bo and Van still weren't back. The Commander looked at his watch. Breathed deeply through his nose. We waited.

A voice spoke from behind us. I jumped; the Commander didn't. "Careful," the voice said.

I turned. It was a lean Hispanic man dressed like a black ops commando. He and the Commander shook hands heartily.

"I was wondering when you guys were coming back. We've had some unwelcome visitors lately," he said.

"Trouble?" the Commander asked.

"Two. Just looking around, but they may be getting suspicious. Not sure how much longer we'll have this place."

"You be careful."

"It's not me I'm worried about." He smiled. "They'll never see me."

"I know." The Commander nodded. "This is Reece." He motioned toward me. "A coma patient."

Black Ops raised an eyebrow but said nothing.

Van and Bo walked up. "Hector!" Van said and hugged him. Bo nodded his greeting. Van continued. "I don't know why the Commander always sends us out to find you since you move like a ghost in here."

"I have a feeling he doesn't expect you to find me," Hector said, "but sends you out for me to find you." He grinned and Van laughed.

"We brought you a box," the Commander said.

"I see." Hector opened it. It was full of medical supplies. He pulled out a syringe. "Thanks."

"If this place gets compromised, you set the signal and get out of here."

"I will. The trucks are wired to burn. But I hate to lose all this if we don't have to."

"I know. Me too," the Commander said. "You come back in anytime you want."

"Thanks, but you know I don't like being cooped up. I'm better out here."

The Commander nodded. "Let's load up."

I turned toward the truck. Hector was beside me. He did move like a ghost. "You can trust the Commander," he whispered. "But be careful back there at the hospital. Don't believe everything they tell you."

The men were loading up. When I turned to ask Hector what he meant, he was gone.

8

We left the warehouse a different way than we had arrived. Van kept the SUV on side streets and back roads. Several times we saw groups of people standing on the road. They turned their heads as one at the sound of our truck but we gave them a wide berth and never came within a hundred yards of them. They left us alone.

"We spent too long in there." The Commander glanced at his watch. "Everyone keep your eyes open. This could get rough."

We kept driving. Everyone on edge.

Several minutes later we were passing through a neighborhood when Bo called out, "Nephs! Nine o'clock!"

The fear in the SUV was palpable. Van spun the wheel around a corner. He punched the gas and took another corner much too fast. We hit a curb and took out a mailbox. Van didn't flinch. We took one more corner and pulled into an empty driveway.

"Everybody out!" the Commander barked. He had his door open before the truck stopped. I ripped my door open and followed. We sprinted across the street and the three of them split up. I followed the Commander. He tried the first door we came to. Locked. The next one. Also locked.

"Here!" Bo hissed.

We vaulted a fence and all piled in the open door together. Bo closed the door behind us just as the sound of two motorcycles split the silence. Bo left the door unlocked.

I followed the men up the stairs. The house was deserted. We made our way to a front room and cautiously peeked out a window. Two men without helmets dismounted their bikes and surveyed the street. No one moved.

They left their bikes parked in the middle of the street and moved to opposite sides of the road. I lost sight of the one on our side of the street. He was somewhere below us. I waited for the sound of the front door opening.

The one on the far side of the street tried a doorknob. It was unlocked. He paused as if considering. He closed the door and moved on to the next house. That door was locked. He kicked it open with very little effort and disappeared inside. We waited in silence. I could hear the Commander's even breathing beside me.

I still couldn't see the man who was searching our side of the street. A bead of sweat ran down my cheek and dripped off my chin. It took a drop of motor oil with it. We waited.

The other man reappeared and continued down the street. He stopped beside our SUV. He walked around it with his nose forward, not unlike a dog searching for a scent. He removed a black glove and placed his hand on the hood. We waited.

I was so involved watching that I almost didn't hear the noise. It took a second to register. It was the sound of our front door opening.

9

No one breathed. Seconds ticked by. No other noise. No foot-steps on the stairs. We waited. My heart pounded in my ears.

Finally, the front door closed. The man appeared on the lawn below us. He continued down the street. The man across the street moved on to the next house as well. We waited as they finished checking each house then got on their bikes and pulled away. The Commander cracked the window open and listened.

"They've stopped on the next street over," he whispered.

We continued waiting. My legs started to cramp, but I still didn't dare move.

"Good call on leaving the door unlocked," Van whispered to Bo.

"They think they're so smart." Bo grinned. His eyes looked crazy underneath the motor oil.

The Commander nodded his approval. "They're looking for us street by street. We'll have to wait them out." He let us get comfortable and told us we'd be taking shifts by the window. He went first. I would go last. I figured he didn't think we would have to wait that long, but wanted to involve me. I appreciated the gesture. Van found some canned beets in the kitchen, and we all shared it. It tasted awful.

I couldn't relax, but Bo had no problem. After he finished his shift, he sprawled out on the floor and went to sleep. Midway through Van's shift, there was a noise outside and Van furtively motioned the Commander over. We all gathered at the window.

An armored truck rolled to a stop in the middle of the street and two men hopped out. Not the bikers. They opened the rear doors and two Naks stumbled out. I saw at least eight more inside. The two men slammed the doors closed and got back in the cab. The sound of grinding gears and the truck pulled away.

The Commander motioned me to be silent. I didn't need the reminder. I could still see Steven coming alive at the sound of Faith's voice. No one spoke.

Bo mouthed the words, "What now?" and the Commander motioned us to wait. None of us left the window. The Naks wandered around the street and yards for a while. They looked bored. Like the one in the basement at the hospital had before Faith woke him. One smelled our SUV but didn't pause. They were ambivalent to everything. For the most part, they even ignored each other. We continued to do what we had done for most of the day: we waited.

At one point the Naks heard a noise. They both turned their heads to listen, and we all froze. But soon they went back to wandering the neighborhood aimlessly. Sometimes one or both disappeared from our sight for a while. But they always came back. The day started to turn to evening, and I could tell the three men were getting antsy about the approaching darkness. Our nerves were frayed from the silent tension. The air turned chilly as we waited.

After a while we couldn't see any Naks. They didn't reappear. The Commander quietly slid the window closed and turned toward us.

"We have to make a move." He whispered so quietly we all had to lean forward to hear.

"What's the play?" Van whispered at the same level.

"One of us will go down first—to be our spotter and see if they're still out there."

No one spoke. We all knew if they were still there, it was a suicide mission. And they probably were.

"I'll go," I said. Not because I was brave, but because I needed to volunteer.

The Commander shook his head. "Not you, Reece."

"I'll go," Van said.

"No, you're our driver. You know the streets. We need you more than me," Bo hissed. "I'll do it."

"Anybody can drive," Van hissed back. "Besides, they'll have a harder time spotting me." He flashed his white teeth in a smile.

"Your call, Commander," Bo whispered.

"You're up, Bo," he said.

Bo winked at Van. "Better luck next time." And he was gone.

10

We returned to the window and watched in silence as Bo exited the front door and closed it behind him without a sound. He crept across the street, moving painfully slow. He stayed so low to the ground, I almost couldn't see him in the dusk. No sign of the Naks. He made it to the truck and ducked behind it. He surveyed the street and then gave us a thumbs up.

We moved down the stairs in single file. The Commander first, then me, then Van. That's when I finally realized none of the men were carrying guns. We paused at the front door and waited for Bo to wave us forward. He did. The three of us sprinted forward as one. We were almost to the truck when I knew something was wrong. I heard it before I saw it. Something was behind us.

I saw Bo jump in the driver's door and heard the engine fire. The truck backed toward us. I took one look over my shoulder. I wished I hadn't. One of the Naks was less than twenty feet away. His orange eyes glowed. I had never seen anything move that fast before.

The truck door flew open from the inside. I dove for the opening. The SUV moved forward before my body was fully inside. I smelled rubber burning. Hands grabbed my shoulders and pulled me all the way in. I grabbed for the open door as the truck lurched forward over a curb. The door slammed shut as the Nak slammed into the outside of it. The door caved inward but held. He grabbed for the handle but we shot forward, and he missed. Broken glass covered me.

The other Nak appeared in the middle of the street in front of us. Bo jammed the accelerator down. The truck screamed forward. The Nak ran toward us. A game of chicken. I looked back and saw the first one chasing us. He was only a couple steps behind. Three other Naks materialized from a side street to join him at a full sprint.

Bo let out a battle cry, and I looked forward. The Nak was three steps away.

Two.

One.

He slammed into the front of our SUV. I saw him fly up and crash into the top of the windshield. He thumped over the roof. It sounded like he was trying to find a handhold. He didn't. I realized why they had taken the roof racks off the top of the truck. Smart. The Nak flew off and crashed into the one behind us. They both tumbled on the asphalt. Blood spewed everywhere. But they didn't stay down for long. Both jumped up and ran after the escaping truck. Now there were six of them.

They kept pace for a while, but when we hit the open road, they couldn't keep up with the SUV. Wind whistled through the broken windshield as we powered back to the hospital. We didn't see anyone else until we neared the maintenance entrance. The Commander keyed his radio and asked for the decoy.

A woman's scream broke the night, and the Naks who were gathered around the fence took off for the woods. The gate opened, and Bo didn't slow down. He finally slammed on the brakes inside the hospital garage, the door closed, and we all piled out.

"See? I told you anyone could drive," Van said.

Bo took in a huge lungful of air and yelled his pent-up emotions at the top of his lungs. His voice echoed off the walls. Van did what looked like a touchdown dance and even the

Commander had to laugh. All I could do was smile. I was worn out. Several people came down to see if we were OK and help unload. Even Faith. The truck was trashed and covered in blood. They asked endless questions, but we were all too excited and exhausted to answer them. The doc swabbed some blood from the SUV and dropped it into a plastic bag.

As I was unloading our cargo, she appeared next to me. "I'm glad you made it back. You'll have to tell me all about it."

"Maybe tomorrow, Doc. I'm exhausted." I couldn't stop grinning. I was still alive.

She nodded and made her way upstairs, presumably to test her find.

After we unloaded, I headed for the roof. The stars were out in bunches. The air was still cool but not cold. I smelled trees. Pine and oak. And maybe even a hint of ocean air. I guess I was even more exhausted than I thought because the next thing I knew it was morning.

I was still alive.

I woke up at 10:37 a.m. on the third day of my life.

11

I found Faith in her lab on the fifth floor. She was bent over a microscope with several tubes of blood spread out on the table beside her. I watched her work for a moment. She moved gracefully, like a tiger in its den, unaware of my presence.

"Good morning," I said. "Sorry, I didn't mean to scare you."

She smiled. "That's OK. Didn't see you there. Sometimes I get lost in my work. How are you feeling this morning?"

"Rested. What are you working on? Is that my blood?"

"No, yours is over there." She pointed to a row of glass-front refrigerators. There were hundreds of vials of blood inside.

"That's a lot of blood. Whose is it?"

"Yours, other patients'. Everyone here at the hospital is in there. Some others."

"I haven't seen any other patients here."

She ignored my observation. "I'm glad you made it back yesterday. I was worried. They aren't usually gone that long on a supply run."

"Yeah, we ran into some trouble."

"Trouble?"

"You're good, Doc. Are you sure you're just a hematologist? I would bet you already talked to the Commander this morning and got the story from him."

"I never said I was *just* anything." She smiled again. "You have questions about yesterday." A statement, not a question.

"What are Nephs?"

"There's someone else who can answer that question better than I can. I'll let him tell you."

"OK, what about the Naks? We hit one yesterday with the truck. We were going full speed and rammed into him head-on, and then he got up and chased us. He should have been dead."

"The virus is called Anak, and the common name for the infected is the Anakim. People like Steven and the humans outside the fence. The security guys call them Naks." I could tell she didn't like that. "Like I mentioned before, as far as we know, they can't be killed. They heal so fast, anything we've tried barely slows them down."

"You mean they're invincible?"

"At the very least they've grown immune to anything we try. They heal remarkably fast."

"Yeah, I saw. But they look just like us."

"Yes, for the most part. Except their skin is a little paler than their average uninfected counterpart, and they move a little differently. When they're not activated by human sounds or smells, they wander around in a kind of hibernation state. The movement is slow and unfocused, like someone who is really tired."

"What's with the smell thing?"

"They have an unusually sharp sense of smell. And we think they can smell our blood." She went back to work as we talked.

"Uninfected blood?"

"Yes."

"If there's a cut or injury?"

"Even if there isn't."

"And the motor oil?"

"The security guys find it helps mask our scent. The same way drug dealers hide cocaine in coffee to hide it from the dogs. It confuses their olfactory sense." She finished working and placed all the vials in the refrigerator. "You asked about the

Nephilim. Are you ready to meet the brains? Try your questions on him?"

"I thought you were the brains," I said.

"It takes a lot of brains to keep all of us alive."

From what I'd seen so far, I couldn't disagree.

12

The brains belonged to a kid. We found him furiously typing on a laptop in a room on the third floor. The doc introduced us. Xavier. A black kid that looked like he couldn't have been a day over eighteen. Glasses and a silver crucifix.

"You're the brains?" I asked. "How old are you?"

"Old enough. How old are you?"

"Twenty-eight," I said. "No, wait—thirty-one, I guess."

"Don't mind him," Faith said, motioning toward Xavier. "X has as a persecution complex."

"Better than a Jonah complex. Or a God complex like you, Doc."

"Cassandra complex. But close."

"You're the shrink," Xavier said, and Faith smiled.

"I thought you were a hematologist?" I said.

"She is, dude, but she also has a degree in psychology. You shouldn't mess with her; she's way smart. Like a super doc. She has two PhDs, and she's only twenty-nine. Kinda makes you wonder what you're doing with your life, doesn't it, thirty-one?"

Faith looked away, but I thought I saw her blush. "X, tell him about the Nephilim."

"Bad dudes. Like, way bad. Have you ever heard of a dude named Arba?"

"No."

"How about David and Goliath?"

"You mean like in the Bible, David and Goliath?"

"Yeah, like in the Bible."

"I've heard the story before. David was the little guy who killed the giant Goliath with a slingshot and a stone, right?"

"Those would be the dudes. Well, rewind a bit. Earlier in the Bible, there's a passage . . ." X's fingers flew over his keyboard as he spoke. I looked over his shoulder. He opened a window on his laptop. The title said "Genesis." He started reading:

"*When human beings began to increase in number on the earth and daughters were born to them, the sons of God saw that the daughters of humans were beautiful, and they married any of them they chose. Then the Lord said, 'My Spirit will not contend with humans forever, for they are mortal; their days will be a hundred and twenty years.' The Nephilim were on the earth in those days— and also afterward—when the sons of God went to the daughters of humans and had children by them. They were the heroes of old, men of renown. The Lord saw how great the wickedness of the human race had become on the earth, and that every inclination of the thoughts of the human heart was only evil all the time. The Lord regretted that he had made human beings on the earth, and his heart was deeply troubled.*"[1]

"That's in the Bible?" I asked.

"Yeah, dude, crazy stuff. But you haven't heard the half of it yet."

I turned to Faith. "What does some crazy passage in the Bible have to do with those guys I saw yesterday? And why were the Commander and his guys so afraid of them? Even more so than they were of the Naks, or Anakim, or whatever you call them."

"Just listen," she said. "Continue, X."

"You know about David killing Goliath, but did you know that Goliath had four brothers?"

I shook my head.

"Few do. Anyway, each of Goliath's four brothers were as big and tall as he was. Do you know how tall Goliath was?"

"Does it matter?" I asked.

"It will." He pulled up another page on his computer—one titled "First Samuel." He continued reading:

"Saul and the Israelite army assembled and camped in the Elah Valley, where they got organized to fight the Philistines. The Philistines took positions on one hill while Israel took positions on the opposite hill. There was a valley between them. A champion named Goliath from Gath came out from the Philistine camp. He was more than nine feet tall. He had a bronze helmet on his head and wore bronze scale-armor weighing one hundred twenty-five pounds. He had bronze plates on his shins, and a bronze scimitar hung on his back. His spear shaft was as strong as the bar on a weaver's loom, and its iron head weighed fifteen pounds. His shield-bearer walked in front of him."[2]

"So Goliath was nine feet tall? I still don't see what that has to do with the men yesterday. They were average height."

"Nine feet tall and incredibly strong. His breastplate alone weighed a hundred and twenty-five pounds. And remember, he had four brothers who were all dudes as big and strong as he was. That's why David grabbed five stones from the stream instead of just one."

"OK . . ."

He looked at me like he thought I should be putting it together. I wasn't.

"Goliath and his brothers were Nephilim, descendants of the sons of God and daughters of men. They were a race of superhumans."

"Sons of God?" I asked. "You mean like angels?"

"Fallen angels, yes." He looked pleased I was starting to get it. I still wasn't sure I was.

"So, fallen angels created this race called the Nephilim . . ."
He nodded.

"And among them was a group of five brothers, all giants. The shepherd boy David killed one of the brothers named Goliath with a slingshot."

Xavier looked pleased. Faith stayed silent.

"Then when he got older, David and his men hunted and eventually killed all four of Goliath's brothers as well," he added as he pulled up another screen titled "Second Samuel." He read:

"Again there was war between the Philistines and Israel. David and his men went out to fight the Philistines, but David became tired. Ishbi-Benob, one of the sons of Rapha, had a bronze spearhead weighing about seven and one-half pounds and a new sword. He planned to kill David, but Abishai killed the Philistine and saved David's life. Later, at Gob, there was another battle with the Philistines. Sibbecai killed Saph, another one of the sons of Rapha. Later, there was another battle at Gob with the Philistines. Elhanan killed Lahmi, the brother of Goliath from Gath. His spear was as large as a weaver's rod. At Gath another battle took place. A huge man was there; he had six fingers on each hand and six toes on each foot—twenty-four fingers and toes in all. This man also was one of the sons of Rapha. When he challenged Israel, Jonathan, David's nephew, killed him. These four sons of Rapha from Gath were killed by David and his men."[3]

He stopped reading and turned toward us. "So, the five brothers were Goliath, who David killed; Saph, who was killed by Sibbecai; Ishbi-Benob who was killed by Abishai; Lahmi who was killed by Elhanan; and the unnamed brother with six fingers, who was killed by Jonathan. History tells us that the unnamed brother was Arba, the most powerful brother, named after his great-great-grandfather."

"OK," I said. "I think I got it. And the father's name was Rapha. But what does that have to do with us now? And again, what does a family of giants in the Bible who were hunted and killed by David and his men have to do with the men I saw yesterday?"

X looked at Faith, checking in. She nodded.

"This next part you might have to see to believe." He punched a few buttons and a video appeared on his screen. "Just push play, dude."

13

The video was grainy, as if it were from a security camera. And it was playing at double speed. I watched as two men rolled what looked like a coffin into view and left it. The coffin was large. And old. There were unfamiliar markings on the outside. The video showed the coffin sitting alone for a while. I looked up at Faith.

"Just watch," she said.

I turned back to the video. Someone entered the room. They pried the lid off the coffin. Inside lay the body of a man partially wrapped in cloth. The man was a giant, at least nine feet tall. The visitor looked around, but the camera still didn't catch any details. I couldn't even tell if it was a male or female. The person leaned over the coffin and did something, but the movements were obscured. The person finished and left, never turning toward the camera. More dead air.

Xavier sped the video to 4x. After what was probably hours, maybe days in fast-forward, something started to happen. The man in the coffin started to twitch. Then he sat up. He looked around, completely calm. Eventually, he removed the cloth and stood up. He was huge. He towered so tall the coffin and the table looked like a footstool. He sat down and waited for something. He was unmoving. Patient. I couldn't believe my eyes. I couldn't look away.

A normal-sized human entered the room. He was reading a clipboard with his back turned to the giant. The giant stood up and leaned over the man. It looked like he whispered something in his ear. Or bit his neck. The man fell over dead. The giant picked him up and tossed him into an empty crate. He sat back down and continued waiting. Not much later, another guy came in. This one on a cell phone. The giant leaned over him as well. Another whisper. Unbelievably, the man seemed not to notice. He wandered back out of the room, very slowly. Another person entered, a woman. The same thing happened, and she wandered away as well.

The giant sat back down, patiently waiting for something. Two people entered at once. He leaned over the girl; the guy tried to run. The girl wandered away. The guy's body was tossed in the crate.

This went on for close to thirty minutes of video in fast forward. About two-thirds of the people wandered away aimlessly afterward. One-third ended up in a box or crate. After what had to be several days of video and close to a hundred people, a woman walked in. Same process. The giant stood up and leaned over her. He towered over her like an oak tree. But this time, after he whispered in her ear, he stood up, leaned over, and kissed her. She kissed him back. He said something to her and she smiled. Then she walked out of the room. Purposefully, not like the others who wandered away aimlessly.

More dead air. Then a woman with dark hair entered the frame. She said something to the giant. He thought about it then responded. They had a conversation that lasted three or four minutes. It looked like the woman did most of the talking; the giant was patient. I wished there was sound. When they finished, the giant smiled. He didn't lean over and whisper to her.

I waited. There was a pause, then both the giant and the woman turned and faced the camera. The recording stopped, frozen on the pair.

The giant had six fingers.

14

"What was that?" My voice rose. I was getting more questions than answers.

"That was the security video from George Washington University three years ago," Faith said. "The coffin was found at an archeological dig in Ethiopia and brought to the university for further study."

"Who, or what is that?" I pointed at the giant on the screen. Faith looked at Xavier to continue.

"One more piece of history you need to know," X said. He pulled the story of David and Goliath back up:

"A champion named Goliath from Gath came out from the Philistine camp. He was more than nine feet tall. He had a bronze helmet on his head and wore bronze scale-armor weighing one hundred twenty-five pounds. He had bronze plates on his shins, and a bronze scimitar hung on his back. His spear shaft was as strong as the bar on a weaver's loom, and its iron head weighed fifteen pounds. His shield-bearer walked in front of him.[4] Goliath stood and shouted to the ranks of Israel. 'Why do you come out and line up for battle? Choose a man and have him come down to me. If he is able to fight and kill me, we will become your subjects; but if I overcome him and kill him, you will become our subjects and serve us.' Then the Philistine said, 'This day I defy the armies of Israel! Give me a man and let us fight each other.' On hearing the Philistine's words, Saul and all the Israelites were terrified. For forty days the Philistine came forward every morning and evening and took his stand. Whenever the Israelites saw

the man, they all fled from him in great fear. David said to Saul, 'Your servant will go and fight him.' Then he took his staff in his hand, chose five smooth stones from the stream, put them in the pouch of his shepherd's bag and, with his sling in his hand, approached the Philistine. Meanwhile, the Philistine, with his shield bearer in front of him, kept coming closer to David. He looked David over and saw that he was little more than a boy, glowing with health and handsome, and he despised him. He said to David, 'Am I a dog, that you come at me with sticks?' And the Philistine cursed David by his gods. 'Come here,' he said, 'and I'll give your flesh to the birds and the wild animals!' David said to the Philistine, 'You come against me with sword and spear and javelin, but I come against you in the name of the LORD *Almighty, the God of the armies of Israel, whom you have defied. This day the* LORD *will deliver you into my hands, and I'll strike you down and cut off your head and the whole world will know that there is a God in Israel.' As the Philistine moved closer to attack him, David ran quickly toward the battle line to meet him. Reaching into his bag and taking out a stone, he slung it and struck the Philistine on the forehead. The stone sank into his forehead, and he fell face down on the ground. So David triumphed over the Philistine with a sling and a stone; without a sword in his hand he struck down the Philistine and killed him. David ran and stood over him. He took hold of the Philistine's sword and drew it from the sheath. After he killed him, he cut off his head with the sword. When the Philistines saw that their hero was dead, they turned and ran."[5]*

"It's the last part that's important." He pointed at the screen. "After David killed him, he took the giant's sword and cut off the dude's head."

"Why is that important?" I asked. "Why cut off the giant's head if he was dead already?"

I looked at Faith.

"That is the correct question," she said.

Xavier jumped back in to explain. "Legend tells us that out of the five Rapha brothers, four of them had their heads cut off after they were killed. David made sure of it just as he did after he killed Goliath. One of them didn't."

I remembered the name Xavier had asked me if I recognized earlier. "Arba."

He nodded. "Arba, the greatest of the brothers, named after one of his forefathers, who was one of the most powerful Nephilim. A bad dude."

"You are telling me that this Arba somehow—"

"Came back to life," Faith finished for me.

"Yes. That's exactly what I'm trying to tell you," Xavier said, pushing his glasses up his nose.

"And that's him in the video?"

"Yes."

"You're kidding me?"

"I wish, dude."

"How?"

"David's nephew Jonathan killed Arba, but it was after David was already old. He was bringing the body to David, but David died before he could make sure the head had been cut off. When David died, his youngest son Solomon took over the throne and with it everything in the kingdom, including the body of Arba, which lay forgotten. Solomon had been too young to understand what his father David and his men had done. Solomon became the most powerful and wealthiest king the nation of Israel had ever known. I mean, this dude was set: He built a temple, parks, theaters, and museums, among other things. Arba's body was placed in one of these museums.

"People came from all over the world to visit Solomon and see his kingdom. Among these people was a woman called the Queen of Sheba. Josephus the Jewish historian identifies her as the queen of Egypt and Ethiopia. She came to see the wealth and power of the famed King Solomon and she brought him gifts. She was amazed by everything she saw, and when she left Solomon gave her gifts in return. The Bible goes out of its way to say that King Solomon gave the Queen of Sheba, and I quote, *'whatever she asked for, besides all the customary gifts he had generously given.'* [6] What she asked for was the body of Arba, which she took back to her own land. As they were prone to do in Egypt, she had the body mummified. And that was the last anyone heard of it."

"Until now," Faith added.

"Impossible," I said. No response. "So, you mean to tell me that there was a race of half-fallen-angel, half-human giants called Nephilim . . ."

They both nodded.

"And among these Nephilim was a family of five brothers who were killed by David and his men."

Still nodding.

"And one of these giants, who has six fingers and six toes, has somehow come back to life four thousand years later because David didn't cut off his head?"

I looked at Xavier. Then Faith. Both nodded.

"Impossible," I repeated. They both just shrugged.

"Who was that in the video that woke him up?" I asked.

"We don't know," Faith said.

"How did they do it?"

"We don't know that, either," Faith said.

"For being the brains, you guys sure don't know a lot."

"We know too much and not enough at the same time," Faith said.

Again, I couldn't disagree.

15

As had become my habit, I made my way to the roof to process. My mind had turned to mush. Too much information. I surveyed the surroundings. Four black-clad men in their usual spots. Beautiful day. A few Naks wandering around outside the fence.

I took a deep breath. Then another. I couldn't believe the world had turned to this. That my life had turned to this. Trapped in a building. Another breath to clear my mind. I felt the air rush into my lungs. I held it there for a moment. Exhaled slowly. Closed my eyes and did it again. The sun felt warm on my skin. The light played shadows on my eyelids. Another breath.

I opened my eyes and felt my pupils constrict to block out the light. I tasted the air. Not salty, but not dry, either. Another breath. This one I held until it hurt. My lungs cried for air. I didn't comply. I held the air in. I felt my pulse start to race. I held it. It hurt. It was good to be alive. I let the breath leave my lungs through my nose. It came out in a rush.

I smiled. I was alive. I stayed there. Breathing. Enjoying it.

Time moved. I did not. I waited until I was ready. Then I turned and headed back inside.

A ding sounded, and the elevator doors slid open. Van and Bo walked out. I didn't feel like putting up with Bo's attitude so I turned for the stairs. I was too slow.

"Hey, Reece!" Van said. Always friendly. "You recovered from yesterday?"

Too late to pretend I didn't see them.

Bo chimed in. "Well, if it isn't our masked hero. Where's Tonto?"

"Yeah, that was something else," I said. "But I'm good. What are you guys doing?"

"Our shift is about to start for over-watch." Van pointed toward the outside door. "Roof duty."

"Good luck," I said, for lack of anything else to say. I pressed the elevator button. I thought of something and turned back. "Why don't you guys carry guns when you go out there with the Naks?"

"Man, for being the teacher's pet she sure doesn't tell you a lot," Bo said.

"Cut it out, Bo," Van said. "It's not his fault. Bullets don't really do much but make them mad. They heal so fast that guns are useless. Unless it's something really high powered, like the elephant guns we use on the roof. But even those just slow them down a little, so definitely anything we could carry is too small caliber to be worth carrying. The more we shoot them with the big guns, the more immune to getting shot they get, so we try not to use those much either."

"So, the Naks can become bulletproof?"

"Pretty much."

"Wow," I said.

Bo spoke up. "You mean the doc didn't fill you in on any of this before she sent you out there with us? It's a wonder you didn't get us all killed. You walk around here like you're special, like the rules don't apply to you. But we're the ones who've been saving everyone for three years. I'm through risking my life for a science experiment."

I couldn't take anymore. "What's your problem, Bo? Have you got a problem with me?"

"Yeah, I've got a problem with you, Kemosabe! My problem is the doctor treats you like our hero, and she's wrong. I'm the one who's been saving everyone for three years! It's my blood that's been spilled to save them. My problem is you're going to get us all infected!"

"It sounds like your problem is with the doctor. Take it up with her. And why do you keep calling me Kemosabe?"

"She really doesn't tell you anything, does she?" He laughed scornfully. "Because you're the Lone Ranger. You're the only one left."

"The only one what?" I asked.

He just walked away, shaking his head.

I looked at Van.

"You better ask the doc about that yourself. And hey, Reece. Little piece of advice," Van said as Bo headed out to the roof out of earshot. "When you're around Doc, don't call the infected people Naks. She doesn't like it."

"Yeah, I kinda picked up on that. Why is that?"

"You know the infected guy in the basement . . . Steven?"

I nodded.

"That's her brother."

16

I stopped by the cafeteria on my way to see Faith. It was closed, but the cook was still there. She was wiping a countertop. A big woman, no laugh lines on her face.

"What do you want?" she demanded, not nicely.

"I'm hungry." My stomach growled as if to emphasize my point.

She wasn't impressed. "Lunch is from noon until two."

I looked at a clock: 2:15. She started cleaning again.

"Any leftovers?"

"Dinner is from six until eight," she said without looking up.

I tried another tactic. "I'm sorry I missed lunch, uh . . ."

I waited. She bit. "Dorris."

"I'm sorry I missed lunch, Dorris. I was with Dr. Richards all morning, and I guess time got away. I'm sure you work very hard all day to feed everyone in this hospital and you don't need me coming around asking for food while you're cleaning up. But I'll eat anything you have left. I'm really hungry."

I could feel her soften a little.

"I'm new here. I've been in a coma for three years, so my timing is a little off."

She perked up at that.

"But I'm really hungry," I repeated.

"I think I might have something in the back you can eat," she said. "On one condition."

I could only imagine what that would be. "Anything."

She drilled me with fierce eyes. "You have to stay and talk with me while you eat."

That, I could do.

She went to the kitchen and emerged moments later with a plate of food. She was a good cook. She cleaned while I ate.

She asked a few questions about the coma, but after that, my part was mostly listening. I learned a lot about Dorris. Before the virus outbreak, she was in charge of the kitchen staff at the hospital. Now it was just her. She wanted to be a musician when she was young, but she didn't have any rhythm. Her first husband died in a car crash. Her second from cancer. Two tries were enough for her. She had four kids, but didn't know where any of them were. Or if any of them were infected. Or any of them were still alive. She wanted to grow old in a cabin in the woods, but didn't think there was much chance of that anymore. Maybe there never had been.

I shared a little about myself. There wasn't much to share. I realized my life boiled down to almost nothing when I laid out all the important parts. I was born unwanted. And I had lived for thirty-one years about the same way. My whole life was almost the same as the last three years had been. Empty. Dreamless.

Dorris brought me a piece of pie. Peach. The best I'd ever had, and I told her so. I didn't realize until later that peaches were probably not as easy to come by as they used to be. She sat with me while I ate dessert.

She made me feel wanted. I liked the feeling.

I finished up and stood to leave. "Thank you for the food, Dorris, and the company. It was wonderful."

She smiled. "I hope they're right about you," she said. "Anytime you're hungry, you come find me and I'll take care of you."

"I'll eat if you make me, but I'll come for the conversation," I said.

I exited the cafeteria feeling better than when I arrived. The feeling didn't last long.

17

The alarm blared in my ears, high pitched and sharp. An electronic, unnatural voice blasted over the PA system:

"All hospital staff and patients, please move to the bunker in the basement." It repeated three times, then fell silent.

People appeared from everywhere, moving toward the elevators. Most of them I didn't recognize. A few I did. Devin. The girl who had offered me the wheelchair. Xavier with his computer. Everyone moved quickly, but no one panicked. Frantic, but in order.

Someone grabbed my hand. Dorris. "Come on," she said. "We have to get to the safe room."

I let her pull me along. The elevators were packed. Small space, too many people. We headed for the stairs. I was breathing heavily, but not from exertion. We made the stairwell and headed down. That's when it hit me. I wouldn't make it crammed in a bunker with a hundred people. Trapped.

I pulled my hand free. Dorris stopped. "I have to go check on Dr. Richards," I said. "I'll meet you down there."

Dorris looked at me with her hard face. "Take care of yourself."

I turned and headed up the stairs, against the flow of people. I walked sideways with my back to the wall, trying not to get swept down with the crowd. The higher I climbed, the fewer people I met. I was breathing heavier from exertion now. No one was left on the top two floors. I headed for the roof.

There were six security guys instead of four. Van and Bo were in the middle of their shift. The Commander was on a walkie-talkie. None of them noticed me. Their attention focused on the fence line. I hid behind an air-conditioning unit.

I strained to discern what was happening. It was hard to see. It was afternoon and still bright. I saw two figures running toward the fence. I kicked myself for not grabbing binoculars on the way up. The pair didn't move like they were infected. Even from a distance, I could tell they were terrified. At least ten Anakim pursued them.

The pair reached the fence. Tried to scale it. Two of the Anakim were close. Very close. The first person to the fence made it halfway up. A woman, maybe. The other one moved more like a man. He was faster; he passed her. He stopped climbing to help her over the top. An Anakim caught his leg. The other person dropped from the fence and started running toward the building. Definitely a female.

Boom. One of the big guns went off. The Anakim jerked backward, and the man resumed climbing. Boom. The gun went off again. The other Anakim left his feet. The guy struggled to climb. His foot slipped, probably broken. Four more Anakim were right behind him.

The girl was almost to the building. Four security guys ran out. She stopped. Turned back. The security guys threw a blanket over her. She started to cry out, but it was cut off. The group carried her as they ran back to the building.

The man was almost to the top. Too late. The fence buckled under the weight of the Anakim. At least five of them.

Boom. Boom. Boom. Boom.

The big guns went off almost as one. I covered my ears. Several more muffled booms. But it was too late. They were all over the poor guy. Tearing. Biting. I looked away.

The guns quieted. They were useless now. I closed my eyes. The man screamed over and over. I tried to block it out. The decoy scream sounded from the woods. I snuck a peek. A few Anakim left. Most stayed.

His screaming stopped. I closed my eyes again. Didn't open them for a while.

18

The hospital remained on lockdown for the rest of the day. Everyone stayed in the bunker. I was glad I wasn't there. I continued to hide on the roof. The Anakim finally left the man's torn body alone and came to investigate the grounds inside the broken fence. The security guys watched with a wary eye. They stayed on high alert and rotated gunmen often. The Commander never moved, continually whispering orders into his walkie.

Eventually, the Anakim lost interest in the hospital and just wandered around. The Commander whispered something into his mouthpiece, and the scream sounded from the woods. This time from farther away. The Anakim took off, orange eyes blazing. While they were gone, three security guys ran out and fixed the fence. One always kept watch while the other two worked. They worked fast. The security guys finished and grabbed the dead man's body and brought it with them as they returned to the building. The Commander was more relaxed with the fence fixed and his men back inside, but he never left his post. It was close to one in the morning when I dozed off, and he was still there. Just watching.

When I woke up the next day, he was gone and all was quiet. The Anakim were once again gathered around the fence, but weren't trying to get inside. There were more of them than before. Four black-clad security guys manned their posts.

I woke up at 11:37 on the fourth day of my life. It was raining.

I let the drops fall on my upturned face for a few minutes. They felt good. Reminded me I was alive.

A few minutes later I heard a scream. It was dampened by the wet air, but it was starting to sound familiar. Too familiar. The decoy. The Anakim took off for the woods. Moments later a black SUV exited the structure. Probably the security guys making a supply run. I was glad I wasn't invited. It was time to find Faith. It was time to get some answers.

I couldn't find her anywhere. She wasn't in her lab. I asked Devin, but he just looked at me like I might bite him. The girl who offered me the wheelchair—her name was Lucy—said she didn't know either. The doc wasn't with Xavier. I asked him if he knew where she was.

"She left," he said. His typing didn't break stride.

"Left?" I asked. "Left where? With who?"

"She left, dude. Gone. She left with the Commander a little while ago." He continued pressing keys.

"Is she coming back? When? How long will she be gone? Where did she go?"

He looked up but didn't stop working. "Whoa, calm down, dude. She'll be back. She just went to check on some lead she got from the new girl."

"What lead?"

"I dunno . . . doctor stuff. Ask her."

"OK," I said. "Call her."

"Can't," he said.

"Why not?"

"We don't use cell phones."

"Why not?"

"Because they can be traced."

"By who?"

"The Nephs."

I took that in. More questions. Xavier kept clicking away on his computer.

"Why do the Nephs want to trace us?" He didn't answer. Didn't even look up. I thought it over for a second. "What are the Nephilim?"

He finally paused and looked at me. "I wondered when you would be back to ask that question."

"Well?"

"They're vampires."

19

I made my way to the cafeteria for lack of anywhere else to go. It was busy. Life at the hospital was back to normal, whatever normal was. A girl sat at a corner table all alone. The new girl. I walked over. She looked young. Probably early twenties. Attractive, in a girl-next-door sort of way. I could tell she'd been crying.

"Mind if I sit?" She shrugged, so I sat. "You must be the new girl."

"I guess."

I reminded myself she had been through a lot recently. "My name is Nick. I'm kinda new here too."

"Rachel."

Dorris had seen me sit down and brought food over. It was different from what everyone else had. It looked tastier. She brought Rachel some too. I smiled my thanks.

I continued. "I was in a coma for three years, and I just woke up the other day. I'm still trying to figure out what happened to the world while I was asleep."

"It's really messed up now," she said.

"Yeah, it is." We sat quietly for a moment, dwelling on that.

"They tied me down, like they thought I was one of the monsters," Rachel said. "Took my blood and questioned me all morning."

"Dr. Richards?"

"The blonde with glasses?" she asked.

"Yeah. She means well. They're just extra cautious around here. They had me strapped to the bed when I woke up. I think they're just making sure our blood is clean. From what I've seen, they don't like to take any chances."

"Yeah, I suppose. The doctor was friendly enough after they took my blood, I guess. It's just been a rough day."

I nodded. Didn't know what to say.

She continued. "That orderly wasn't very nice."

"The tall one?"

"Yeah."

Devin, I assumed. "He never is."

"They brought Pete's body back. I think they took his blood too."

"Your friend?" I guessed.

She nodded. Looked like she might cry again. Took a breath. "I only met him a couple days ago. But he saved my life. He helped me over the fence." The tears came now. She put her head down. I didn't know what to do. I looked around for help. No one noticed. I just waited helplessly. After a while she stopped. "I'm sorry." She wiped her eyes.

"Don't be."

She took a deep breath. "It's been a rough few days."

I couldn't have agreed more. Didn't seem appropriate to say it, so I didn't. "What did Faith ask you about?"

"Faith?"

"Dr. Richards."

"She wanted to know how and why I came here. I told her I heard about this place from another hospital up north. I lost my family to those monsters." She looked like she might cry again. She held it back but looked like a dam about to break. "And I just left and headed south. Ended up at a hospital several hours north of here, but they aren't doing as well as you are here. Someone told me about this place so I came. I met Pete on the road the day before yesterday. He offered to help me find this place."

Dorris brought us dessert. Rachel hadn't touched her food.

"Where was the other hospital?" I asked gently, my elbows on the table.

She shrugged. "I'm not good with directions and there's no GPS. Several hours north somewhere."

"Do you know why Faith—Dr. Richards—left here? Do you know what she was looking for?"

"No," Rachel said. "But she seemed really interested when I told her I met a coma patient there. Like you, I guess."

I turned that over in my head. A coma patient. Interesting.

"Did you see Pete? Did you see what those things did to him?" Her questions interrupted my thoughts.

"No," I lied. "They locked everyone in a bunker in the basement."

"He saved my life."

"I know," I said for lack of anything else to say.

"Do you know what they did with his body?"

"No, I'm sorry, I don't."

"He saved my life," she said again. The dam broke. I sat there and let her cry. Her shoulders shook, but the tears were silent. Her head in her hands.

I sat and talked with her about nothing. About everything. Her family. Where she was from. Dorris cleaned up and closed the cafeteria, but still we sat. Faith was gone, so I had nowhere else to be. Sharing helped. Rachel was wounded, but I saw a strength deep inside her. As we talked, it rose to the surface.

She would be all right. Maybe I would be too.

20

Faith still wasn't back when I woke up the next morning, so I decided to take matters into my own hands. I needed some answers. It looked like I needed to find them myself. After breakfast, I came up with a plan. I thought about asking Rachel to help as a lookout, but decided against it. She'd just arrived so I figured I could trust her, but she'd just lost her friend and might not be up for it. I would have to do this on my own.

I made my way to the fifth floor. Most of the rooms were dark. Fortunately, Faith's lab was empty. Unfortunately, it was also locked. This was going to be tougher than I thought.

I would try Van first.

I found him on a treadmill in the fitness room. He was really moving. I was thankful Bo was nowhere to be seen. I greeted him, then asked, "Do you know when Dr. Richards will be back?"

"Nope. We never know," he said, not breaking stride. "Could be today, could be several more days."

I waited as he took a breath.

"Depends on what she's looking for and what she finds. Just look for them around noon each day. She's with the Commander, and he believes noon is the safest time to travel."

"I left something in her lab the other day, but I think the door is locked."

"Yeah, she has the key. She likes to keep it locked."

I said nothing, a tactic I read about somewhere that can cause people to volunteer more information to fill the silence.

He obliged. "There's a master key in the security office, but it's probably best if you just wait until the doctor gets back."

"OK, it's nothing important. I'll just wait for her."

I knocked his walkie-talkie off the stand and acted like it was an accident. I scrambled to pick it up.

"Oops, sorry about that," I said. I flipped it off as I set it back in its place. He didn't seem to notice. "Thanks, Van."

He nodded. I saw him turn the treadmill up a little faster as I exited.

I was going to need help.

I hunted Rachel down and described the plan to her. She only agreed to help if I also got the key to let her into the morgue to see Pete's body. She said Devin told her that's where it was. I knew it was a mistake, but I agreed.

The security office was on the first floor, down the hall and around the corner from the fitness room. I leaned against the wall across from the security office. Rachel went inside. I could hear through the open door.

"Excuse me," she said sweetly. "Do you know where Van is? I need to find him."

A pause. I assumed the security guard on duty was checking a schedule. "No, he's not on duty for another hour, so I'm not sure where he is. But he has to be around the hospital somewhere."

"Could you call him for me? Please? I need to know where he is." She drew out 'please' into more syllables than it should have been. She was perfect. I imagined the guard trying to work up the nerve to say no to the helpless new girl.

"All right," he finally said. I silently willed him to use the walkie-talkie. I had never heard them page any of the security guys over the intercom before. I hoped I was right.

"Van, what's your location?"

No response.

He tried again. "Van, are you there? Come in, Van."

Still no response. Van hadn't noticed his radio was off. So far so good.

"I'm sorry, sweetie, his walkie must have died," the guard said. He sounded like he was from the south. That was good. "Did you check the fitness room? He usually likes to get in a run before his shift."

"No," Rachel said, still super sweet. "I'm new here. Can you show me where the fitness room is?"

"It's on this floor, right around the corner."

"Pleeeeease?" Again, she drew it out. She was great. I imagined puppy eyes.

I heard a sigh. Then a chair slide.

Perfect. Game time.

Rachel followed him into the hall. I pretended not to pay attention to them as they passed. She winked at me as she went by. I waited until they rounded the corner before I dashed into the office. The plan was for Rachel to keep him busy with questions while the office was out of sight. From what I had seen so far, she was capable. I figured I had maybe sixty seconds. No more.

I took a quick survey of the office. A desk. A laptop. A row of monitors. Three filing cabinets. Some type of intercom system. A bank of walkie-talkies. An unplugged coffee maker. A cage full of shotguns that looked like an addition to the original office. It was padlocked. Fifty seconds left.

The desk. I darted to the desk and pulled open drawers. The first was filled with junk. Paperclips, Post-its, bubble gum. Papers. Under the papers, a snub-nosed .38 revolver. I thought about taking it. I didn't. Thirty-five seconds left.

Next drawer. Bingo. A metal box. I pulled it out and set it on the desk. Inside were hundreds of keys. They were numbered.

Not good. Twenty-five seconds left. I tried to remember the number to the lab. I pictured the doorway in my head. I couldn't recall a number. Had there been one? Twenty seconds.

Fifth floor. Her lab was on the fifth floor. My hand floated across the row marked five. Fifteen seconds. Which room? There were dozens. Ten seconds. I looked up. Nothing yet. But the guard would round that corner any moment. Five seconds. I wracked my brain for a number. Still nothing. Time up.

I had to get out. There were two keys that weren't numbered. I grabbed them both. Slammed the box closed and dropped it back in the drawer. Loudly. But if Rachel hadn't been able to distract him long enough, then silence wouldn't do me any good anyway. There was no place to hide. I slid the drawer closed and peeked out of the office. I could hear their voices around the corner. He sounded apologetic but firm.

I leaned back in my spot just as he rounded the corner, hustling back to his office. I ignored the instinct to dart away, knowing it would only draw unwanted attention. I stayed planted. He entered the office, and I waited for an alarm to sound. None did. I breathed a sigh of relief and walked away. It wasn't until I got to the elevator that I remembered my promise to Rachel. I had forgotten to get the key to the morgue.

Oh well. That problem would have to wait. I had answers to find.

21

There wasn't a room number on the lab. Luckily the first blank key I tried worked. I stuck the other one in my pocket. I eased open the door to the lab. It was dark. I could hear the low hum of the refrigerators. I left the lights off and closed the door before I turned on the flashlight I had borrowed from a maintenance closet. I locked the door behind me. I didn't want to take the chance of someone walking in.

I swept the light back and forth, trying to decide what I was looking for. The blood was as good a place to start as any. I opened the glass refrigerator door and pulled out a random vial. It looked normal to me. Not that I would know if it wasn't. I looked for a label. It only had a number: 1383. I put it back inside and pulled out another: 962. It also looked normal.

I moved to the other side of the fridge, grabbed one that looked like it had letters on it. A name: Steven. I turned the vial sideways; the blood barely moved. Other than that, it looked like all the rest. I picked up another with my other hand: 241. This one was thick as well. Extremely thick. It didn't move at all in the tube. Like Jell-O. I put them both back.

I looked around for mine. No other names. All numbers. I had no idea what my number would be. The last one? No, the second or third to the last one? I found the three highest numbers—1437, 1438, and 1439. No way to tell if any of these were mine. They all looked normal. None of them looked extra thick.

An image flashed through my mind of Faith writing everything down on her clipboard. I needed to find my chart. I replaced the blood and looked around for patient files. Four large filing cabinets stood against the side wall opposite the lab table. I pulled open a drawer. Tons of patient files. All numbered, no names. I pulled a random one out. It was full of facts. But that was it, just facts. Height, weight, race, blood type, a medical history, a brief description of the person's personality in medical jargon at the bottom. Nothing to distinguish it as any specific person that I could see. I pulled out another. Same thing.

I closed the filing cabinet and moved to another. This one had a word printed in small letters on the front. COMA. Bingo. I pulled a file out. Again, no distinguishing characteristics. Just medical facts and a number. And the numbers were random, no apparent order. Many numbers in the sequence were missing. Another file. Same thing. There were no personality traits on these, but that made sense if they were all coma patients.

I noticed when I closed this one to put it back in the drawer, it had been stamped with one word on the outside: Deceased. Stamped in red ink. Impersonal. I pulled the first file back out. Same stamp. Deceased. I pulled a few more random files out of the cabinet. Every one of them had the stamp. Weird. Nothing on the notes written on the inside of each one told me why. Most of it didn't even make sense to me. All doctors' jargon and medical words I didn't know. I noticed Faith's handwriting in most of them. It was an interesting cross between a female's bubbly lettering and a doctor's illegible scrawl.

I closed this filing cabinet and opened a third. I hurriedly shuffled through dozens of patient files, not even bothering to open them. Not one of them was missing the red stamp. Red block letters stamped on every single one: Deceased. I closed this cabinet and checked the front for COMA. It was there.

The same word was printed on the third cabinet. That made three out of four marked COMA. Creepy.

I opened the last filing cabinet marked COMA and searched for the highest number I could find. Found it. It was numbered like all the others, number 1437. The same number as one of the vials. But the numbers on this file were crossed out and a name was handwritten over them. Nick Reece. My file.

I held the flashlight with my chin and used both hands to read the file. Inside were tons of handwritten notes—all Faith's. I read, trying to decipher words and phrases. In the notes section, she had written: control issues, claustrophobic, intelligent, abandonment, no family history. I smiled. My life boiled down to bullet points.

The medical portion of the chart was even harder to decipher. One phrase caught my eye. "Elevated cytotoxic T cells" was written out in bold and underlined, followed by "Mutated cells?"

I didn't know what T cells were, but it seemed important. There were a bunch of other words I either didn't recognize or couldn't read. There were also a bunch of numbers, but none of them were highlighted so I assumed they were normal.

I heard footsteps in the hall. I clicked the flashlight off. The footsteps got louder. Closer. I slid the file back home and closed the drawer quietly. Listened. The *click-clack* echoed off the walls. Boots maybe? But the footfalls sounded light. Was it Faith? I hoped not. The footsteps stopped right outside the door. I didn't wait for the sound of a key to slide into the lock. I dashed to the door, grabbing a chair as I went. I flipped the lights on with one hand and unlocked the door with my other. I sat back in the chair and tried to look bored.

The flashlight! I realized it was still in my hand. I slid it in my back pocket, out of sight, leaned back, and closed my eyes.

The door opened.

A female voice. "Hello?"

Not Faith.

I opened my eyes. It was Rachel. "What are you doing?" she asked.

"Nothing," I said. "I thought you might be the doctor. I wanted her to think she left the door unlocked, and I was just in here waiting on her to get back."

Rachel nodded. She closed the door behind her and asked. "What did you find?"

"How did you know where I was?" I hadn't told her what room I was trying to get into.

"I guessed. You seemed interested in the doctor and what she found out," she said. "Two and two."

I was going to have to watch this girl.

"Did you get the key to the morgue?"

"No," I said. "I couldn't steal two keys. If too many went missing they might notice." She looked like she was about to get upset, so I cut her off. "I have another plan to get into the morgue. We'll get in and see Pete's body. I promise." The lie seemed to appease her. Now I had to come up with the promised plan.

As it turned out, getting into the morgue was much easier than I thought it would be. The hard part was getting Van to scan his key card so the elevator would go down to the basement. I caught Van just as he was heading up to the roof to start his shift. I told him I wanted to see Steven again. He looked suspicious, but when I promised I wouldn't touch anything, he finally relented. He exited the elevator with a warning to be fast and not to get him in trouble. I promised.

I picked up Rachel on the way down. Steven was in hibernation mode when we exited the elevator, and I wasn't sure if Rachel even noticed him. I hoped she wouldn't. I didn't need any more trouble from her. The morgue itself was already unlocked.

I guess they figured that anyone with access to the basement would have no interest in stealing anything from a morgue.

They were wrong.

Pete's body was gone.

22

I dropped Rachel off and went to see Xavier. I still needed answers. I opened my mouth to greet him when Devin burst in behind me.

"We have a problem," he said. He was short of breath.

"What?" Xavier asked.

"The blood of the dead guy we brought in with the new girl—" Devin noticed me and cut himself off.

"Yeah?" Xavier saw Devin looking at me. "He's cool," he said. "What about the new guy's blood?"

"It's not clean."

"Anak?" Xavier asked.

"No. Something else."

"Crap." Xavier said. "Where's the body?"

"The morgue," Devin said. I didn't disagree with him. They would find out soon enough.

Xavier lifted a bunch of papers from his desk and fished out a walkie-talkie. He keyed it and asked for Bo. Xavier told him the situation. Devin left in a rush to meet Bo in the morgue. Xavier turned the radio back off. He returned to his computer and started typing furiously. I think he forgot I was there.

Xavier pulled up screen after screen as I watched. I didn't know what he was doing, but I could tell he was a genius with the computer. His hands moved like lightning across the keyboard. I finally cleared my throat. He was so involved he didn't even notice. I waited. I decided I might learn more by watching and listening.

Bo marched into the room, followed by Van and two other security guys.

"Did you secure the body?" Xavier asked.

"The body is gone," Bo said.

Van glared at me. I shook my head and mouthed, "Not me." No one else paid any attention to me.

"Gone?" Xavier asked. "Gone to where? Where is he?" He pushed his glasses up on his nose.

"I don't know," Bo said. "Any word from the Commander or the doc? Did she move it before she left?"

"No, no word. But they can't call, so unless they're close enough to use these . . ." He held up his radio.

"I tried. No luck," Bo said. Then to Van and the other two: "OK, take two men each and search this entire hospital. Search every floor. Every room. Every closet. Every bed. That body has to be in here somewhere. Find it." He thought for a second. "Van, pass out the shotguns. Go."

The security men left. Bo stayed. I grabbed Van's arm as he was leaving. I spoke low so that no one would overhear. "I swear I didn't touch the body, Van. I didn't touch anything. It was gone when I went down there."

He nodded. He wasn't happy. "You better not be lying. This better not come back on me."

I held up my hand. "I swear it wasn't me."

He turned and left.

A phone rang. I hadn't heard one in so long it sounded foreign. Apparently, Bo and Xavier hadn't either. They looked confused. It rang again.

Xavier pulled up a screen on his laptop. A number flashed across the screen. "The Commander's emergency phone."

Bo stood frozen. This had to be bad. Really bad. It rang again.

"Answer it," Bo said.

Xavier pressed a button. "Hello?"

Static.

We waited. A voice spoke. Female. Indistinguishable. It came through the computer speakers. More static.

The voice spoke again. "X, are you there?" It was Faith.

"Faith," Xavier said. "You shouldn't be calling. They can track you. You should be on the secure line. They can track you on this line." He spoke a mile a minute and his fingers moved even faster across the keyboard. "I'll try to jam it, but you shouldn't have called. You should have used the radio, Faith, not the phone."

"Xavier. Xavier!" Faith's voice came through as a frantic whisper. A whisper yell. It cut Xavier off. "They're here. Can you hear me? They're here. You have to give Nick a message for me."

"Who's there, Faith?" Bo cut in.

"The Anakim—" Her voice was cut off by static. "Bo, Xavier—" More static. "A message for me . . . Nick a message for me."

"I'm here." I spoke up. I stepped closer to the speaker and repeated. "I'm here, Doc. What's going on?"

Static. Then, "I was right, Nick. I was right about you. I have to be—"

She was lost in static.

Xavier pressed a few buttons and the static stopped momentarily. "—find me."

"Where are you, Faith?" Bo again. "Tell me where you are."

"I don't know. We came north. You have to trace me, X. Trace this cell."

"Already trying," Xavier said.

"Find me, and tell Nick where I am. Nick, you have to find me." She sounded frantic, scared. Her voice was still a whisper yell.

"Where's the Commander?" Bo asked.

"He's gone," Faith said. "He . . . " She started to say something else but instead whispered. "They're here." And went silent.

Nobody spoke. We just listened. We heard scraping. A muffled noise that sounded like Faith had covered the phone with her hand. More muffled noises. We waited quietly for another sound. A scream maybe. Or the phone to go dead. My heart pounded. More scraping and some banging. I tried to imagine what was happening. Faith hiding under a table? In a closet? I heard fabric rustling. Like the phone was placed in a pocket. Muffled footsteps and then a click. A door being latched?

No one spoke. We strained to hear. Xavier turned the volume up. We kept waiting.

Finally, her voice spoke again. This time even more quietly. "Nick?"

"I'm here," I said. I whispered, too, for some reason.

"Nick, you have to come find me. We drove north to find the hospital Rachel was at. I'm not sure how far we came, or where I am. Have X trace this call."

"The Nephs are going to be tracing it, too, Faith," Xavier said.

"I know. Nick, you have to find me before the Nephilim do. You are the only one that can do it. I was right about you. There are three more like you—" The static returned.

"Doc?" I whispered frantically. "Doc? Faith?"

More static. Xavier's hands flew over the keyboard.

Her voice came back. "Nick. You have to come." She cut herself off. The phone was muffled for a moment. I heard a muffled scream. Rustling and then static. I waited. Her voice came back one more time. "Find me," she hissed.

Static filled the speaker for a few seconds. Another scream. The phone went silent.

She was gone.

23

"Get her back," I said.

Xavier worked the keyboard. He ignored me.

"Get her back."

"I'm trying, dude."

I waited.

"It's not going to happen. She's gone."

"Can you trace her? Where is she?"

He didn't respond, kept pressing keys. I took a breath and waited.

"Crap," Xavier said.

"What?" asked Bo.

"I didn't get her exact location. Only traced it to within a triangle of three cell towers north of here."

"How large of an area?" I asked.

"Few miles, probably." He pushed his glasses up with one hand. The other didn't break pace on the keyboard.

"Why can't you get closer?"

"Her cell is off. She must have turned it off so the Nephilim couldn't trace her exact location either." He turned to me. "She's counting on you to find her first."

Van burst back in the room. Devin followed him in. Van had two shotguns in his hands. He gave one to Bo.

"No sign of the body anywhere," Van said. "We've searched every floor. It isn't in any room, any bed, any closet. There's no trace of it anywhere."

Bo thought for a second. "We should initiate lockdown. I have a bad feeling about this."

"Are you sure?" Van asked.

"Yes, we should put the hospital on lockdown and redo our search. Go through every nook and cranny of this place until we find that body. It has to be lying around here somewhere. Or someone had to have taken it and hidden it. We'll find it."

"What if it isn't?" I asked.

"What do you mean?" Bo asked.

"I mean what if the body isn't lying around here some-where?" I said. "You guys know more about this stuff than I do, but what if the body isn't lying around because he isn't dead at all? Could he have come back to life like the Arba guy in the security video? Devin said his blood wasn't clean."

"No. Impossible. There hasn't been any other evidence of anyone else coming back to life," Xavier said from where he was still working on the computer.

"Well, maybe he wasn't really dead then," I said.

"No way," Van said. "Did you see what the Naks did to him? He had to be dead."

"But do we know for sure? I mean, the Anakim recover incredibly quickly. How fast would a Nephilim recover if he wasn't really dead?"

Everyone looked at each other. No one wanted to consider it.

"We're not sure," Xavier finally said. "I'm not sure if anyone knows how fast they recover. No one has lasted long enough to find out."

"Besides, I took his blood myself," Devin said. "There's no way he was still alive. No way."

"Did you check to make sure he was dead, or did you assume he was?" Bo asked.

"He was horribly mangled by the Anakim. There's no way he was still alive," Devin said.

"I asked if you checked," Bo growled.

Devin shook his head.

Not good. I looked longingly at Van's shotgun. He shook his head.

"Van," Bo said. "Initiate lockdown."

Van nodded and brought his radio to his lips. He said something. A voice responded. Van asked them to repeat it. They did. Van turned to Bo with a look of terror on his face.

"What?" Bo demanded.

"Steven got loose."

The sound of a shotgun round being chambered grabbed at my ears. I was trying to keep up. Steven was loose in the hospital. Pete was probably a Nephilim and still alive. And Faith was in danger and I had to save her. My head was spinning.

"Lockdown. Now," Bo demanded.

Van said something in response, but it was drowned out by the alarm sounding. Too late for lockdown.

Devin ran. Van yelled something into his radio and dashed out of the room. Bo grabbed Xavier and started to pull him away from his computer. Xavier pulled his arm away and continued punching buttons on the computer. Bo yelled at him. Xavier kept typing. Bo kept yelling. The alarm kept blaring.

Xavier jumped up and grabbed a paper off a printer. He marked it with a red pen. Bo grabbed his arm again and started to drag him out. Xavier used his free hand to grab his laptop. As they passed me Xavier said something to me. My ears were still ringing with the alarm. I couldn't tell what he said. He waved the paper at me. I took it. Once again, he jerked his arm free. He leaned in close.

"Here's where she is!" he yelled, pointing at the paper. It looked like a map. I could see a red circle he had marked. "She's somewhere in here. Find her!"

Bo pulled him out the door.

24

I stood there, trying to figure out my next move. With Steven loose, the first thing I needed to do was make myself invisible. I knew I wouldn't find any motor oil in Xavier's computer lab so I looked for an alternative. I stuffed Xavier's map in my pocket and busted the printer open. I pulled out the toner cartridge. I dumped it on my skin. Not enough. I looked through the cabinets for more. I found a box of refills in the closet. I broke more open and covered myself in toner. Then shoved a handful of extras in my pockets. It would have to do. I hoped it worked.

Now I needed a plan to get out of the hospital so I could find Faith. It wouldn't be easy with Steven and Pete on the loose, but I had no other option. I would have to try. The alarm kept blaring. No voice over the intercom this time.

I made my way toward the stairwell. It was hard to hear anything except the siren in the hallway, but as soon as I closed the fire door and entered the stairwell, it went quiet. The muffled alarm barely made its way in. I crept down a level to the next landing. There was a twisted body on the steps. I turned it over. A security guy. I didn't recognize him. Not that I would have. His body was mangled badly. I snagged his radio as I went by. I wished he had a shotgun. He didn't.

I heard a sound on the landing below. First floor. I couldn't take the chance of it being Steven. I darted back up three floors. Whoever it was heard me. They followed me up. Fast. I hit the fifth-floor door running. It flew open with a crash. The alarm pounded in my ears. I didn't break stride as I looked for somewhere to go. To hide. At the end of the hall I turned left. Toward Faith's lab. I tried a door on the left. Locked. The next one was locked as well. The lab it was then. I patted my pocket for the key. I heard someone running down the hall behind me. The key was out and in the lock. Wrong key. I reached in my other pocket. Bingo. I slammed the door and locked it behind me. I had to hide. I looked around but there wasn't much cover.

The refrigerators.

I pulled them out from the wall. The glass tubes rattled against each other inside. I ducked in between two refrigerators and pulled them back in front of me as best I could. I was dead. I could feel it.

The door crashed inward, and Steven rushed into the lab. His orange eyes glowed in the darkness. He picked himself up and looked around. I shrank back and made myself as small as I could. He looked confused. He was covered in blood. It wasn't his. No way he wouldn't see me soon. He sniffed the air. I hoped the toner worked. He started to make his way toward the refrigerators. I froze. This was it. Every muscle in my body clenched. I was about to die, but I wouldn't go down without swinging.

He stopped. Sniffed again. As if he smelled something he didn't like. I tried not to breathe. His orange eyes searched back and forth. I couldn't stand it any longer. I started to shake. I tried to stop myself, but I couldn't. I took a few shallow breaths. Willed myself. Steven remained standing there.

Sweat trickled down my face, leaving streaks of toner. If he came any closer he would smell me for sure.

A scream sounded from down the hall. It was cut short, but Steven heard it. His head spun around so fast I was sure his neck would break. He took off down the hall. I pushed the refrigerators out but didn't move. I finally stopped shaking. I waited until my breathing evened out.

I had to come up with a new plan. I couldn't go back that way. A new thought occurred to me. If I could make it to the roof, then maybe I could somehow make it down on the outside. Avoid Steven and Pete altogether. It was worth a try.

After I snuck out of the lab, I made my way up the stairs. It took a while because at any sign of trouble I either hid or went the other direction. Either Steven was really fast, or Pete was helping him. Or both.

On the floor below roof level, I heard a noise from my pocket. It startled me. The radio: "Bo, he's trying to open the doors. I think he's going to try to get the Naks outside the fence in here." He . . . Pete?

I heard the shotgun go off. A groan. Another gunshot.

Bo responded, but the voice didn't answer back.

A thump.

Bo demanded a report. There was none. I could hear screaming and a few more gunshots, but they were muffled. It sounded like the security guy was down and had fallen with the talk button depressed. More sounds came through but no response from the voice. I turned the volume down and pushed open the door to the roof.

There were only two security guys manning the guns on over-watch. I went to an empty corner and looked for something to let myself down with. I couldn't find anything. The Commander was smart, though, so there had to be a rope or something stored around here in case of an emergency. I kept looking.

I found it. A wooden box in the back corner hid a rope inside. The rope was already anchored to the roof. I tossed it over the side. The rope had a knot tied every few feet. Hard to climb down, harder to climb up. The Commander was smart. It was just long enough to touch the ground. I started down. It was a good thing I had no fear of heights.

A quarter of the way down, I heard a noise. A yell. Or more like a wail. It came from the front of the building. I looked toward the fence line. The Anakim all turned as one. Every eye went orange. At least I imagined they did. It was hard to see that far out. They tore at the fence. It hardly resisted. Dozens of the infected sprinted toward the hospital. More came from the woods to join them. Someone inside thought to sound the scream from the woods. It was too late. They didn't even slow down.

I stopped climbing. I hoped they wouldn't see me. The rope swayed slightly with my weight. I flexed every muscle to stop it. Dozens rushed by, ignoring me, trying to find a way inside. They threw themselves against windows and doors. Dozens more crashed in behind them. They were inside. More screams to match the decoy in the woods. I still didn't move. One last group made for the entrance. I willed them not to see me. I closed my eyes as if I could make myself invisible.

The rope jerked. I looked down. One of the Anakim had spotted me. He grabbed the rope and started to climb. Hand over hand. He was strong. I clawed my way back to the top and pulled myself over the ledge. I panicked. He was halfway up. Climbing fast. I scrambled around looking for anything to cut the rope with. I patted my pockets. No pocket knife. Nothing I could use. I looked around on the roof for a scrap piece of metal. Again nothing. The roof was clean.

The Commander was smart. He would have thought of this. I checked the box. There was a small hacksaw in the bottom. I grabbed it and dove toward the rope. Mistake. He was three-fourths of the way up. Seeing me made him move faster. I hated to cut my lifeline, but I started sawing. He was two floors down. Closing fast. The rope started to fray. I sawed faster. I could feel the heat of the friction on my hand. Halfway through the rope. He was one floor down.

I thought about running. Too late now; he would catch me. I had to finish cutting the rope. Three-quarters of the way through the rope it started to pop. Strand after strand. He was only a few feet away. The powder from the printer cartridge stained the rope as sweat ran down my fingers. Almost there.

The rope snapped. I looked over the edge. The Nak was still grasping the rope in his hands. His orange eyes showed no fear. Or remorse. Only anger. He slammed into the ground. Bloody and twisted. He laid there for a few seconds while I caught my breath. By the time I had recovered, so had he. He hopped up with a growl and jumped through a broken window into the hospital.

No doubt coming to find me.

25

I had to find another way out of the hospital. A vehicle from the loading bay was all I could think of. I pulled a fresh toner cartridge from my pocket and reapplied. Neither of the security guys were on the roof now. One of the guns was still there, but I figured it would be too big to carry. I took a breath and steeled myself to go back down into the hospital.

The first floor down was silent. Eerie. At least the alarm had been shut off. The noise of my shoes on the tile echoed off the walls. The next floor down was almost as quiet. But I could hear faint sounds of carnage from the floors below. I stepped as quietly as I could. At one point, I thought I heard the sound of someone quietly breathing, hidden somewhere behind a desk. I hoped they made it. I doubted they would.

I avoided the elevators. I couldn't stand the thought of being trapped in there. I zigzagged from stairwell to stairwell, from floor to floor, hoping to avoid running into anyone. Or anything.

For three floors, I succeeded. On the fourth floor down, I didn't.

The growling of several Anakim echoed through the stairwell. They were coming up fast. I exited the stairwell and found a broken bed frame that I used to bar the door. I made my way down the long hallway to the other set of stairs. Out of nowhere a man appeared. He stood at the end of the hallway, between me and the stairs. I froze, but he saw me.

No place to go. I couldn't return to the stairs behind me. He had seen me, so hiding in a room would do no good. He just looked at me. No smile. Almost no expression on his face at all. His eyes weren't orange. I was relieved. I shouldn't have been.

They were black.

He took a step toward me. Slowly. Confidently. Like someone afraid of nothing. I knew who this was. Pete. A Nephilim.

I backpedaled. One step. Two. He didn't move any faster. Or slower. I tripped over my own foot and fell.

Terrified, my mind went blank. I scooted backward. No thoughts, no plan. Just fear. He took another step.

Precise. Calm.

I vaguely heard the Anakim pounding on the door behind me. From somewhere far away, I heard a *ding*. My mind was a dry-erase board that had been wiped clean. Fear was the only thing left written on it.

He took another step. His heel fell heavy on the tile.

A strong hand grabbed my arm and pulled me up. Vise-like. I snapped out of it, turned. It was Bo covered in motor oil. He had a shotgun in his hand. His eyes looked crazier than ever. I saw an open elevator behind him. He pushed me toward it. My legs felt heavy.

"Go find Faith!" he yelled. I think I nodded. He turned toward Pete, who was moving faster now. Bo smiled. A teeth-bared smile. I pressed the button for the loading dock. The doors started to close. Bo wasn't coming. He turned and tossed me his shotgun.

As the doors closed, I saw Bo draw a pistol and run forward with a yell. Muffled gunshots, but I was moving downward.

Too far away to hear how long the yell lasted.

26

When I exited the elevator at the loading dock, Van was there. He had his shotgun pointed at the elevator doors when I stepped out. He turned it away when he saw it was me, but didn't lower it.

"Where's Bo?" he asked. I didn't respond.

There were dead bodies strewn all around—blood everywhere.

"Where's Bo? Have you seen Bo?" Van demanded again. His shotgun held at the ready, like something might jump out from anywhere at any moment. I heard pounding on the outside of the metal loading-bay doors.

"He's on level six. I saw him on level six," I said. "But, Van, I don't think he's still there . . ." My voice trailed off.

"What? Where's Bo? Tell me, Reece."

"When I left, he and Pete were fighting. Bo was . . . Bo's crazy."

Van jumped into the elevator.

"Van. No, don't. It's too late," I said as he stuffed shells from his pockets into the shotgun.

"I have to." He pressed a button.

I tried one more time. "Come with me."

He shook his head. "I can't. You go, Reece. Good luck." The elevator doors closed.

"You too." I doubted he heard me.

There were three black SUVs sitting in a row, the last one still wrecked from our excursion. I pulled open the door of an undamaged one. There was a dead body inside. Someone trying to escape. I pulled the body out and hopped in with my shotgun. I turned the key. Nothing. I tried again. Still nothing. It was dead.

I tried the next SUV. The doors to this one were already open. At least three dead bodies. It was hard to tell which parts belonged to who. I only moved the one in the driver's seat. This truck was dead too. Couldn't be a coincidence. I popped the hood and looked under it. I knew very little about car repair. I hoped whatever was wrong with it would be obvious. It wasn't. I tried the third SUV, hoping for a different result. No luck. I could still hear the Anakim pounding on the garage door. They weren't giving up. It was heavily dented but still standing. So far.

I looked around the loading dock for another mode of transportation. The pounding became background noise. I was more worried that someone, or something, would bring the elevator back down. Or that the door to the stairwell would crash open, and Anakim would pour through. I tore through the dock, furiously looking for anything I could use.

I found what I was looking for under a tarp in the back. Two motorcycles. I took the black one. I loved the Commander. He was always thinking ahead. I rolled it to the middle of the loading bay. I searched for a light switch. I found it by the stairs and flipped it off. It took a moment for the big incandescent lights to power down. While they did, I grabbed a gate opener from one of the SUVs and straddled the bike. I hoped it hadn't been sabotaged like the trucks. The lights went out.

I said a little prayer before I turned the key. I wasn't sure to whom. It started. Part one down. Now came the risky part. I made sure there was a round chambered in Bo's shotgun. There was. I pulled a handful of printer toners from my pocket and held them, took a deep breath, and pressed the button to raise the bay door.

The gate started up. It wasn't slow, but it wasn't fast either. This would be close. I could see the Anakim's feet as they continued pounding on the door as it raised. It was a good thing they weren't smart. Not one of them got on their hands and knees and crawled under. The gate was at waist level before they figured it out. My heart pounded in my throat. This was it. All or nothing.

A couple of them ducked under the door. More followed. It took a moment for their eyes to adjust to the darkness. Before they spotted me, I made my move. I tossed the toner into the air above them, shouldered the shotgun, and pulled the trigger. I pulled it twice more in a heartbeat just to be sure. When I lowered the gun, the air was filled with printer toner. It hung in the air, like a snowstorm of black powder. All over the Anakim. I gave it a moment for the powder to coat their nostrils as they inhaled.

I revved the bike. The tire started to smoke. I let it whine in a burnout. Smoke surrounded me. I popped it into gear. The bike shot forward. I closed my eyes and ducked. I couldn't see anyway. I felt the bike brush against several Naks, but I didn't slow. A hand grabbed at my arm, but the fingers didn't find a hold. I lost my grip on the shotgun and heard it clatter to the floor. I felt sunlight hit my eyelids. I opened my eyes. I had made it. I looked back. The door continued its ascent. I didn't want to think about how close I had come to not timing my exit right. Several Naks ran out into the sunlight to give chase, but I had too much of a head start. I gunned the bike down the driveway.

Bodies covered the lawn. People who had tried to make a run for it. None of them moved. I looked forward and changed gears. The bike was fast. Fifty yards out in the middle of the drive I saw the shape of a crumpled person. I didn't slow. The form separated into two; one of them stood up and turned. Orange eyes.

The drive wasn't wide enough to go around him. And the bike wouldn't make it in the grass. I was going to have to play chicken and hope for the best. Much like in the SUV, the Nak was more than willing to play. He started running toward me. I dropped the bike into its highest gear. I had a bad feeling about this, but no other options. He was fifty feet away and closing fast. I tightened my grip on the handlebars and braced for impact.

He was ten feet away when an invisible hand yanked him backward. I saw him fall before I heard the gunshot. He tucked and rolled. I accelerated and was gone.

I looked back. A man waved from the top of the hospital. It looked like Van, but I was too far away to be sure. I smiled as I flew past the downed fence. MERCY GENERAL HOSPITAL, the sign said.

I still had to find Faith. I still had to find out why I was special. And I still had to find out who the other three people she was talking about were.

But I was still alive.

It was 4:37 p.m. on the fifth day of my life.

Book II
The Four

Part I

Faith
Two days earlier

1

The Commander and I left the hospital and headed north. A few raindrops pattered on the windshield. It was a light Southern California type of rain. It wouldn't last long. But I liked the rain, and not just because the Nephilim didn't.

We sat in silence as I wondered how we were going to find Rachel's hospital. The Commander was confident we would, but he was always confident. That was just his style. That's why I didn't worry about it. The hard part was convincing the Commander it was worth the risk of the trip. But we trusted each other's judgment so here we were, driving north.

I hoped Rachel's information was correct and there really was a coma patient alive at the other hospital. So far Nick Reece had been the only one.

The Commander interrupted my thoughts. "You like him, don't you, Faith?"

"Who?" I asked.

"Reece."

I felt my cheeks flush warm. I looked out the window. "He's an interesting case. Hopefully, he's what I've been looking for."

"Do you think he is?"

"I hope so. It's unbelievable how fast he recovered from his coma, which could be a good sign. On the other hand, that recovery time could point toward infection even though he hasn't exhibited any other signs. If this other patient exists, and if we can find her, then I can get more information."

"We'll find her." Always confident.

Minutes passed.

I couldn't resist. "What do you think of Nick Reece?"

The Commander smiled. "Hopefully, he's what you've been looking for."

I wanted to ask for more. I didn't.

"I'm not sure he's ready for what he'll have to go through if he is, but I guess none of us are ready and we've been in the middle of it for three years," the Commander said. "You know more about his mental state than I do."

"He'll be OK." I wasn't sure if I fully believed it or if I just wanted too—badly. "He'll be OK." I hoped.

"Is that your professional or personal opinion?" I knew the Commander wasn't judging, just asking.

I thought it over. "Both. I want it to be true, and I believe it is. He has a certain . . ." I searched for the right word, "strength inside."

"Yes," the Commander said, "he does."

We sat in silence for a while as the miles ticked by. I fell asleep.

Sure enough, the rain had stopped by the time I woke up. Evening had started to fall. I felt the Commander's tension as soon as I woke.

"Where are we?" I asked.

"Hopefully close," he said. "I saw signs for a hospital a mile back. If it's not the right one, we'll have to find other shelter for the night."

We were on the outskirts of a city, or possibly a town, depending on the size requirements to earn the title of city. I'm sure at one time it was heavily populated, but not anymore. Still, groups of people wandered around in the streets. It took another half hour to find the hospital because the Commander had to use side streets and evade infected people several times. I knew the longer we were on the road, the more he worried about being spotted by the Nephilim. I was too. This was the furthest from my hospital I had been in three years.

We spotted the hospital and pulled into a parking garage across from it. The security gate was broken. We drove to the second floor, and the Commander stopped the SUV in an open area where he angled the car toward the exit. He left the keys in the ignition. We got out and surveyed the building. It looked deserted. No security men around the entrances or on the roof and no lights in the windows. Nobody was home as far as we could tell.

"Maybe this is the wrong hospital," I said.

The Commander kept watching for movement and didn't respond. He stood like a statue. Darkness continued to fall. Finally, he said, "We should go in and check it out."

I nodded.

"I can't leave you here alone," he said, "so you'll have to come with me."

"OK." I would feel safer with him anyway.

He retrieved a gun from under the floorboard in the back of the SUV. It looked stranger than any of the hunting guns my brother always used. Duct tape had been wrapped around the handle, and the barrel had been cut short. I looked at him questioningly.

"Just something I've been working on," he said. "It's a modified shotgun. Pistol grip. Modified ammo. Might not work any better, but it's worth a try. I'll at least feel safer with it." He motioned to the trigger with his finger. "Just point and pull."

If he would feel safer with it, than I would too. I nodded and instinctively reached up to rub my necklace between my thumb and finger, a habit I had developed that somehow made me feel safer. I knew it was a nonverbal, self-comforting mechanism, but I had stopped caring. Everyone has something.

The Commander made his way down to the first level. I followed close at his heels. I tried to match his movements. If he moved, I moved. When he stopped, I stopped. He moved more quickly and quietly than I would imagine someone of his size could. I had left the hospital with him before, but we were never alone or this far from help. I felt my heart rate quicken as we reached street level, where the Commander again paused and watched.

Before we moved, the Commander motioned me to pull the hood of my black sweatshirt up over my blonde hair.

"Stay close," he whispered.

I nodded at the back of his head.

We dashed across the street. I stayed so close to the Commander that I almost tripped over his heels. He flattened himself against the wall. I did the same. I felt my core getting warm. Probably more from adrenaline than from exertion. My heart rate was elevated. Our motor oil was wearing off.

The hospital still looked deserted. No lights. No movement. We made our way to the front entrance. The lobby was empty. We watched and waited. Still nothing. We went inside. I stayed close. The Commander smelled of motor oil and sweat. It was a strange combination.

The elevator was dead. We didn't try turning on the lights, but the whole first floor was empty as far as I could see. I followed the Commander to the stairs. We took them one step at a time. Slowly. We inched our way up with the Commander's gun leading the way.

At the second landing, the stairs were blocked with sandbags from floor to ceiling. They smelled like coffee grounds. Someone had been here at some point. The entrance to the second floor was also blocked with sandbags. The Commander pointed. I followed his finger. There was space at the bottom of the bag pile just large enough for a person to crawl through on their belly.

I looked at the Commander. He held up his hand for me to wait. He got down on his stomach and peered through the hole, gun gripped firmly in his hands. I waited.

Eventually, he stood back up and leaned close. I felt his whiskers scratch my face. "Nothing," he whispered. "But someone is here. I'll go first."

He got down to crawl through but turned back. I was scared. He could tell. He smiled a calming smile. "Follow me," he mouthed.

I watched as he laid on his belly and inched through. He was gone. Into the darkness. I strained to hear anything. Nothing. I got down on my belly to look. Nothing but darkness. I couldn't see the Commander. I dared not call out. I waited the moment it took to convince myself I had the nerve to follow and then started to crawl through. I scooted slowly, using both hands and feet to move forward. The strong smell of coffee beans was suffocating underneath the bags.

My hand exited the tunnel first, and I felt a strong hand grasp my arm. I hoped it was the Commander's. I still couldn't see anything. My head and shoulders popped out next and I looked around. I spotted the Commander. It looked like he was asleep. A man stood on each side, grasping his arms. I started to call his name but electricity shot through my body. I was paralyzed. Nothing but pain. Then nothing at all. Darkness took me.

2

I woke up tied to a metal folding chair. My hands were tied behind my back—tight. I could feel the rough rope where it had already chafed the soft skin of my wrist. My ankles were tied even tighter. I couldn't feel my feet.

I looked for the Commander, but I was alone in the room. Sponge ceilings and tile floors. The space had once been a hospital room but was now devoid of any furniture except for my chair. The window was boarded over with plywood. Even the spaces where the wood met was covered with duct tape. There was a lone mirror on the wall, but it wasn't at the right angle for me to see myself. I almost called out, but knew it wouldn't do any good. Whoever had grabbed us was in charge, so I needed to retain whatever control I could over the only thing I could control— myself.

I tested the ropes again. They were too tight to move. Someone wasn't taking any chances. Even my torso and calves were duct taped to the chair. I didn't see any cameras, so I would have to wait until someone came in and realized I was awake. I waited silently.

Hours went by. I figured it had to be close to midnight, but no one came in to turn off the lamp that stood in the corner. I tried to sleep but couldn't. I was thirsty. I was hungry. And I was scared. I almost dozed off a couple times from exhaustion but always jerked back awake. My arms fell asleep. I needed to go to the bathroom but held it. I wondered how long I would have to hold it. I wondered how long I could. I started to cry. I told myself not to, but I couldn't help it any longer. Tears ran down my cheeks, and I couldn't even brush them away.

I had no idea how long it had been when the door finally opened.

A man walked in and knelt down in front of me. He was unremarkable in every way—the kind of guy you would have trouble picking out of a lineup. He waited for me to speak. I tried to compose myself.

"Where is my friend?" I was thinking clearly enough not to call him by name.

"Don't worry about your friend," the guy said. "You just worry about you right now."

I was glad I had stopped crying hours ago, but I could feel the streaks still on my face. "Who are you?" I tried to regain some control.

"My name is not important. I need to know about you. Why are you here?"

"To find someone. I heard about this place from someone who showed up at my hospital."

"Where is your hospital?" he asked.

"South," I answered.

"Where south?"

"I don't know, just south," I said. I wouldn't have told him if I had known.

"I know of no functioning hospitals to the south," he said.

I just stared at him. He wasn't very bright.

But then again, I was the one who was tied up.

He spoke again. "I saw a movie once where a detective said if you have a handful of suspects for a crime and don't know which one did it, then you lock them all up in a cell overnight. In the morning when you return, you look to see which one is sleeping. The guy that's sleeping, he's your guy, because he's the only one who knows he's guilty so he's got no reason to stay awake all night worrying about it."

I realized what he was trying to tell me.

He filled me in anyway. "What I'm saying is this, I need to know if you're infected. You obviously aren't one of the Anakim or you wouldn't have found your way in here. But I need to know if you're a Nephilim. I obviously couldn't just ask so I put you in here and watched you overnight."

I looked for cameras I might have missed. He saw me looking. "No cameras, just one-way mirrors. Low tech." He pointed at the mirror. "If you were a Nephilim, I don't think you would have had such a rough night."

I didn't point out that if I was a Nephilim, I might be smart enough to fake discomfort.

He continued. "Still I can't be a hundred percent sure, so I need you to convince me before I can let you go."

"I can do better than that," I said. "This is a hospital, and I'm a hematologist. I can prove it to you."

3

It took me a while to convince the man to let me prove I wasn't a Neph. He wouldn't untie me, but eventually he brought in a woman who drew blood from my arm. She had trouble finding my vein, but the guy—she called him Zack—wouldn't allow her to loosen the bonds. I talked her through it. She obviously had very little nursing experience.

She brought in a microscope, and they examined my blood. I told them what to look for and explained how Anak manifested in the blood. They knew nothing about the virus. I couldn't imagine how they were still alive. I had her mix my blood with various chemicals and test it. Each time Zack wanted to know what he should expect to see before he let her try the mixture. He was afraid of the blood and put on latex gloves before he picked up the vial to examine it. I talked them both through what to look for, but my patience was wearing thin. I had to go to the bathroom so badly it hurt, and I couldn't feel any of my extremities. I told myself to remain calm for a little longer.

The nurse drew some of his blood to compare with mine. They looked similar.

Finally, he sent the nurse away. I thought he might be about to untie me.

"Do you believe me now?" I asked.

"One more question," he said. He took an inkpad out of his pocket and made a mark on my forehead with his finger. Then he pulled the mirror off the wall. I could see a window into the next room, but I couldn't tell who or what was in that room. He crouched down and held the mirror in front of me. "Tell me what you see," he said.

"I know what you're doing," I said. "As far as I know it's a myth that vampires can't see themselves in mirrors."

"Just tell me what you see."

"This is stupid," I said sharply. My patience was gone. "I've proved to you scientifically that I haven't been infected with the Anak virus. I could feel you draw an X on my forehead so I don't need a mirror. And if I were a Nephilim I would pretend to be dumb enough for you to believe me. Untie me right now!" My voice was a scream. He seemed taken aback by my loss of control. I softened my voice. "I have to go to the bathroom."

He stood in front of me for a moment.

"Finally," he said. "Let's get those ropes off you."

4

They were primarily using the top few floors of the hospital. Only about thirty or so people were living there, and most were afraid to go to the lower levels. There was really just one I was concerned with finding—the coma patient.

They eventually let the Commander out of his bonds, but only after I proved his blood was also clean. It appeared he had an even rougher night than me. His face was bruised and his eye swollen, but he didn't volunteer any information and I didn't ask. He obviously hadn't gotten any sleep either. Zack didn't return the Commander's gun, and with the mood the Commander was in that may have been the wisest move Zack had made in his life.

They fed us a meager breakfast while everyone watched us warily. The people were a mixture of races and ages with one thing in common. None of them looked healthy. They were on edge and keyed up. They were worn down psychologically. Tired from living in fear. Adrenaline receptors fried. I sympathized. I had seen the same in individuals who had arrived at our hospital, but these people were way worse than our group.

We split up after eating. Me to find the patient, the Commander to find what other information he could gather. We met a couple hours later on the top floor to share what we had learned.

I went first. "I found the coma patient. Her name is Eva Lee, and she was on the same flight as Nick Reece."

"You tested her blood?"

"Yes. It's a different blood type than Nick's but otherwise very similar. She has elevated levels of cytotoxic T cells. And they're mutated, similar to Nick's."

"What difference does the blood type make?"

"It only makes a difference for cases where blood needs to be mixed, like during a transfusion. There are four basic blood types: A, B, AB, and O."

"What type is Nick's blood?"

"AB. The same as mine," I said.

"And Eva's?"

"B."

"Is B rare?"

"It's not the most common blood type, but it's not exactly rare either. It's most commonly found in Asian Americans like Eva."

"Does this help or hurt your theory about Nick?"

I thought about it. "I'm not sure yet."

"Is Eva willing to come back with us?"

"Not yet. I'll need to spend some time with her. She feels safe here. But I'll eventually be able to convince her. She's only been awake for a few days, and she already hates this place."

"I don't blame her," the Commander said quietly. "When did she wake up?"

"Four days ago." As I said it, I realized something. That was the same day Nick woke up. I didn't know how I missed that. It could mean nothing, but it could mean a lot. Two people who went into a coma on the same day from the same plane crash don't just happen to wake up on the same day. I needed to find out more.

The Commander had said something, but I was lost in thought and missed it. I asked him to repeat it.

"I learned something interesting about your coma patients as well."

"Yes?" My mind was spinning. What was the link?

"This place had a trauma center. Three years ago, when the outbreak started, there were at least a dozen people in comas that called this place home. Over the last three years, all of them died. Eva is the only one who woke up."

A person dying in a coma was not that uncommon, but still it raised questions. "All of them? Without any testing?"

"Without testing. They all died on their own."

I thought about that. Trying to piece things together in my mind.

"I found one more thing you'll want to know," he said. "The hospital intake form for all the people that were taken to hospitals from Nick and Eva's flight." He pulled a piece of paper from his pocket and handed it to me. "It lists the specific hospital each patient was taken to after they didn't wake up from their coma after a reasonable amount of time."

I looked it over. Four names. Nick Reece. Eva Lee. Beck Hastings. Asher Geere.

Nick's name said Mercy General beside it.

The Commander pointed at the address beside Eva's name. "This is the hospital where we are."

I nodded.

He pointed to another name. Beck. "I think this guy is at the hospital Rachel was at before she came here. Remember she said she had been at two hospitals, both north of us?" He pointed at the address below her name. "This hospital is even further north of us."

I looked at the fourth name. Asher Geere. There was no hospital listed under his name. Instead, a word was written in the space: "Undisclosed." I looked back at the third name. "We should find this Beck Hastings."

"I agree we should find him, but I think I should go alone," the Commander said.

I disagreed. I absolutely didn't want to separate. I told him so.

"You should stay here with Eva. She won't leave with us, so you stay and convince her to come back to our hospital. I'll bring Beck back with me, and we'll all four head home."

The Commander and I usually agreed on the important things, but when we differed, we had an unspoken arrangement that if it was his area of expertise, then we would do it his way. But if it was in my area, then we stuck to mine. I knew that arrangement was why the Commander had risked danger to help me find Eva. So, I also knew I would have to defer to his choice on leaving now. I nodded.

The Commander sensed I needed reassurance. "You'll be safe here. They aren't the brightest group, but they're very careful. They have a good setup. None of the infected will be able to find their way in."

"OK." My fingers found my necklace.

"I better get going. It's almost noon."

"Be careful."

"I will." He pulled his emergency cell phone out of his pocket and held it out. "Here, take this. You know you shouldn't use it unless you absolutely have to."

"No. You should keep it."

"Take it," he said. "I'll be back soon. Take it."

I did.

"Be safe, Al."

He nodded and left. My fingers were still rubbing my necklace.

5

The Commander left the hospital, and I spent the rest of the day trying to gather information. For the most part I was unsuccessful. I was an outsider and everyone was too afraid to talk to me. I ended up spending most of the day with Eva, but since she had only been awake for four days, there was very little she could tell me. She did remember exactly what time she woke up from the coma. She remembered because the first thing she had asked was the time and date. She woke up at 4:37, the same time as Nick.

That couldn't be a coincidence. I wondered what it meant. I had no clue. I had never heard of anything like it before—two people who had gone into a coma at the same time and woke up at the same time.

We sat in the community room drinking coffee. People ignored us. Eva's mind was still trying to grasp what was happening in the world outside.

"Why can't the president or the military do something?" she asked. "They have to have some type of plan, right?"

I pondered how much to tell her. Her mind was still fragile. "As near as we can tell, they never had a chance. It all happened in a matter of hours. All communication, including phones, the Internet, satellites, television, and even radio were shut down first, so by the time the rest of the country realized there was a huge problem, it was already too late."

"But what about the rest of the government? Don't they have an antidote for the virus? Can't they do something?"

"Sweetie, there is no antidote. As far as we know, there is no government anymore." I kept my voice soft and even. "That's why we're trying to figure this thing out. That's why we need you to come back with us to the other hospital. It's much safer there. And I'm working on a solution."

"I'm safe here. They told me that none of the infected have ever gotten in here. They said the infected are too stupid."

"None have gotten in yet, but that doesn't mean they never will." I could tell I was losing the argument. Eva needed to feel safe, and she felt safe here. I changed tactics. "Do you have family, Eva?"

"No, it's just me."

"I'm sorry to hear that." I reached out and touched her hand. "I have one brother. His name is Steven, and he's infected. I'm trying to find a cure to save him. To save everyone who is infected, and I need your help for that."

"Do you think there is a cure?"

"Honestly, I don't know. But I have to try." I was getting through to her.

"How far away is this other hospital?" she asked.

"A few hours south. Al will take us there. We'll be safe going with him."

I could tell I almost had her convinced. I didn't get the chance to finish the job. I heard a commotion behind me, and rough hands grabbed my shoulders.

Someone yelled, "They're here!"

Everybody panicked.

6

A voice I recognized said in my ear, "I knew I couldn't trust you two. He must have let them in." It was Zack's voice. I twisted to get free, but his grip was strong. "Now they're inside."

He dragged me out of the room. His fingers dug hard into my arms. He was stronger than he looked. He pulled me down several flights of stairs to an abandoned floor. It was dark. We passed screaming people, but no one paid us any attention. I briefly wondered if I'd lose Eva, but at that moment I needed to worry about myself.

Zack dragged me backward down a dark hall. I kept trying to pry myself free to no avail.

"What are you doing?" I yelled.

"You're with them. They won't kill me if I have you."

"No! Let me go." I kept struggling. "I'm not with them. I'm not a Nephilim. They'll kill both of us. Let me go! We have to run." He wasn't listening.

He had the Commander's gun in his hand, and he punched me hard in the stomach with it. The wind left me. I choked for air. Gasping as he dragged me along.

"Your friend left, and the infected suddenly find their way in." He was yelling now too. "You're both working with them." I heard a noise behind us. Footsteps were coming fast. I was still trying to catch my breath. Zack kept yelling. "But I have you, so they're not going to get—"

He was suddenly cut off.

His hand left my arm. Torn away violently.

I looked. I saw orange eyes in the darkness. I screamed. But nowhere near as loudly as Zack did. The monster had him.

The Commander's gun had fallen to the floor. I picked it up and ran down the hall. I turned a corner and dashed into a room. Slammed the door behind me. I pulled the curtains open, but the window was covered with plywood. Nailed on. It was probably too high to jump anyway.

I could hear screams from outside the room. Lots of screams. More than just Zack's. I went into the bathroom and huddled down in a corner of the shower. My hand bumped against something in my pocket. The phone. I pulled it out. The Commander had said, "Don't use it unless you have to." I had to. I inserted the battery and held the power button. It lit up, powering on. It took forever.

I pressed the first saved number and waited.

Two rings. Three. Someone picked up.

"Hello?" Xavier.

"Xavier. Hello. Can you hear me?" I spoke softly so the Anakim outside the room wouldn't hear me.

No response.

I tried again. "X, are you there?"

His voice came back mixed with static. "Faith. You shouldn't be calling, they can track you." Static. Then, ". . . try to jam it, but you shouldn't have called. You should have used . . . " Static. " . . . Faith, not the phone."

"Xavier. Xavier!" I cut him off. More loudly than I should have. "They're here. Can you hear me? They're here. You have to give Nick a message for me."

"Who's there, Faith?" Another voice. Bo's.

"The Anakim are here. They're in the hospital. You have to find Nick, give him a message."

I waited. No response. Reception was bad in the bathroom. I tried again, frantically: "Bo! Xavier! Can you hear me? You have to deliver a message for me. You have to give Nick a message for me."

I heard a faint response. I pressed the earpiece closer. The voice spoke again. It was Nick. "I'm here, Doc. What's going on?"

"I was right, Nick. I was right about you. I have to be right about you. I know I am. You have to come find me."

"Where are you, Faith?" Bo again. "Tell me where you are."

Where was I? "I don't know. We came north. You have to trace me, X. Trace this cell."

"Already trying," Xavier said.

"Find me and tell Nick where I am. Nick, you have to find me." I was whispering loudly again. I paused to listen for other sounds. More screaming.

"Where is the Commander?" Bo asked.

"He's gone. He . . ." I started to tell them where, but I heard a noise. A crash. Something was pounding on the door to the room. "They're here," I whispered and covered the phone with my hand. My heart raced, my mouth dry. I held my breath.

More pounding. Anakim? I stuck the phone in my pocket. Slowly, I scooted to the door of the bathroom and closed it with a click. It would further kill my reception, but I had to do it.

I took a breath and tiptoed back into the shower. "Nick?" I whispered.

"I'm here," he whispered back.

"Nick, you have to come find me. We drove north to find the hospital Rachel was at. I'm not sure how far we came. I don't know where I am. Have X trace this call."

"The Nephs are going to be tracing it too, Faith," Xavier said.

"I know," I whispered back. I might not make it that long. "Nick, you have to find me before the Nephilim do. You're the only one that can do it. I was right about you. There are three more like you. The Commander went to find the third. I need you . . ." I trailed off. No sound from the phone. Had I lost them? I waited. Nothing. I tried again. "Nick. You have to come." I heard a sound. The hospital room door opening? I covered the phone again. A scream. A voice in the room. "Dr. Richards, help!" It was Eva's voice.

"Find me," I hissed into the phone. A scream came from the room. I switched the phone off. I took the battery out so the Nephilim couldn't trace me. If it wasn't already too late.

7

I opened the door with the gun firmly in my grasp. It felt awkward. I had never used a gun before. "Just point and pull," the Commander had said.

Eva stood by the open door. She looked panicked. Terrified. Someone materialized behind her from the darkness and I realized what. A Nephilim. So that's how the infected had gotten in. He smiled when he saw me. It was a pleasureless smile.

"Doctor, help me," Eva said. The Neph's fingers dug into her arms. I could see red welts appearing on her china-like skin.

I didn't raise the gun.

He leaned over her like he was going to whisper something in her ear. She kicked violently to no avail. Her foot hit an oxygen can and knocked it over. It rattled on the floor as it came to rest. Eva's eyes were wide. Brown and white. The Nephilim bit her neck, not deep but right over her carotid artery. She screamed. He straightened up and licked his lip. Slowly. Looking at me.

Eva kicked again, and this time the Nephilim shoved her away. She stumbled toward me, and I tried to catch her. The virus would just be entering her blood stream. Not good. She stumbled and fell in a pile at my feet.

The Nephilim took a step toward me. A controlled step. I had nowhere to go. He knew it. Another step. His black pupils drilled into mine. My mind froze. But only for a second. I thought about Nick for some reason. I wasn't sure why. I didn't have time to analyze it. I remembered I had the gun. I raised it. The Neph didn't flinch. He wasn't scared of it. Not good.

I remembered the oxygen can on the floor. I could shoot it. But we might all die. I decided it was worth the risk. It was better than taking my chances with the disease. And it was probably too late for Eva anyway. One more step. Three more between us. I let the gun barrel float down to the canister.

Just point and pull.

I pulled the trigger.

Two things I didn't expect happened. The first was the sound. The gun roared and there was an explosion and then all I could hear was ringing in my ears. The second was the recoil. The gun barrel kicked up, and I missed the canister on the ground. But the spray of ammo hit four other oxygen tanks.

It was the recoil that saved me. The gun kicked so hard it knocked me to the floor. One of the tanks shot over where I had just been standing and lodged into the wall beside an emergency fire hose. Another tank shot straight up through the roof, showering the room in white powder. Probably wreaking havoc on the floor above. The third tank crashed through the window, taking the plywood with it. The last tank took out the Neph at the knees, propelling him backward into the hallway and out of sight.

I lay there stunned, but only for a second. The muzzle flare from the gun had lit a fire. Flames spread quickly through the room fed by the exploding oxygen. I yelled Eva's name. Miraculously, she was unharmed, except for the virus spreading through her body. We both stood and frantically looked for an escape route. The window was now open, but we were several floors up. If jumping didn't kill us, it would at least break our legs. I remembered the fire hose on the wall. Somehow the protective glass was still intact. I looked around for the gun to break the glass. At some point, I had lost my grip on it. I wasn't sure when. It was nowhere to be seen. Lost in the debris. I used my elbow to smash the glass.

I pulled the hose to the window. Eva joined me. She was stronger than I had judged. We were three floors up. No other options. I wrapped the hose around my wrist and Eva did the same. We held onto each other with our free hands.

We scooted out the window together.

We fell fast. The unwinding fire hose slowed us a little, but not much. I realized we might die from the fall after all. Then we hit the end of the hose's reach. We jerked as it topped out. The hose tore into my hand, squeezing it until I thought it was broken. All our weight pulled at my arm. We bottomed out, and I felt our weight release as the hose rebounded slightly. I let go. Eva did too.

We were only about five feet from the ground, but it felt like a mile. We landed in a pile, and it took me a moment to realize I was still alive.

I stood on unsteady legs and pulled Eva up beside me. She was wobbly. The virus was spreading through her system. The faster we moved, the more her heart would pump, and the faster the virus would spread. For her sake, I knew we shouldn't run. But we had to get away. We hobbled away from the hospital toward the neighborhood behind it.

I looked back at the hospital. Flames licked at the windowsill outside the room we'd escaped from. Smoke billowed out too. I saw a shape materialize. The Nephilim. Standing framed in the window.

We ran.

8

We hurried farther into the subdivision. Eva wasn't doing well. She leaned into me as we moved. I hurried her along, but I knew the virus had spread through her bloodstream by now.

I thought about leaving her. It would be safer for me. And it was possibly my only chance of survival. I decided to stay with her. My theory was about to be put to the test. Would she become an Anakim? Or turn into a Nephilim? Or would the virus eventually be too much for her body? Would I be forced to watch her die?

I had to stay with her. I had to know. So we ran.

Eventually, she couldn't keep running any more. So we walked. Her footsteps dragged, but still we walked. My ears were still ringing. I couldn't hear anything, so I wasn't sure if she could either, but I encouraged her anyway. Quietly, in case there were Anakim within earshot. I hadn't seen any outside of the hospital, but it was only a matter of time till more showed up. We kept walking. I wasn't sure where we were going. Except away from the hospital.

The ringing in my ears grew monotonous. I was on edge and afraid we would walk right into a group of infected. Darkness was falling, making it harder to see. I had to find somewhere for us to wait out the night. I found an abandoned house and dragged Eva inside with me. I bolted the door behind us. I was exhausted. My body had taken a beating in the last twenty-four hours. I used the last of my strength to shove a desk in front of the door. It probably wouldn't even slow them if they found us, but it made me feel a little better. Very little.

I took Eva to the back of the house and laid her on the bed. There was running water, so I placed cool, wet towels on her. She was fading in and out. Like she had a fever. I was surprised she wasn't already gone. I knew she would be soon. I stayed awake nursing her as long as I could but eventually fell asleep next to her.

I woke up well over twelve hours later. It was noon or later. Eva was still sleeping. She was pale but alive. Her body was doing its best to fight the virus. She was much stronger than I would have guessed. I replaced the towels and let her sleep.

I couldn't find any food in the kitchen. The cupboards were bare, and there was nothing in the refrigerator. I decided to try the house next door. It was locked, but I found a spare key under a rock in the flowerbed. People were predictable, if nothing else. The key was rusty, but it worked. I went inside. The home was in disarray. It looked like the owners had left in a hurry and had a hard time figuring out what was important enough to take.

Most of the furniture didn't make the cut, but the walls were bare of the usual family pictures and artwork. I checked the kitchen. The food didn't make the cut either, but everything in the refrigerator was rancid. I gagged and shut the door. I checked the closet of a child's room and found some Halloween candy scattered on the floor. I took what I could and headed back to Eva.

As I crossed the lawn, I realized my hearing was back. That was good. Unfortunately, I noticed because I heard something very bad. The sound of a motorcycle in the distance. The Nephilim usually rode motorcycles. We didn't have much time. We had to get moving.

I woke Eva, and we ate hurriedly. She didn't have an appetite, but I made her eat anyway. We both needed the energy from a sugar rush. Eva was incoherent but able to move. We moved.

I still didn't have a plan. All I knew was to get further away from the hospital and the sounds of the Nephilim. Hopefully, I could look for a car that worked. It was unlikely but possible. Eva still couldn't run, but we moved as fast as possible. We started to see pockets of Anakim down the street. Neither of us spoke. Not even a whisper. Eva's slow movement may have helped. The Anakim in the distance didn't bother us. I knew we wouldn't be safe for long.

We continued deeper into the neighborhood, but Eva was having more and more trouble. I knew her heart was pumping hard as her blood thickened. Her head started to roll from side to side. She wouldn't make it much further.

I saw some of the infected down the street. I turned the corner before they spotted us. I kept us close to the houses for cover. Eva moved slower than ever. I could hear the Anakim on the next street over. My hand reached for my necklace. We weren't going to escape in time. We were about to be trapped. We needed to hide again. I tried one door. Locked. I couldn't risk making noise by breaking in. We hobbled toward the next one.

An Anakim appeared down the street. I pulled Eva down behind some shrubs. My heart pounded. We were trapped. It was only a matter of time. I thought about Nick again. I liked the thought. I held my breath as the Anakim passed down the street. I had one hand over Eva's mouth. Just in case. The other pinched my charm.

Then I noticed something. At first, I thought I was imagining it. There was a light in the window across the street. It flashed on and off. Then again. One last flash and it went dark. Strange. Someone else was alive. But it could be a trap. A Nephilim. I had to take my chances. Eva was fading fast. I raised my hand and waved at the open window. A hand waved back.

I checked the street. It was empty. Both ways. I pulled Eva up on her feet, and we stumbled toward the light. Eva's legs dragged. I supported her as best I could.

I glanced to my left. Anakim. I dragged Eva as fast as I could. My pulse raced. I looked again. Orange eyes. They had spotted us. We had no protection. Even if we made it to the house, we were dead. I stole one more peek. Too far. We'd never make it.

I moved fast.

The Anakim moved faster.

Book II
The Four

Part II
Nick

1

I wasn't sure exactly where I was going, but I knew Faith was north so I headed north. The hospital faded in the distance behind me. The only home I had known since waking. The motorcycle had a full tank of gas. I expected as much from the Commander. The miles ticked by. It was strange. The whole world looked empty. Deserted. I stayed on the highway and kept the bike wide open for mile after mile.

Occasionally, I would see a town from the interstate. Usually, there were people wandering around. Anakim I assumed. Each time I zoomed by without slowing; I didn't want to find out for sure. I had gotten a late start from the hospital, and the later in the day it grew, the more people I saw outside. I figured soon I would have to find a place to hide out for the night and regroup. I kept my eyes open.

Twice I saw other vehicles on the road. Both were headed in the opposite direction. The first was a red sedan, carrying three people. They drove frantically. I didn't see them in time to hide. They saw me but didn't slow. They had the pedal to the metal and roared past. Uninfected humans I guessed. I hoped. They probably had the same thought about me.

The next vehicle I saw was a motorcycle just like mine. All black. I was coming over a hill so I saw the rider before he saw me. I reacted quickly and pulled off the road behind a road sign. I downshifted and hit the brakes so fast I lost traction on the gravel. The bike went down, and I bailed, hands over my head, instinctively protecting my face. Fortunately, I laid it down on dirt. I slid for a second then came to a stop. Unhurt. The bike slid further and stopped the same way, scuffed but unharmed. I hoped. I lay there and listened for the sound of the other bike passing. It did without slowing. I breathed a sigh of relief and brushed myself off. Got back on the bike and continued north.

After that I kept the bike at a steady pace. Not quite as fast. I kept a wary lookout for other vehicles. The sun started to dip below the horizon. I passed several more residential areas, but none of them looked inviting enough to spend the night. I knew I had to find somewhere soon. I pushed on.

The air cooled down. I thought about stopping and sleeping on the side of the road but was afraid a Neph might drive by. I couldn't chance it. A road sign promised a town up ahead. Only two exits, so it was small. That was good. I passed the first exit without taking it. One more mile to the next. I watched as the buildings passed. There were a couple restaurants, a grocery store, a pet store, and a hardware warehouse. As well as two gas stations. No movement. I figured it would be my best option. I was hungry and tired.

I was so distracted with finding a place to bed down that I completely missed seeing the oncoming motorcycle until it was too late. Another bike just like mine crested the hill in front of me. Driving straight and steady. Head forward. It was a Neph for sure. I saw it too late to hide. My heart rate spiked. My body flooded with adrenaline.

I kept the bike steady. Stared straight ahead. My mind begged me to speed up. To run away. I refused. I kept the bike's speed even. No faster. No slower. I passed the exit without flinching. My heart pounded in my throat. As he passed, he looked over. I knew I had to meet his gaze. I tried to keep my face expressionless. Emotionless. No fear.

He didn't blink. I didn't either. He continued on. I resisted the urge to turn and look. I also resisted accelerating. I stared straight ahead and kept the bike at a steady speed until I cleared the next hill. Until the sound of the other bike faded into the evening. It finally did. I went one more mile before I slowed. A bead of sweat dripped from my nose.

Against every instinct, I turned the bike around and drove back to the exit. I figured if they had some type of sentry system, then it was better if I was in an area that had already been covered. I pulled into the gas station. I had to figure out how to turn the pump on manually, but the first station was empty so I tried the other. I topped the bike off then searched for food. Nothing. I grabbed two bottles of motor oil and left.

All the buildings in the shopping center were covered in dust. The windows were all dark. I left my bike hidden in an alley between two stores. I checked the restaurants but found nothing promising, so I made my way to the grocery store. It looked deserted. The windows had the clean look of freshly installed glass, and I could see canned goods inside. The place looked spotless except for few dark smudges that stained the concrete in front of the building. Something felt off.

I was starving, but I scouted the building, looking for a less obvious entrance. They were all boarded and chained except the front. I poked my head around the corner. It was deserted. I waited. Eyes and ears open for anything strange. Darkness continued to fall. Finally, I decided I couldn't wait any longer. I made my way to the door. Slowly. I listened for any noises. I heard nothing. I saw no one.

I had just reached for the handle when I heard a sound behind me. A growl.

2

I turned. A dog stood ten feet away, teeth bared. I realized I hadn't seen any animals since I woke up. His growl continued. Low and threatening. I almost laughed. After all I had seen, a dog was hardly a threat.

"Scram," I hissed and turned back to the door. As I reached for the handle, his growl deepened.

He was crouched low on his front legs. He looked to be some type of shepherd mix—a mutt.

"Scram," I hissed again. "I found it first."

I put my hand on the door handle. I felt the dog lunge forward. I spun to face him. I wasn't about to get bit in the backside. He was five feet away now, teeth still bared. I could see his gums. I stared him down. He didn't continue forward, and his growl stopped, but his teeth were still showing.

I took a quick glance around for danger. There wasn't anyone in sight. I felt bad for the animal. Who knew the last time he ate.

"Fine," I said. "There's plenty for both of us. Calm down."

I reached for the door one last time. The dog lunged forward. I briefly wondered if animals could be infected. I didn't think so. His teeth clamped around my calf. Not hard. I spun, and he lost his grip. I kicked at him but missed. He was quick. I quietly cursed him. He growled at me again. Still low. I hoped he wouldn't start barking. He lunged at me again but pulled up short when I cocked my foot back. He scampered backward.

I was hungry. I was also mad. More mad than hungry now. Stupid mutt. He lunged at my other leg, and I was quicker this time. I kicked him in the side. He yelped. High pitched.

He growled again, louder now, but I no longer cared. I had to get out of the open. The stupid dog would draw attention. I headed away from the grocery store. His growl lessened but didn't go away. He followed me about ten feet back. If I turned, he paused but didn't stop tracking me. I heard sounds from the other side of the complex. I snuck into one of the empty restaurants and hid. The stupid dog disappeared behind a dumpster. Probably looking for nonexistent scraps. He had ruined both our dinners. I checked my calf. There were red marks, but luckily he hadn't broken the skin.

The restaurant was filthy, but empty. It would work for the night. I took the florescent light bulbs from the ceiling fixtures. I laid them out on the floor just inside the entrance as a makeshift alarm system. If anyone entered they would crush the bulbs and the sound would wake me. It wouldn't be much warning, but it was the best I had.

I found an old newspaper to sleep under and curled up on a booth in the back. I went to sleep with my stomach growling louder than that stupid mutt.

I woke to the sound of screams.

3

I startled awake. The screams were real. They came from outside. I quietly crept to a window. It was hard to see through the dust, but I found a relatively clean spot. It was foggy, but I couldn't risk being seen.

I saw a red car. Possibly the one from the road yesterday. I couldn't be sure. There was also a black Jeep. I counted eight people. Half of them were male, half female. Five of them moved like Nephilim. Calculated and in control. They were outside the grocery store looking in. Three of them moved frantically. Still human. And uninfected for now. I could see them just inside the store. All of them were screaming at the sight of the Nephs.

Three Nephs went inside. Two stayed outside by the door. The humans scattered. One of them was caught quickly. A girl. She screamed as one of the vampires leaned over her neck. She went limp. One of the other humans crashed into the glass window, trying to escape. The glass fractured as his body crashed through. He was probably dead before the Nephilim got to him. Two other Nephs caught the last human. They held one arm each and dragged her out of the store. One of the guards walked up and leaned over her. She went limp for a moment. They held her up. Her eyes turned orange for a moment and then went flat. They let her go, and she wandered away.

I realized I was barely breathing. I didn't move. The window was dark, but I didn't want any movement to give away my presence. I waited. The Nephilim were discussing something.

One pointed toward the window. Another one pulled out a cell phone and spoke into it. I couldn't hear what he was saying. As he was talking, two of them climbed back into the black Jeep and drove away.

I saw movement on the ground. The first girl who had been bitten stood up. She looked around slowly. She no longer looked scared or frantic. She said something, but I couldn't tell what it was. One of the Nephs smiled. It was the first time I had seen any emotion from any of them. The smile looked out of place. Unnatural.

The guy with the phone said something to the group. They nodded. Two motorcycles stood by the entrance of the shopping center. All four Nephs walked over and got on. The two guys on the front, the girls behind them. They gunned the bikes and shot off down the interstate.

I stared at the broken window of the grocery store and realized what had happened. The food was a trap. That's why the front window was clean. The Nephilim must have had the door hooked up to a silent alarm. The stupid dog had saved my life.

Another thought occurred to me. Now would be my only chance to snag some food. It only took a second to talk myself into believing it was a good idea. Then I was moving, and it was too late to stop. I was too hungry. I peeked out the door of the restaurant to see if there were any Anakim in sight. I didn't see any. I listened. I couldn't hear any. I needed to take my chance now before the Nephs returned to reset the trap. Which could be any moment.

I darted across the parking lot. The glass from the window crunched under my shoes. I didn't use the door in case whatever alarm they had set up was still functioning. I went in through the broken window. Cans were spilled all over the floor. I ignored them. Instead I scooped up a bunch of the ones stacked neatly on the shelves by the window. A few were opened and partially eaten. The humans had at least gotten one last meal before the Nephilim arrived. I left the open ones as well. I filled my arms with as much as I could carry. I wanted to go back for more but wasn't sure I had time.

I took my loot and ran for the home improvement warehouse. I left it inside and hurried back out for one other thing. The motorcycle. No way they would miss seeing it when they came back. Even a quick search would discover it. I rolled it into the warehouse and hid it under a tarp. I grabbed a bag of dirt and dusted the door and walkway to erase my tracks as I went inside. The dust would also be useful to show me if anyone came looking for me.

I took my stash deep into the building and sat down with my back to a lumber pile. I pried several cans open and ate fast. Spam. Protein. I felt on edge. I jumped at every noise, real or imagined. I knew the Nephilim would be back at any moment to fix the window and reset the trap.

Halfway through the third can, I heard a noise. I froze and waited. Seconds later, the dog stuck his nose around the corner. He wasn't growling this time. I wondered how he had gotten in. He watched me. Somehow, I knew he wouldn't bark. I took a little mystery meat and held it out to him. He just stared at it. I moved closer. He backpedaled. He was unsure of me. We had an uneasy truce, but we weren't friends. I set an open can down and went back to my spot and continued eating. He moved a step closer and watched me. He made no move toward the open can.

"Go ahead. It's for you," I said. He just watched me. "Fine, suit yourself." I continued eating.

His eyes followed my hand motions. Every time I took a bite he watched. He looked hungry. I scooted the can a little closer to him with my foot. I motioned toward it. "Eat. That's for you."

He appeared to understand what I said. Slowly, he lowered his head and started eating. He never looked away from me. His eyes watched me warily as he ate. He ate fast. Really fast. I finished my can of Spam and opened two more. One for each of us. I set his can down a little closer to my leg than the last one. He waited until I started eating before he inched closer and started on the second can.

I was full, but I opened one more can for him. This one I sat right beside me. He waited before he came over. He just watched me watching him. Examining me. He was smart. Finally, he moved beside me and started eating. He was really hungry. I didn't touch him while he ate, but eventually when he finished and raised his head, I reached out to pet him. He let me. I moved slowly so I wouldn't startle him. He was definitely some type of shepherd mix. One eye was blue.

We sat like that for a while. He seemed to enjoy the company. I wondered what terrible things his mismatched eyes had seen. Eventually, he got comfortable with me and stopped skirting away every time I flinched. When I crawled toward the front of the warehouse to check the situation outside, he followed me.

Two Nephs were cleaning up the store and replacing the glass. I noticed there were no dog tracks in the dirt at the entrance. Again, I wondered how the mutt got in. I snuck back deep into the building and waited. The dog kept me company.

4

When I next checked outside it was almost noon. The glass front of the grocery store was as good as new. With plenty of food in sight for the next unsuspecting hungry human who wandered by. The dead body was gone. Just one more dark spot on the concrete. There wasn't a Neph or Nak in sight. I remembered Van saying the Commander liked to travel at noon. I figured I should follow suit.

There were tracks in the dust outside the door. The Nephilim had searched the area. I was lucky. I rolled the motorcycle out from its hiding place and prepared to continue north. I found a backpack to keep my leftover canned food in and slung it over my back. I hated to leave the dog. He followed me out of the warehouse and watched as I prepared to leave.

I bent down and patted his head. "I never told you thank you. You saved my life yesterday. Thanks. I owe you and I wish there was more I could do to pay you back, but this is the best I have." I opened a can of food and left it for him. He ignored it.

He watched me mount the bike with his mismatched eyes. "Good luck," I said.

I started the bike and pulled out of the parking lot. He followed me at a trot. I pulled onto the interstate and twisted the throttle. He ran behind me for as long as he could but eventually he couldn't keep up. I kept going and told myself not to look back. He ran until he couldn't and then he slowed to a trot. But he didn't stop trying. I topped the hill and then didn't look back. I gunned the motorcycle until the wind bit my face.

I continued for almost a minute before I stopped. I knew I shouldn't, but I couldn't help myself. I turned around.

The dog had just topped the hill as I came back over the next one. He continued toward me. When I pulled up next to him, he sat. His tongue hung from his mouth. It had a black spot on it.

I smiled. "Well, you just don't give up, do you?"

I imagined he would tell me that was how he had managed to stay alive this long.

I guided the bike back toward the shopping center but kept it at a slow pace. Second gear. The dog followed behind at a trot. I wasn't sure what I was going to do, but I would figure something out. I couldn't leave him behind. But I needed to work fast. I was really pushing my luck by returning.

I found what I needed at the pet store. A dog crate. I took the top off and tied it onto the back of my bike with some rope. It looked awkward, but it would serve its purpose. The dog watched me work. I tried to hurry.

"What do you think?" I asked him when I finished.

He didn't respond.

I shrugged. "I guess you're going to need a name if you're coming with me. Do you have a name?"

Again, he didn't respond. Stupid dog.

"Fine. How about Blue? Any problems with the name Blue?"

He just stared. "Blue it is then. Get up here, Blue." I pointed at the makeshift ride. He tilted his head but didn't move.

Blue was medium-sized and I guessed about sixty pounds when I picked him up and set him on the open crate. He didn't resist. I hoped he would stay put once we hit the open road. That would be his choice, I guess.

I popped the motorcycle into gear and headed north. He seemed content to watch as I drove. He stayed put. I opened the bike up wide. There was no way I would be mistaken for a Nephilim with a dog strapped to the back of my bike. I was really pushing my luck. But Blue had saved my life. The least I could do was return the favor.

We headed north. Toward the red circle on Xavier's map. I hoped I wasn't too late.

5

Just inside the red circle on the map, I passed a sign for a hospital. How many hospitals could be in a three-mile radius? It had to be the right one. I followed the directions it gave and could tell something was amiss as soon as I arrived. I slowed the bike to a crawl within sight of the building. The dog growled behind me, so low I almost didn't hear him. He hopped off his perch and trotted away. I almost yelled at him but changed my mind. Instead, I followed him on the bike. I figured he probably had a better nose for danger than I did.

I was right. The dog led me behind a building, where I stowed the bike. We peeked back around the corner and watched. Dozens of Anakim appeared. They looked to be headed toward the hospital. I felt the breeze and realized the dog had led us downwind of them. No wonder he had survived so long. I kept watching. More and more of the infected wandered by, and they all headed in the same general direction. The hospital.

I heard a motorcycle. A lone rider appeared. A Nephilim. He zigzagged behind the infected, channeling them. Herding them. Pushing them toward the hospital. The Anakim were still in their hibernation state, but if there were any humans at the hospital, the Anakim wouldn't stay that way for long. There were hundreds of them. One got loose and started to wander our direction. Blue scooted backward. I didn't.

The Neph noticed he had lost one. He gunned the bike and cut him off, much like a sheepherder would do. The stray was directed back toward the group. They continued toward the hospital.

I tried to figure out what to do. I had to find Faith somehow. But if she was still in the hospital, then it might already be too late. I decided to circle around and try the back of the building. But I would have to leave the bike. The Nephilim might hear it.

I turned and trotted away from the hospital. The dog followed warily. I made a large semicircle and came at the hospital from the back, toward the residential side. I moved as quickly as I could. I assumed the Neph had gathered every infected soul for miles and the way would be clear. I hoped so anyway.

The hospital looked even worse from the reverse side. Plywood was torn away and windows broken. The wall around a window on the third floor was black from an explosion or fire. A fire hose dangled from the window. It was flat. Unused.

A couple twisted bodies lay on the ground outside the hospital. Not Faith's, I hoped. Through the windows I saw a few people wandering around. Whatever had happened here was over now. I was too late. The Neph herded more of the infected toward the hospital to destroy anything that might be left, which couldn't be much.

I retreated into a neighborhood to regroup and figure out my next play. There was no way anyone had survived in the hospital. Faith was gone. I needed to come up with a new plan. I was on my own. Just the dog and me.

6

I broke into a house and made myself at home. I had left the backpack with the bike, but I found an unopened can of peanuts and a couple cans of tuna in the pantry that Blue and I ate. I was halfway through the second can when I realized something. The only time I had seen the Nephilim use the Anakim was when I was trapped in the house with the Commander, Bo, and Van. They had used the infected to flush us out when they didn't know where we were. That led to another thought.

The Nephilim on the bike had been herding the Anakim toward the hospital, and I had assumed they were using them to kill anyone left alive. That couldn't be right. There were already infected people in the hospital, so why bring more? Unless someone had escaped and the Nephs were using the Anakim to flush them out.

Faith? Had she escaped? Unlikely. But possible. If she did manage to get out, the only place to hide would have been this neighborhood.

I dropped the can of tuna mid bite and sprinted to the front of the house. Sure enough, Anakim filtered down the street. I was right. The Neph had pushed them past the hospital into the residential area. I ran to the back of the house and exited the back door without bothering to close it behind me. The dog followed as I sprinted from yard to yard, heading deeper and deeper into the neighborhood. A couple times I had to double back at the sight of a Nak. Blue always spotted them before I did and let out his low growl. His keen sense of smell was coming in handy, and I learned to listen more for his growl than for the sounds of the infected.

We jumped fences and broke though shrubs, making our way deeper into the neighborhood. Blue was a great jumper, but twice I had to stop to help him over fences that were too tall. I hated getting so far away from my motorcycle but didn't have a choice.

I figured we had to be almost a half mile away from where we started before we stopped to rest. Blue didn't need it, but I did. I found a house that looked safe and broke in. The front door was locked but the side door already had a broken lock. We went in, and I barricaded the door after us. The place had been looted. Broken furniture everywhere. I pulled Xavier's map out and guessed at our position. If I was right, we were further from the bike than I thought. Blue did a sweep of the house with his nose but didn't growl. After his inspection, I figured this place to be as good as any to hole up and come up with a new plan. I still needed to find Faith. If she was alive. But I had no idea where to start. She could be anywhere.

I heard a sound outside. Blue growled. I crept over to the window and looked out. A group of Anakim was coming down the street. Unfocused. Wandering. My pulse raced. I watched as they wandered along. Neither fast nor slow. Several disappeared from sight. More appeared. I ducked low and crawled around broken furniture to a different window to get a better view. I stayed out of sight.

Blue understood the danger. He crouched low and crawled behind me. Also staying out of sight. I stole a peek from my new vantage point. More Anakim wandered by. I held my breath. I noticed something else.

Two people who didn't move like the infected crouched low beside a house across the street. Two women. The Anakim hadn't seen them. Yet. They were trying to get into a house. One of the two was having trouble moving and required help from the other to walk. She stumbled a lot. The healthy one tried a door. It was locked. She didn't try to break in. I watched as they stumbled to the next house. Also locked. I wanted to attract their attention but there was nothing I could do. An Anakim wandered by, and the women hid in some bushes. The Nak moved on. I waited. So did they.

Blue didn't make a sound. He stayed crouched—every muscle tense. I felt the same way. I tried to think of some way to help them hide.

The flashlight. The flashlight from the hospital was still in my back pocket. I pulled it out and checked to make sure the coast was clear before slowly opening the dusty curtain a bit. The pair was straight across from me. I eased back from the window so I was deep in the room and flicked the beam on and off. Fast. Toward the ceiling so the light could only be seen with a direct line of sight. I did it again. On and off. Once more.

I crawled to the window. There was movement from the bushes. I saw a hand wave. They had seen my signal. I checked again to see if the street was clear. No Anakim in sight. But I knew they were close. We would have to hurry. I quietly slid the window open and motioned the pair to come over. The bush separated, and the duo slowly made their way across the street. I motioned them to hurry, but the sick one slowed them down. The other one was helping her along. They were both a mess. The helper finally looked up. Our eyes met. It was Faith.

I motioned her to hurry. I looked down the street. Several Anakim appeared. They were still unfocused. So far, they hadn't noticed the pair who had just crossed the street. My pulse spiked. If the Anakim saw them, we were all dead. The pair slowly crossed the lawn. Faith's partner was an Asian girl who looked ghostly. Sick. Her head hung limply.

I silently willed them on. *Faster!* I looked toward the Anakim. One moved our way. Faith must have sensed it. She started to trot, dragging the other girl. I leaned out the window and urged them forward. Behind me I heard Blue growl. I knew we were in trouble.

An Anakim appeared from the other side of the street. Orange eyes. We were in big trouble. I had to get the women inside. I reached out and grabbed the Asian girl. Faith pushed her up from below. She was in. Faith grabbed the windowsill and pulled upward. I grabbed her wrist to help. There were now two Anakim with orange eyes. Closing in fast. Faith wasn't going to make it. Her feet scrambled against the brick siding, looking for traction. She had a white-knuckle grip on the ledge. She looked into my eyes. I saw stark fear. I let go of her wrist.

I reached down and picked up a broken table leg. The two Anakim were less than ten feet away. I wasn't quite sure what I was doing until I had done it.

I crouched on the windowsill for a split second.

Then I jumped.

7

I snarled as I jumped. A guttural sound that came out involuntarily.

Four orange eyes glared back at me. Pools of anger and hatred.

I clutched the table leg in my hand like a battle-ax. It was the ultimate game of chicken.

My feet hit solid ground, and I knew I was dead. I landed face-to-face with a nightmare. Two living, breathing monsters.

I almost bumped noses with the closest one. I expected to feel pain as they tore into me. I expected a quick, excruciatingly painful death. But something else happened. He drew back. It was a subtle movement, but it registered in my mind that I had never seen an Anakim move backward before. Ever. For anything.

The second one did the same thing. He flinched.

Neither Anakim moved forward; instead they backpedaled. One tripped over his feet and fell. The other scooted away from me in a trembling shuffle. I saw something in their eyes I had never seen there before. Fear.

The words were out of my mouth before I knew what I was saying. Before I even knew I was talking. All my pent-up fear and rage spewed out at once. "You think everyone should be afraid of you?" I spat it at the one on the ground. He struggled to get away. "You think you're the one to fear? You think it's you?" My voice was iron. "It's not you, it's me!"

He ran.

I gripped the chair leg, breathing hard. Angry from living in fear. Angry from having to sneak around in silence. Angry from seeing people hurt. I walked to the middle of the street, still carrying my club. Several Anakim watched me, all with orange eyes. I took a deep breath and yelled as loudly as I could. Deep and long. "IT'S MEEEEE!"

They scattered.

8

I went back into the house knowing the rules had changed. The Anakim were afraid of me.

Faith tried to make the other girl comfortable on the floor. She looked really sick. I saw a red mark on her neck and guessed why. Faith was a mess, her blonde hair tousled and her face dirty. Somehow, she still managed to look beautiful.

Our eyes met. "Thank you," she whispered.

I nodded.

"Did you know they would be afraid of me?" I asked.

"No." As she talked she wiped the other girl's face with a wet towel. "I knew you were special. I just didn't know how."

Special. I liked the sound of the word on her lips. Especially referring to me.

"Who is she?" I asked.

"Do you recognize her?"

I looked closer. "No. Should I?"

"She was on your flight. She woke up from her coma five days ago at the exact same time you did. Her name is Eva Lee."

"She was bitten by a Neph." Not really a question, but Faith nodded anyway.

"Is she going to turn?" I asked.

"I'm not sure. Her body is fighting the infection. I've never seen anyone last this long. Her blood has some of the same markers as yours."

I heard a noise outside. "We shouldn't stay here. The Nephs will find us eventually. They might already know we're here."

"I know," she said.

"What happened to the Commander? Where is he? Is he alive?"

"I'm not sure. He left yesterday to find another guy from your flight. Beck Hastings?"

I shrugged. I didn't recognize the name.

"We were supposed to wait at the hospital for him. He's coming back for us. To take us back home to Mercy."

I realized she didn't know about Mercy General being overrun. "I have bad news, Faith . . . home is gone." I told her about Pete, how he had tricked us to get inside the hospital. How he wasn't really dead.

Tears filled Faith's eyes. I didn't tell her about Steven. I just told her Pete let the other Anakim inside. But she was smart. She knew I wasn't telling her something.

"Steven?" she asked.

"I don't know."

She looked down and wiped the sweat off Eva's forehead. Her shoulders trembled. I let her cry. She asked about several other people, but I always gave her the same answer. I didn't know. It was mostly true.

When she turned back to me she looked lost. White streaks ran down her face where the tears had cleaned a path. "What are we going to do now?"

"Survive." I said it with more courage than I felt.

Her emerald-green eyes peered into mine, searching for reassurance. She blinked. Her eyelashes brushed a tear free, and I knew I'd do anything to keep my promise.

9

Our plan was to hook up with the Commander. That meant we had to go back to the hospital and wait for him to show up.

I carried Eva over my shoulder, and Faith stayed close on my heels. Blue followed about ten steps back. He didn't seem to like Eva very much. I listened for his growl, but he was quiet. None of us spotted any infected. I wondered if we were lucky, or if they had some way of communicating with each other and the word was out on me. Either way, we arrived at the hospital without incident.

Faith hid Eva behind a concrete pillar in the parking garage across the street, and I went to check out the hospital alone. I wondered if the Commander had come and gone already. Possibly. Or possibly he was dead. There was nothing to do but wait and see if he showed up.

I did a lap around the hospital. It looked the same as it had earlier in the day, with one notable exception. The broken windows had been fixed. They were covered with plywood like all the others on the upper floors. My guess was there were Anakim trapped inside, left there by the Nephilim for anyone who might come back. From what I knew now, they liked to set traps.

I pondered how to warn the Commander. He was smart enough to sneak back into the hospital without me spotting him. I couldn't risk him going in. I had to think of a sign he would recognize but the Nephs wouldn't.

The delivery dock at the back of the hospital gave me an idea. A truck. I remembered the conversation between the

Commander and Hector at the food warehouse. Hector told the Commander the semis were wired to burn if he got compromised. I needed to find a semi. And something that would burn.

Before I left on a scouting trip, I helped Faith and Eva hide in an abandoned van in the parking garage. The dog wanted to come with me, but I told him to stay and watch the girls. He tilted his head to one side, as if trying to understand, and I took that as agreement. I don't think he liked it, but he stayed.

Finally, I found what I needed at a gas station about a mile away. The truck was a small U-Haul box truck filled with furniture but out of gas. Whoever had been driving didn't get the chance to refill it. I did it for them. Before I left the station, I hosed everything in the back of the truck with gasoline. I figured the furniture would make good kindling.

It did.

I rejoined Faith and her fading patient. We watched the truck blaze and waited for the Commander.

Unfortunately, the Nephs showed up first.

10

They came with the darkness. Nephilim of all shapes and sizes. Male and female. They came in trucks and on bikes. There were at least fifty of them. More than I had ever seen in one place before. Something was going on. And it wasn't good.

We watched from the parking garage. They piled out of the vehicles. The light from the burning truck danced on their expressionless faces. They promptly put the fire out. Darkness reigned.

Half of them disappeared into the neighborhood where we had been only hours earlier. The rest of them waited. We did too. To move now would be suicide. There were too many eyes that might spot us. Eva was in the van, still unable to move. Faith crouched beside me watching. Blue had disappeared, probably under a vehicle somewhere. Or gone already. He was smarter than we were.

Faith tapped my shoulder. I looked over and saw the steel back in her eyes. She motioned toward the Nephilim and then put up both her hands, fingers wide. Ten. She pulsed them once. Twenty. Again. Thirty. Then only three fingers on one hand. The other one still had five showing. Thirty-eight.

I looked back at the Nephs. They were milling around, waiting on something. Or someone. Thirty-eight of them.

I looked back at Faith. She lowered one finger. Thirty-seven. Another finger. Thirty-six.

I looked back to the Nephilim who were still milling around. Then at Faith again. One hand was fisted. The other had only two fingers showing. I didn't understand. I shrugged. She leaned close—so close I felt her soft lips on my ear.

"There are fewer." She pointed at the Nephs again.

I did a quick count. Twenty-eight. I realized what Faith was trying to tell me. They were disappearing. Melting into the darkness. Spreading out. Searching for us? Searching for me?

We had to move. We didn't have a choice anymore. They would soon find us.

I hauled Eva from the van and threw her over my shoulder again. She was delirious. Moaning. Faith tore a piece of cloth from her shirt and gagged her mouth. It was our only option. I looked around for Blue, but he was long gone. Smart dog.

We made our way to the other side of the parking structure. I tried to walk quietly, but my footsteps echoed off the concrete. I winced at every noise I made. Eva was light, but carrying her was awkward. Again, Faith followed closely behind. She moved noiselessly.

We arrived at the stairs, but we had moved too late. A Nephilim was right below us. She paced the street for a moment, peering out into the darkness. She hadn't spotted us.

She took a few steps and paused. After an eternity, she moved a few steps the other direction and paused, waiting on something. Her back was to us. I willed her to walk into the night. She stopped pacing, and her breath hung in the cool air for a moment. I thought she might leave. She didn't. Instead another Neph joined her. It was a man built like a bulldozer. They stood together for a moment, but I couldn't tell if they spoke. They were both armed.

Eva grew heavy.

A third woman joined the group. Dark hair. Also armed. The three of them turned and started up the stairs.

My mind raced for another way to escape. I scooted backward so the Nephs wouldn't spot me as they mounted the stairs to the first floor. They arrived on the first landing, and one of them stayed at the stairwell. The other two disappeared. I assumed searching the first floor. We were trapped. Three more floors and they would find us.

I sensed Faith wasn't behind me anymore. I turned. She was gone. I dared not call her name. I looked around. Nothing. I started to panic.

A hand tapped my shoulder.

It was the Commander. Where had he come from? He motioned silence with his lips, then pointed downward. He wanted me to follow him down the stairs. I shook my head furiously. He motioned more emphatically. Tapped two fingers on his wristwatch. Then motioned down the stairs again. I shook my head again.

Faith was standing behind him, ready to descend the stairs. I shook my head once more. One simple, strong motion. Side to side once. No. Down was death. Faith stepped out and grabbed my arm. Her nails dug into my skin. She pulled me downward. We followed the Commander.

The Nephs were on the second level now. With one still guarding the stairs and the other two out of sight. We were crazy to head toward them. Faith's hand didn't leave my arm. We moved slowly. Step by step in the wrong direction. Toward the Nephilim.

We reached the third floor as they finished searching the second. They started up. We were about to be trapped.

The Commander ran. His movement was quick but silent. Faith let go of my arm and followed. I tried to keep up. Eva felt heavier than ever. Her head bounced as we ran. Lolling from side to side. Her arm hung limply. I wondered if she was dead, but there was no time to check. And as much as I wanted to, I didn't drop her.

We skirted the wall and turned a corner, and I saw where we were headed. There was a suspended walkway. The Commander darted across first. Then Faith. I followed with Eva.

11

The bridge led to another smaller parking garage on the far side. It was further away from the hospital, and the Nephilim hadn't made it over to check this one yet. But I was sure they would soon.

We stopped on the first floor. I set Eva down to rest. She wasn't moving. Faith checked her pulse. "Her heart is still pumping. Barely."

The Commander turned to me and whispered. "Good thinking, Reece, burning the truck. Thanks for the warning."

I nodded.

"I saw the smoke from a mile out, parked the SUV three blocks from here, and came in on foot. By the time I got here, the Nephs had just put it out. I spotted you guys, but it took me a while to make my way over." He looked at Faith. "Are you OK?"

She nodded. "Did you find Beck Hastings?"

He nodded yes.

"Where is he?"

The Commander's response was drowned out by the sound of a helicopter. We all looked up but couldn't spot anything in the darkness. We could tell from the sound it was landing close by. Probably on the hospital roof or the parking structure we had just left.

The Commander motioned for us to move. Good idea. The helicopter would provide sound cover. I picked up Eva, and we moved out. We followed the Commander in a tight formation.

I sensed something moving in the darkness parallel to us. Keeping pace. I didn't say anything. I hoped it was my imagination. I stared hard into the darkness, but whatever it was stayed just beyond my eyes ability to see into the gloom. I spurred the group faster toward the truck. Whatever it was kept up.

All my attention was on the thing in the dark beside us. So, when it growled, I recognized it immediately. If I hadn't been so in tune I might not have heard it above the drone of the helicopter blades behind us. It was Blue's growl. It had to be. Then I realized something else. He only growled for one reason. Danger.

I looked back. A Neph was following us. It saw me turn and closed fast. I heard the vehicle start in the distance. The Neph moved effortlessly even as she covered distance twice as fast as we were. Her steps were precise. The Commander and Faith started to pull away. Eva slowed me down. I couldn't keep up while carrying her. But she was still alive, so I wouldn't drop her. But I knew I'd never make it before the Neph overtook me.

The SUV had almost reached the Commander and Faith. I couldn't tell who was driving. I put my head down. Pushed my legs faster. They were burning. I was at my top speed. I looked back. The Nephilim was almost on top of me. I wasn't going to make it.

I heard the roar of the engine. The SUV passed me in a blur. The wind of it passing ripped through my hair.

The truck slammed into the Nephilim. The sound of her body burying itself into the hood was loud. The driver slammed on the brakes, and the Neph flew forward like a rag doll. She rolled across the pavement into the darkness.

The Commander ran past me. He grabbed Eva and yelled something. Probably about getting in the truck. My mind was spinning. I thought I was dead. Faith raced past me and

I followed. We were all three in the truck when I remembered Blue.

"Blue!"

The other two doors slammed shut, but not mine. The truck spun around.

"Blue, run!"

The truck gained speed. The Neph stood back up.

Blue dashed out of the darkness and sprinted after us. We didn't slow down. My door was wide open.

"C'mon boy."

The SUV was moving too fast. He wasn't going to be able to catch it. I leaned across from the rear seat and yelled at the driver. "Stop. Stop the truck!" The driver didn't listen. The Neph was once again after us. Blue was trying his hardest. I yelled again. "Stop the truck!"

The driver tapped the brakes. Barely. But it was enough. Blue jumped for the door. I caught him in my lap and pulled the door closed. "Go!" I yelled at the driver, but he didn't need to be told. He already had the pedal on the floor.

We rounded a corner and hit the open road.

"Thanks," I said. The truth was if I was in the driver's position, I probably wouldn't have slowed. But he did.

"You're welcome," the driver said, and I realized it wasn't a he. Beck Hastings was female.

12

The next several miles passed in silent tension. No one spoke. Everyone watched the road or the sky for activity. None. We took side streets and smaller roads. Winding around, headed anywhere but back.

At one point the Commander had Beck pull over, and he switched places with her. After he took over, our general direction became south. He avoided the interstate. He turned the running lights on but left the headlights off. Visibility was poor so he went slowly. We crawled along uneventfully. I fell asleep.

When I woke, it was light outside. The Commander was still driving. We were still headed south. Blue had crawled into the back of the SUV and was asleep. Eva's legs were laid across mine and Faith was cradling her head. I saw her chest rise and fall. She was still hanging on. Somehow.

A horrible smell filled the vehicle.

"What is that smell?" I asked.

"It smells like death," Beck said.

"That's exactly what it is," the Commander responded. "It's a graveyard. Remember the virus kills two thirds of people on contact. That's millions of dead bodies. The Anakim eat them, so the Nephilim pile them in mass graves to make the Anakim easy to find when they need them."

"That's horrible," I said.

"They probably also do it to minimize the spread of disease," Faith added.

"That's ironic," Beck said.

The Commander chuckled. I joined him. It felt good to laugh. Beck and Faith smiled too. It helped relieve the tension.

"We need to find a pharmacy so I can get medication for Eva," Faith said when we quieted.

The Commander met her eyes in the rearview mirror. He nodded.

"Will that help her?" I asked.

"I don't know," Faith said. "But it's worth a try. I don't know what else to do."

"What's the status at Mercy, Reece?" the Commander said.

The way he asked it was strange. I got the feeling he already knew the answer. I filled him in. When I finished, his jaw muscles were clenched, but he said nothing.

"You already knew something happened at the hospital, didn't you?" I asked.

He gave a small nod.

"How?"

"I learned a few things at Beck's hospital up north. They have a good communication system in place."

"To communicate with who?" Faith asked.

"There's a network of uninfected people across the country who are in touch with each other."

"How do they get away with it without the Nephs discovering them?"

"Instead of trying to outsmart the Nephilim with technology, they've gone old school."

"What do you mean?" Faith asked.

"Morse code. They call it the wire."

"How does that work?" I asked.

"They hide messages in unencrypted viruses and files. It's smart because the Nephs aren't checking every software virus for a secret code since they created most of the viruses themselves."

"Can we find the location of the uninfected people they communicate with?"

"No. No one knows for sure anyone else's exact location, but my guess is hospitals are some of the most popular places for the uninfected to gather," the Commander said. "Apparently, we weren't the only ones to realize how self-sustaining a hospital can be. But no one shares too much information about numbers or locations because they're afraid of a trap."

"Why aren't we headed north to Beck's hospital?" I said. "Since Mercy is gone."

Faith and the Commander shared a look in the rearview mirror.

"All my work is at Mercy," Faith said. "Commander, you heard about Mercy on the wire?"

"There were rumors that a hospital had been overrun, and by the location, it sounded like it could be Mercy General."

"Who put the message on the wire?" I asked.

"No way to know." The Commander turned the truck off the highway.

"It had to be someone who knew about the hospital," I said.

No one spoke. I drew the conclusion for them. "So, it had to be either a Nephilim or a survivor." *Or someone who was both.*

13

The first three pharmacies we found had already been ransacked. We stayed in the vehicle. I imagined how it must have been three years ago when the virus first appeared. People probably flocked to pharmacies the same way they flooded to hospitals, trying to find anything to combat the outbreak.

We kept driving. We passed a warehouse store.

"What about there?"

"Where?" the Commander asked.

"There. They usually have discount pharmacies inside those bulk warehouses. We might have better luck trying that."

The Commander looked at Faith. She nodded.

We circled the building twice, looking for anything that might suggest a trap. We saw nothing to warn us off.

I offered to take Faith inside so she could find what she needed while the Commander waited with Eva, Beck, and the dog. Everyone agreed.

The Commander dropped us off at the front of the building. He swung the truck around so it was angled toward the parking lot exit but where he could also watch the building entrance. He left it running.

I examined the front door. The glass had plywood covering it. No lights shone between the cracks. Everything was dark inside. As best as I could tell, the front door didn't have an alarm, but I wasn't taking any chances. Instead of using the front door, I moved to the side where there was a tire repair center entrance.

Faith followed me. The Commander followed us in the SUV. He parked at the same angle relative to the new door.

There were two clues that we shouldn't have entered the building. I missed both.

The first was that the plywood was on the inside of the glass. I saw it, but the meaning didn't register as I broke the glass with my foot. Then I kicked in the plywood. I entered, and Faith followed. I switched on my flashlight and saw the second thing I should have taken note of but didn't. There were bloodstains on the floor. Bloodstains that someone had tried to clean up.

We crept inside. I used the flashlight to guide us. Five tire irons were laid out on the counter. Each had been placed the exact same distance from the next. I picked up the middle one without registering that clue either. I wasn't sure what good the tire iron would do, but I felt better with a weapon in my hand. I transferred the flashlight to my left hand. I kept the beam low.

We passed the electronics section. A layer of dust covered everything. We moved deeper inside. I spotted the sign for the pharmacy near the back. I led us toward it. Faith stayed close. I could hear her breathing through her mouth. Her nose was clogged. The dust must have been getting to her.

We made our way through the food section. That's when I noticed something was off. All the food was gone. Nothing else in the store had been touched, but the food shelves were empty. Strange. The freezer doors hung open. Nothing remained inside. Not even empty crates or boxes.

Something wasn't right.

Hungry humans would have taken whatever they could find. But not cleaned up after themselves like this. And organized humans would have taken other things they needed off the shelves, not just food. Something wasn't adding up. Another trap? Who would take all the food and leave everything else?

I paused and listened. Faith stopped breathing. I thought I heard something from the other side of the building. I kept listening. Silence. Maybe I had imagined the noise. I looked at Faith. She shrugged and shook her head. I knew we needed to keep moving. If there was an alarm, the Nephs could show up at any time.

But instead of moving, I clicked the light off and waited. I closed my eyes so they would adjust to the darkness faster. It also helped me focus on my other senses. I listened again.

There was someone—or something—else in the building. I could feel it.

I had to make a choice. Continue on to find the medicine, or leave. We were as far in as we were out, so I decided to keep going. Plus, Eva was on my flight, and she might have blood like mine. I wanted to save her if we could.

I clicked the flashlight on. We crept deeper into the building.

The pharmacy was undisturbed. I checked inside, and then guarded the entrance while Faith went in to find what she needed. I could hear her rummaging around inside. Less than five minutes later, I felt a tap on my shoulder. She signaled she was ready to go. She must have found stuff she could use because she had a bag over her shoulder.

I nodded, and we quietly started to make our way back to the tire center. I took a different path. Maybe I would come across something else we needed. Faith stayed a half step back. I could hear her breathing again. We passed through the home goods department. I scanned the shelves for anything that might come in handy. There was a whole isle of vacuum cleaners. I wondered if anyone bothered cleaning anything anymore. What was the point? I spotted Christmas decorations. I smiled. The storeowners had gotten an early start on Christmas, and now it had been Christmas in here for three years.

I led us to the clothing section. I had been wearing the same clothes since I woke up. The mannequins watched us with hollow eyes. Creepy. We were halfway through the clothing department when I sensed Faith wasn't a half step behind me anymore. I heard her breathing pattern change. A sharp intake of breath.

I turned. Tire iron still clutched in my hand. Faith stood frozen, eyes wide. A slender white arm was wrapped around her shoulders. The long silver blade of a hunting knife pressed against the smooth white skin of her neck.

14

I froze. My grip tightened on the tire iron, but I didn't raise it. My jaw clenched.

A face materialized over Faith's shoulder. Eyes first. They weren't orange. Or black. I noticed the hair next. It was long and stringy. Then the face. Pale—that unnatural pallor people get when they haven't been exposed to sunlight in years. He blinked. It was a quick frantic blink. His eyes swam. I wasn't quite sure where his focus was.

Faith looked like she was about to make a move. I subtly shook my head no.

"What are these intruders doing in my home." His voice was whiny and unfocused, like his eyes. "Stealing my treasures. Disturbing my sanctuary. Polluting my carpet." They were statements, not questions.

I held up my left hand, palm out in peace. My right still gripped the tire iron. "We just needed a few things," I said. "We were about to leave."

His eyes darted side to side. "Disturbing my sanctuary. Polluting my carpet." He could have been talking to himself.

The knife pressed a little harder into Faith's neck. She let out a small yelp of pain. A drop of blood appeared.

"No," I said, palm still out. "Don't. We just want to leave. Can we leave?"

His eyes darted all over the place.

He mumbled. "Disturbing . . . polluting . . ."

"We're sorry," I said. "Will you let us leave? We'll leave you alone."

"Polluting my carpet. Polluting my carpet."

The floor was concrete. He was crazy. If he pushed the knife any further, I would take my chances and rush him.

I tried another way. "We came to make a trade. We want to trade with you for your treasures. Will you trade with us?"

"Polluting my carpet, my carpet." His eyes darted up and down now.

Faith spoke. Her voice was strong, but calm. "We're sorry we polluted your carpet. It was dark so we didn't see." She nodded toward my feet. She spoke to him again. "We'll clean up your carpet for you. We won't pollute your carpet anymore."

She nodded at my feet again. I noticed he was barefoot. I understood.

"I'm going to take my shoes off," I said before I bent down. No sudden moves. "So, your carpet isn't polluted anymore." I slowly removed my shoes and held them in my left hand. "See?" I spoke as if I were talking to a child. "My name is Nick. And that's Faith. Can Faith take her shoes off so she doesn't pollute your carpet?"

His eyes roamed before they landed on me again. He nodded. One quick jerk of his head downward.

"Can you move the knife so she can take off her shoes?" I asked. "So, she doesn't pollute your carpet?"

A sideways head jerk. No.

He left the knife at her neck as she knelt down. While she removed her shoes, I examined him. He was skinny. Probably not more than a hundred pounds. His shirt hung on him like a blanket. His skin was gaunt but clean. As if it was scrubbed every day. Like the floors.

Faith finished removing her shoes but didn't stand. Smart. He had less leverage that way. And kneeling was less threatening. The knife remained at her throat. I thought about rushing him.

"Now your carpet isn't polluted anymore," she said. "Does that make you feel better?"

A sharp nod yes. His eyes went up and down with the movement of his head.

I remained silent and let Faith do the talking.

"Now can we make a trade?"

A pause. Another nod.

"What's your name?"

His eyes moved side to side. So did his head. "Two Bit. They call me Two Bit."

Faith was smart enough not to ask who "they" were.

He filled us in anyway. "The doctors call me Two Bit. Can you hear them calling me? Two Bit, Two Bit. Can you hear them?"

"I like your name, Two Bit. That's a good name." Faith's voice remained calm but with an authoritative edge. "Would you like to make a trade, Two Bit? We came to make a trade with you."

He tilted his head as if listening to the advice of someone we couldn't see.

He nodded. Up and down. "Trade."

I stayed quiet and let Faith do her thing. She slowly removed the bag of products she had taken from the pharmacy and held it out to him. The knife hand relaxed slightly. He took the offered bag with his other hand.

"We came to make a good trade with you, Two Bit." As she spoke, she slowly used both hands to remove the knife from her neck. He let her.

She stood up but stayed close to him. She didn't move to me. As if she was on his side not mine.

"Nick and I want to trade you this magic metal bar for your collection." She held out her hands, motioning toward my tire iron. I hesitated to give up my weapon. Now that he was exposed and I saw how frail he was, I could take my chances. Faith shot me a look. I extended the iron. She took it.

She held it out to Two Bit. Palms up like an offering.

His eyes floated over it. Then to Faith. Then back over the gift.

"Will you trade us?" Faith asked.

"A Two Bit trade," he said and cackled. Faith smiled with him like she understood the joke. Maybe she did.

Two Bit reached out his hands to take the offering. He realized his hands were full. He seemed to have forgotten he had the knife in one hand and the bag of medicine in the other. Faith took both from him and gave him the iron.

He turned it over in his hands and examined it. Probably looking for the magic. I hoped he didn't recognize it as being from his tire sanctuary. He didn't. And whatever magic he was looking for he must have found because he smiled an ear-to-ear smile.

"Thank you, Two Bit," Faith said.

"Thank you, Two Bit," he responded, the smile still in place. He held out his hand for his knife.

"Will you trade for this too?" she asked.

He gave a quick shake of the head. Still smiling.

"Are you sure?"

"No more trade," he responded.

She handed the knife back to him.

"Come with us," Faith said. "We have something else for you." She reached out to lead him by the arm, but he pulled back, so instead, she motioned him to come. We made our way to the exit. I led the way. Faith followed me. Two Bit hesitantly followed her.

I exited through the broken glass. Faith said something to Two Bit and then followed. He stayed inside. He was careful to avoid the light spilling through the door.

The Commander pulled the truck up. I watched as Faith took some canned goods from the supply the Commander had in the back of the SUV. She gave it to Two Bit. They shared one final smile, and he scurried back into the depths of the warehouse, prizes in hand.

We climbed into the SUV, and the Commander sped away. Faith rummaged through the bag and pulled out a bottle and a syringe to help Eva. Antibiotics? When I looked over at Faith, her head was down, but I saw a tear run off her nose and drop onto the seat. I reached over and placed my hand on her knee. It felt awkward. I left it there anyway. She didn't seem to mind.

15

We drove down the coast. The sky was clear. The roads weren't. Abandoned vehicles were scattered everywhere. It looked like people had just abandoned their lives here. Other areas had been cleared. Why not here? It made me wonder.

I asked.

"The Nephilim haven't had a chance to clear everywhere yet," the Commander said. "They've spent the last three years searching for humans, clearing areas, and rebuilding infrastructure, but there are still some places they haven't gotten to."

"Wouldn't it have been safer to use a hospital in this area?" I asked.

"We felt it was better to stay in an area they had already searched. Plus, you play the hand you're dealt. It would have been tough to move everyone."

Blue barked. My pulse spiked until I realized it was a different noise than his warning growl. He barked again. He probably needed a bathroom break. I asked the Commander to stop. He nodded.

Faith spoke up. "I need a stable place to work on Eva." She had a makeshift fluid bag hanging from the ceiling that swung as we drove. "Maybe we could find a place to stop for the night."

The Commander nodded again. He drove on for a while, searching for a spot that looked safe. I patted the dog's head so he knew we'd stop soon. He was quiet. After we pulled over and let Blue relieve himself, we kept driving, searching.

As evening fell, we saw more Anakim in the streets. As usual. After the experience back at the house, I wasn't as afraid of them as I had been. But I was still unsure what the current rules were between us. They hadn't been afraid of me before. Not until I jumped out the window and attacked them. Had it been a fluke?

The Commander pulled the truck to a stop. I stepped out of the SUV and stretched. Blue hopped out and sniffed the air. He didn't growl.

To our left stood an abandoned high school. All cinder block and steel. A high chain-link fence surrounded it. Diagonally across the street was an old cathedral. Blue chose the church and darted off. We followed him.

Blue did a lap around the building to investigate. The Commander and I helped Faith carry in Eva. Beck grabbed the rest of our food and followed us.

The big front door opened easily. The sanctuary smelled of old pews and hymnals. The Commander looked around and immediately chose the high ground—the balcony. Faith laid her patient out on a pew and went to work. Eva looked dead. I had felt the faint rise and fall of her chest as we carried her in, so I knew she wasn't. But she had to be close.

"Stay here and keep an eye on them," the Commander whispered.

Holding the shotgun at ready, he headed for the bell tower to scout the area. Beck followed him.

I watched Faith work. It felt nice to relax a little, and besides, Faith still looked beautiful to me even with the dirt and grime. After a while, she said, "Nick, I need you to tell me the truth." She didn't look at me. "What happened to Steven?"

I knew we would get back to that topic eventually. I thought of what to say, took a deep breath, and answered honestly. "Pete let him loose in the hospital. He killed a lot of people. He almost killed me."

Faith took it in without comment. I was only confirming what she must have guessed.

"Thank you," she said.

I knew she meant for deciding she was strong enough to handle the truth.

Silence. Not uncomfortable.

I broke it. "How's Eva?"

"Alive. But back in a coma."

"Is that normal?"

She looked at me. "Define normal."

I smiled. "Stupid question?"

She pulled out a syringe and used it to draw liquid from a bottle.

"Tell me, Nick, what did you do before all this?"

"I liked to surf, play volleyball, and go for *long* walks on the beach," I said, sounding like a dating site. "You know, guy stuff."

She smiled. "How long?"

"Long." I drew the word out. "Maybe I could show you sometime."

"Maybe." She stuck the needle in Eva's arm. "What else did you do?"

"You mean to pay the bills?"

"I mean to pay the bills."

"You don't think I could just skate by on my looks?"

"Could you?" She looked up and smiled.

"No."

"Few of us can."

My turn to smile. "I worked for The Man."

"Doing what?"

"What I was told."

"What you were told," she repeated with a smirk. "Yeah, I bet."

16

It happened while I was on watch in the bell tower. Sometime past one in the morning. At first, I thought it might have been my eyes playing tricks on me in the darkness. I felt it as much as saw it. A shadow separated itself from the other shadows.

Blue was keeping me company. Or he was taunting me with sleep. He lay with his head on my leg, oblivious to the world.

I peered hard into the night. It was surprising how dark it got without the lights of a big city filling the sky. I saw it again, for sure this time, a shadow that moved. It made its way to our vehicle. The dog didn't notice.

The shadow paused. Melted into the shape of the SUV. I watched. Whoever, or whatever, it was, was patient. Minutes ticked by without further movement. Its movements were too focused to be an Anakim. Was it a Neph? Or someone uninfected? Or my imagination? I watched and waited.

It moved again. Slipped along the side of our vehicle. Dark hair and dark clothes against our black truck. The hair was short, so I assumed it was male. Though I had made that mistake when evaluating Beck. He tried the driver's door. The Commander had locked it. The visitor was prepared. He drew a slim jim from his sleeve. It took him almost no time to open the door. He was experienced.

The interior light came on as the door opened. He was quick to shut it off. But in that split second, I saw his face. Definitely male. I considered my options. Alert the Commander, or go down and handle the situation myself, or wait and observe.

I waited.

I could see his outline moving around in the vehicle, but it was impossible to tell what he was doing. He was inside the SUV for no more than two minutes. He emerged without taking anything as far as I could tell. Not that we had left much inside to take. He moved to the front of the vehicle and raised the hood. Whatever he did there only took him thirty seconds. He lowered the hood without making a sound. Dropped to his knees and looked under the vehicle. Another thirty seconds. I still couldn't guess what he was doing. It was pitch black. I focused hard at the darkness. I spotted him rise to his feet. Then he disappeared back into the shadows.

The dog never stirred.

17

The next day came without incident. I told the Commander about the late-night visitor, and he checked the vehicle but found nothing amiss. Most likely it was a survivor looking for supplies. Good luck to him. We all needed it.

I spent most of the day in the cathedral sleeping, eating, or talking to Faith as she nursed Eva.

After a dreamless nap, I woke to find Faith watching me. I liked the feeling. But on further examination, she didn't seem to be looking at me as much as she was looking through me, lost in thought. Bummer. The Commander and Beck were gone, probably on watch.

Faith spoke. "Blood transfusion."

I rubbed sleep from my eyes. "Huh?"

"Eva. I think I need to do a blood transfusion. The disease is in her blood, and her blood is fighting it. Giving her some clean blood might help."

"You think so?"

"Couldn't hurt."

"They teach you 'couldn't hurt' in medical school."

"They did." She smiled.

"Whose blood will you use?"

"It needs to be clean. It also needs to have the same markers that Eva's has."

"Special blood?"

She nodded.

"Mine?"

She shook her head. "It needs to be the same blood type. Or a universal donor."

"You said there were three others like me. Coma patients who woke up."

"Yes."

"Why is that unusual?"

She paused. "Because all the rest of the coma patients since the infection outbreak have died."

"Except me and Eva."

"And Beck. And I'm assuming another individual named Asher Geere. Do you recognize the name?"

"No. The fourth survivor from my flight?"

"Yes."

"So, you need one of our blood types to match Eva's? Mine doesn't and Beck's doesn't."

"Correct."

"So maybe this Asher's will?"

"I would bet on it."

"Why do I get the feeling you know more than you let on?"

"Because I do."

"Then we need to find Asher Geere."

"Yes."

"How?"

"I have no idea."

"So, there are limits to your knowledge?"

I smiled. So did she.

18

Blue and I went outside to sniff around. Well, Blue sniffed and I mostly just looked. There wasn't much to see. It was quiet. We did a lap around the school across the street. It was a large school with lots of buildings and a fence all the way around.

We walked slowly. The dog stayed within ten feet of me. I didn't force him to stay close; he just did. I didn't adjust my pace. I would walk and he would sniff. As soon as I got a few steps ahead of him, he would dart past me and continue investigating.

I spotted them before Blue did. He didn't even growl. He was slipping. A person stood in the window of a building about a hundred yards inside the fence. The man didn't move. I didn't either. He didn't smile. I didn't either. He didn't blink. I didn't either.

I couldn't make out any distinguishing characteristics from that far away. But it probably wasn't the same person from the previous night. The person stood completely still. It was unnerving. I stood and watched him watching me. Blue stood frozen too.

All three of us stayed that way for a while. The person could have been a statue. I waved. Nothing. No movement at all.

It must have been over ten minutes of staring before we moved on. I looked back. The window was empty.

19

I was uneasy that night in the bell tower. Blue wouldn't come up with me, so maybe he was too. I wasn't sure why, but something didn't feel right.

I had told the Commander about the person in the window. We kept an eye on the school all day but never saw any movement. Still, something didn't feel right.

And it didn't take long to figure out my instincts were correct.

They came quietly. So quietly I wasn't sure when they arrived. Or where they had come from. The only warning I had was from Blue. He gave a single bark. And even that came too late. The bark sounded from the darkness somewhere. Then it was silent again. I knew it was trouble.

I stared into the darkness but saw nothing. No reason for a bark. But I knew there was one. They were here. I didn't know who, but I could feel I wasn't alone.

I made my way down the spiral staircase from the tower. I saw no one. Nothing hiding in the darkness. I made my way to the balcony where we had made our home base. It was slow going. Too dark to move fast. I paused to listen at every sound. All of them imagined. I listened for Blue. I wanted to call for him, but I didn't. I wanted to call a warning to the Commander, but I didn't. I knew it was too late. I could feel someone there already. Lurking somewhere in the darkness around me.

I stopped to look, my eyes straining. Nothing. I kept going. I made it to the balcony. I crouched down and felt my way along. I counted pews in my head. I was close. I wondered where the Commander had camped out. I knew he wouldn't be in the same place as he had been the night before. I decided to find Faith first. She would be by Eva. I got down on my hands and knees as I moved. I sensed someone in the darkness. Watching me.

I felt along until I found Eva's pew. It was empty.

Maybe I had miscounted. I tried the next pew. Also empty. So was the next one. I started to panic. They were gone. I couldn't stand it any longer. I whispered into the darkness, "Faith. Commander."

Nothing. No response. Not even the sound of movement. I tried again. A little louder. Still nothing.

Something hit me. Hard. It glanced off my shoulder. Somewhere in my mind, I knew they were aiming for my head. If they had been accurate, I wouldn't be thinking at all. I was moving before the thought could form. I ducked and rolled. I felt something else hit my shoulder. It didn't give. A pew. I was on my stomach. I crawled under. Sensed something in the darkness above me. Kept crawling. Three pews later I stopped.

I could hear them moving in the darkness. Looking for me. I couldn't tell how many there were but more than one. They didn't speak. Not even a whisper. I held my breath and waited. They kept searching. I briefly wondered if Blue was OK. I hoped he had gotten away. I needed to move before they found me. I crawled forward, toward what I hoped was the stairs. But I had lost all sense of direction in the darkness.

I bumped into something. It moved. It was someone's leg. Hands grabbed me. I twisted loose. They grabbed me again. Someone held my leg, and they started dragging me. I had to get loose before the others came to help. I kicked in the dark. Missed. I kicked again. This time my foot connected with something solid. I heard a grunt. The grip on my leg loosened. I pulled my leg free. Started to get up.

Something solid hit me again. This time across my back. It felt like a baseball bat. Pain shot though my body. I dropped and rolled. I heard the bat hit a pew. Wood splintered. I crawled sideways in the darkness. Came up against something solid. A wall. I felt my way along. I could hear people scrambling for me in the darkness. Three people? Four? I wanted to head for the door again. I resisted the urge. I followed the wall until I came to the balcony rail. I tried not to remember how far down the drop was to the first floor. I didn't have another choice. I needed to jump and hope for the best. I told myself I wouldn't break my legs. I pulled myself up by the rail.

Two things happened. My head exploded in pain and everything got darker. I wasn't sure which happened first.

20

I opened my eyes to find myself in a gymnasium. The wall was painted with a school mascot—the Vikings. Most likely I was in the school across the street from our church. Faith was nowhere to be seen. Neither were the Commander, Eva, or Beck. Or Blue. I was alone. There was a faint buzzing sound and my head pounded.

I was also chained to a post. I pulled at the bonds. The restraints around my wrists were handcuffs, but with a longer chain. Like the type used for ankles. I could stand up and move a couple feet away from the post if I desired. I didn't. There was no point.

I examined the post. It was a structural beam that ran from the concrete floor to the ceiling. I wasn't going anywhere anytime soon. I started sweating. I tried not to think about my lack of mobility. I had to stay coherent. Had to keep my mind clear. I took a deep breath and reminded myself how big the room was. My head hurt. So did my back. I reached up to feel my head and found blood. Judging by how dry it was, I had been out for a while.

I wondered if everyone else was OK. I hoped so. Especially Faith. I sat and considered my options. I came up with none. There was nothing I could do but sit and wait. And try not to remember that I was in restraints. Again.

So I sat. And waited.

It didn't take long. Two men entered from a small side door. They walked across the gym and headed toward the far wall. They didn't look my way as they passed.

I watched them. They ignored me.

"Hey," I said.

No response. Nothing to indicate they heard me. They could have been deaf.

They came to the double doors on the far wall and paused. One man at each door. They nodded at each other. Then they pulled the doors open at the same time.

Nothing happened.

The two men turned and walked opposite directions. Neither of them crossed in front of the open door. They didn't run, but they didn't walk either.

"Hey," I said. Louder this time. Still no reaction. They exited separate doors on either side.

"Hey!" I yelled. That was a mistake.

I heard a noise from the open double doors. A grunt. Or a moan. Human. But somehow not.

I scooted to the side to get a better view. I didn't see anything. Then all the sudden it was there.

An Anakim.

He came tumbling out of the double doors like a junkyard dog. Orange eyes. He spotted me immediately. I wished I hadn't yelled. My heart rate spiked. Adrenaline flooded my veins. Fight or flight.

The Anakim was huge. At least three hundred pounds. His eyes were wide. Like a dog excited for a meal. An easy meal. One chained to a post. I jerked at the chains, not that it did me any good. I couldn't run. Fight it was. Time to see if my blood really was special. It had worked once before.

The Anakim barreled toward me. He moved fast for how big he was. I blinked, and he was halfway across the gym. I blinked again, and he was three quarters. I stood up. His eyes were locked on me. Showing fear wouldn't help. I stared back.

His eyes seemed to grow brighter. More orange. Somehow my stare made him angrier. I didn't go to the end of my chain. But I didn't back up either. I just stood there and waited. He kept coming. I wanted to close my eyes. I didn't.

He was almost on me. He was so excited he was trembling. Ten feet away. He lunged. This was going to be bad. I braced for impact. At the height of his jump he stopped. Like he hit an invisible wall. He fell straight down and landed with a thud. He didn't pause. He kept coming. Clawing at the ground. Straining for me. Only he wasn't moving forward. Something held him back. He clawed the air. His mouth opened and closed on nothing. I was out of reach. Even if I had been at the end of my chain, I would have still been out of his reach.

A drop of dirty sweat dripped from my chin. I was filthy, still covered in dirt, printer toner, and motor oil. I wondered if he would have been afraid of me if he had been able to smell me. Or maybe if I had lunged at him. I exhaled. Loudly. The sound enraged him further. He pulled harder. Moving side to side, trying to get free from whatever held him. I finally saw it. He had a chain around his waist. Not a small chain like the ones I wore, but a big chain, like the ones used in shipyards. The chain held him taut. Straining with all his might. I moved to the side. He moved with me. Snarling. Straining. Hoping he would get me with just one more total effort.

Then, slowly, he started to move backward. He didn't want to. He resisted. Still straining toward me. He tried to dig his feet into the gym floor. No luck. He kept straining. The chain must have weighed thousands of pounds. He had dragged it behind him with no effort. It stayed tight as he slid backward. I was glad it held. He wasn't. Seeing his meal slowly get away was more than he could bear. He strained until I thought his body would break in half. His backward movement stopped for a moment.

I stopped breathing. I heard an engine whine. He started backward again, even though he still strained toward me. Orange eyes enraged. Finally, he disappeared. Dragged back though the double doors. I could no longer see the Anakim, but I could still hear him fighting his bonds.

My mind must have heard another door opening, but I was concentrated on the double doors. Suddenly, a man stood beside me before my mind registered him fully. He got my attention fast; he pointed a gun at my head.

21

After a certain point, some people stop being afraid and get angry. I had reached that point. I had been stalked and beaten in the dark, chained to a post, and threatened with an Anakim. Now a stranger was pointing a gun at my head and I had had enough.

"Shoot me or let me go," I growled.

The man made a show of pulling the hammer back. The cylinder rotated. The click bounced off the high ceiling.

I set my jaw. Watched for his finger to whiten on the trigger.

"Don't miss," I said.

"I won't." I believed him.

He drew a long knife from his waist with his other hand. He held it like he had used it before. His finger tightened.

"Wait," I said. "What happened to Faith?"

He didn't respond.

"The woman. Blonde hair. What happened to her?"

Still no response, but the gun didn't go off.

"The blonde woman. Is she OK?"

I could see his eyes peering over the sight of the gun. They were steely gray. They examined me. He lowered the gun slightly. Only about an inch. But enough so I felt I was talking to him, not the gun.

"What do you care?" he said.

"I just want to know she's OK."

He spun the knife in his hand. It looked like a circus trick. He didn't seem to notice he was doing it. The gun stayed steady.

He didn't respond further. I could feel my blood beginning to boil again. "Tell me she's OK!" I yelled at him like a weapon of my own.

He blinked. The knife stopped spinning. He lowered the gun hammer with a click. He dropped the gun to his side, then turned and walked away. His cowboy boots echoed off the floor.

"What about the others? Are they OK? Answer me! Are they OK?"

But he was already gone. I was yelling at the walls.

22

I sat for an hour. The hour felt like ten hours. My back hurt and my head hurt and the buzzing sound didn't help. The same two men who had opened the double doors had come back and closed them. They ignored me . . . again. I went over my options and still came up with none. I had stood to stretch when the man with the knife came back in.

He handed me a syringe and an empty vial. "Fill it."

Resisting would lead nowhere. I stuck my arm. The vial filled quickly. I pulled the needle out of my arm and held them out for him to take. He was careful. He stayed at the end of my radius and took the vial with his left hand. His right hung loosely by the knife handle. It looked relaxed. I knew it wasn't.

He nodded and exited without an explanation. I sat back down.

I was tired of waiting. But I had no choice. I tried to make myself comfortable. Something in the air bothered me, but I couldn't place what. I tried to lie down, but the chains put my shoulders in an awkward position. I tried reclining against the post, but my back was still too tender. I ended up lying on my side with one hand behind me. That's how I was positioned when the knife guy appeared again.

He came over and stood inside my range. I didn't stand up.

He waited for me to talk. A power play. I knew I could wait longer. I did.

"You're lucky," he said.

"It definitely feels that way."

He smiled a humorless smile. "I need to see for myself. Stand up."

I didn't.

He nudged me with his toe. Not hard. "This is no place for cowards. And I have no use for people without the skills for survival and no time for a nonconformist. Get up."

I thought about tackling him. But his hand hovered near the knife. I put the thought away. For now.

I stood up.

"Despite failing our test, she was able to convince us you're not a Nephilim."

Faith. God bless her.

"The woman. The blonde woman," he said. There was something behind his words. "She also made other claims, but I'm going to need to see about those for myself."

"Where is she?"

He ignored the question. I knew he would.

"So you're going to show me what you can do. For real this time."

"Or?"

"There is no *or*."

"There's always an or," I said.

"We'll see." Another humorless smile.

He pulled a key from his pocket and dropped it on the floor by my feet.

I never noticed when it happened, but the double doors were wide open again. I heard a noise.

"By the way," knife guy said as he walked away, "we've taken off his restraints as well. It's only fair."

23

I scrambled for the key and unlocked my cuffs. The Nak made his entrance as they clanked to the floor. He was bigger than I remembered. He remembered me too. His orange eyes were wide. I noticed he didn't have a chain around his waist to hold him back. I had two choices: challenge him to see if he was afraid of me, or run.

I ran.

Halfway to the exit I stopped. I knew the door would be locked. I turned the other direction. I needed to loop around and get to the double doors. The Nak was only steps away. Spittle bounced off his chin. He grabbed for me. I dodged quickly to the side. He was fast, but his size made him less agile. Still, he got a piece of my shirt. I left it with him.

He kept coming. I dodged back the other way, away from the doors. The shirt inspired him. He came full speed. At an angle. I was moving as fast as I could. He was moving much faster. His full focus was on me.

My mind calculated his angle and speed. I knew I wouldn't make it to the exit before him. His angle was better. And he was faster. I came up with a new plan. I adjusted my path slightly. He adjusted his to match. He knew he was going to win. I could see it in his eyes. His head was craned my way. That's what I was hoping. He didn't even see it. He ran head first into the steel beam I had been chained to. The beam bent. At first I thought it might snap in two, but it held. I felt the building shake. The

Nak went down hard. I noticed the buzzing again. I realized what had bugged me. It gave me another idea.

He was up as fast as he went down. A small head shake to clear the cobwebs and he was after me again. I never broke stride. When I reached the double doors, I kept going. I could have taken the exit but I didn't. The Nak could catch me in the hallway just as fast as he could in here. Possibly faster.

I reached the far wall and stopped. I made sure not to touch it. The buzzing was louder. I turned to face the beast. He was coming full speed again. It was probably his only gear. I couldn't imagine a three-hundred-pound human that could move that fast. I stood my ground. He covered the distance quickly.

I told myself to wait until I could see the whites of his eyes. I'm not sure if I did. He was almost on top of me. His arms were wide to grab me. I dove to the side. Covered my head and rolled.

He may have flinched at the last second. Or that may have been my imagination. Either way he hit the wall hard. A grunt. Concrete dust filled the air. The lights went dark for a moment. Then flickered back on. The Nak crumpled into a pile on the floor, unmoving. He was surrounded by parts of the crumbled wall. I could see his shoulders rise and fall. He was out cold.

I heard a door open. Boots clicked on concrete. It was the man with the knife. He made his way over to me, ignoring the mess.

"Welcome to the remnant," he said, holding his empty knife hand out to shake.

I punched him in the face.

24

The Commander, Beck, Faith, and I sat on the front row of the school auditorium, listening to a woman give us our mandatory introduction. She looked like she could have come with the school. And she took her job on the rules and regulations committee seriously. Too seriously.

She explained a lot of things I had already heard from Faith and Xavier about the Anakim. She explained that other than occasional rolling power outages, the Nephilim did a good job of rebuilding and maintaining infrastructure. They were able to do this with only a fraction of the manpower because of their higher IQs.

Then she rattled on about the rules and guidelines for living with the remnant. They had a lot of rules. I only half listened. The seat was too small for me. And my body still hurt from my meeting with the baseball bat at the church. Faith shifted in her seat beside me, probably thinking about getting back to Eva. Beck sat stock-still, taking it all in. The Commander sat still, too, but I knew his mind probably raced with plans.

The room got quiet. Principal office lady stared at me. Apparently, she had said something that required a response. I had no idea what. I told her that.

"I said, everyone will be required to do his or her part without complaining. Will that be a problem?"

"What will that part be?"

She took my question as agreement. It wasn't.

"Everyone will be assigned jobs according to his or her talent, or lack thereof. Those with specific training, such as the doctor, will be assigned posts in congruence with their talent. Anyone without a special skill," she looked at me, "will be assigned lookout duty as we've lost a couple members of our watch team."

"Congruence," I repeated.

She ignored me. "Are there any questions?"

"Who will assign jobs?"

"Saul. He's in charge of operations at this post," she said. "I understand you've met."

Saul. The knife guy.

"Yes, we hit it off," I responded. I spotted a small smile from the Commander out of the corner of my eye.

The Commander spoke up. "How many people are a part of the resistance?"

"As I stated before, we are called the remnant. There are seventeen people at this outpost. If I were to include you four, that number would be twenty-one."

"Are there others?" Beck asked.

"Yes. There are other outposts spread around the states. Most of them about the same size. We try to keep the groups small to avoid detection. Larger groups lead to a larger drain on the power grid. Larger power drains get noticed by the Nephilim."

"How many people total?" the Commander asked.

"About a thousand, give or take. We lose a few and add a few every week. Though the additions are slowing as of late."

"Lose?" Beck asked.

"A war is not without its casualties."

"A thousand is not very many."

"That is why it's important that every new member do his or her part."

"When will I be able to attend to my patient again?" Faith asked.

"I'm told your patient has little chance of survival. Your time will be better spent helping patients who have a fighting chance."

"That's not true. I have to save her."

Principal lady gave Faith a hard look. "Doctor, your patient has come in contact with the virus. We are lucky she hasn't turned already. There is no chance Saul will let you spend your time trying to save someone who may then infect us all."

Faith returned the look. "I don't believe it's any of your or Saul's business who I spend my time helping."

"Doctor, I thought we would have understood each other by now. You are either with us, or you are against us. In this war, there is no room for middle ground."

25

Immediately after orientation, they hustled me off to my post as lookout. They said it was because they were shorthanded, but I figured they probably wanted to keep our group separate for a while. Except Beck. I could tell they thought she was harmless. I had the feeling they were wrong. She was assigned to watch with me.

Our post was the third-floor window of a classroom, the same window where Blue and I had seen the person standing the day before. I stood while Beck sat on a chair and waited. We were doing thirty-minute shifts. There was nothing to see. Nothing. There weren't even any Naks wandering around outside.

I heard boots coming down the hallway. Saul. I didn't turn as he entered the room. He stood beside me. I still didn't turn. Instead, I stared at the uneventful street.

"How did you know the gymnasium walls were electrified?" he asked.

I didn't answer.

"I thought you were a Nephilim at first. The way you evaded us in the church and the fact you weren't afraid of the Nak." I could feel him looking at me. "But then the way you asked about your friends, I could tell you cared about them. The Nephilim don't care about anyone, not even each other."

I looked at him. The skin around his eye was a deep purple color. I didn't feel the obligation to respond. So I didn't.

He continued unfazed. "The doctor told me the Anakim are afraid of you. But I didn't see that in there. I saw you outsmart the Nak. I saw you find his weakness. But I didn't see him afraid of you. Are they?"

I could sense Beck listening intently.

"Some have been," I said.

"But not all?"

I shrugged. He spun his knife absentmindedly.

"What about the Nephilim? Have any of them ever been afraid of you?"

I thought about the fear I had felt in Pete's presence. He didn't need to know about that. I shrugged again.

He evaluated my non-answer.

"We are in a war, Reece. You are either with us or against us." He turned to go. His steps landed on the tile hard, heel first. Deliberately, I felt. He spoke over his shoulder as he exited. "Sorry about your head."

I should have said I was sorry about his eye. But I wasn't. So I didn't.

Beck joined me at the window when he was gone. I hadn't noticed before but her eyes were light brown. They matched her short hair perfectly.

"They keep saying 'you are either with us or against us' like it's their motto," she said.

"Maybe it is," I answered.

"I've been observing . . . "

"And?"

"And you don't like Saul very much."

"You've got a sharp eye."

"I do, don't I?" She smiled. "Why not? These people may be our only help."

"He beat me with a baseball bat then chained me up as Nak food. Why would I?"

"Good point. So, is your blood special?"

"Faith tells me it is."

She looked out the window. I waited.

"Mine too," she said.

I nodded. We both gazed outside. The view hadn't changed.

"Why do you think they have us on watch duty when there isn't a Nak in sight and they have motion sensors all the way around the school?"

I scanned the perimeter. She was right. She did have a sharp eye.

26

I was starting to feel like Beck and I were prisoners rather than guests. The next day we were back on useless watch duty together. In the same room, with the same view of nothing. We hadn't seen the Commander or Faith since the orientation. I had asked about them and was told the Commander had left with a team for a scouting mission. I hadn't seen anyone leave, but I wasn't given any more information, even though I had asked multiple people. It was like they had their own orientation meeting and everyone was on the same page about what to tell me. I was told Dr. Richards was attending to her patient and couldn't be disturbed.

So it was just Beck and I taking shifts at the window.

"Do you get the feeling we're being quarantined?" she asked.

"I just had the same thought." I had my feet propped up on a desk. It was her shift. "Do you think the Commander really went somewhere with them?"

"I never heard a vehicle leave," she said.

"Me either. They could have left on foot."

"We've been watching the gate."

"We have."

"There could be another gate."

"There could."

"Are you just repeating me?"

"I am."

"Do you think Eva will turn?" she asked.

"She hasn't yet," I said.

"That doesn't mean she won't."

"It doesn't."

"Will she?"

"She might."

"I hope not," Beck said.

We switched positions. It was my turn at the window. I sat where I could still see the street. Sitting was against their rules. But it wasn't against mine. The street was still empty. We hadn't seen an Anakim for days. Something seemed strange about that. There were always at least a few wandering around the gate at the hospital. But there were none here. I knew I should make something of that fact, but I didn't know what.

"Do you think there's any hope?" Beck asked.

"What do you mean?"

"Any hope of getting back to normal. There are millions of infected Anakim who are all stronger and faster than us and possibly unkillable. There are hundreds of thousands of Nephilim who are all smarter than us. And there are maybe what, a few thousand humans left, caught in the middle? Seems kind of hopeless to me."

She was right. I didn't want to say something patronizing like, "There's always hope." She waited. I said it anyway.

"Always?" she asked.

"Always." It was probably a lie. But it was a lie I believed.

"Thanks."

I didn't know what else to say. So I didn't say anything.

A movement in the street caught my eye. I stood up. Watched for more movement. There it was. It was Blue. He was sniffing around the gate. I watched. He was careful not to touch it. He took another step, nose to the ground. He moved cautiously. I hoped no one else spotted him.

"What is it?" Beck asked.

A couple more sniffs and he was gone. I couldn't see where he went.

"What do you see?"

"Hope."

27

The next morning was more of the same. I still hadn't seen the Commander or Faith. As usual breakfast was delivered to our lookout room. I was midway through a bowl of what looked like oatmeal but tasted like mud, trying to figure out a plan. So far, I had nothing. All I had figured out was someone had put extra salt in the oatmeal to mask the poor flavor. They failed. I reached for my bottle of water in retaliation. I didn't notice it on my first sip. Or my second. But by my third I did. Someone had written on the inside of the label. I peeled it off to read.

Five words.

Third-floor men's room. Noon.

Who would have left me the message? I tore the label to little pieces as I pondered. There was only one way to find out.

The next few hours crawled. At three minutes till noon I asked Beck to cover for me and made my way to the restroom. The hallway was empty, but I spotted little cameras in the corners of the ceiling. I bet they worked. Someone was watching. High school was a dangerous place.

I pushed open the men's room door and went inside. It was empty. The first stall had an out-of-order sign on it. I chose the next one and closed the door behind me. Everything looked normal. Complete with the usual bathroom stall scribbles. I sat down and waited.

It didn't take long. Someone entered. I saw their feet move along. They paused in front of my stall. I didn't say anything.

Whoever it was shuffled for a moment as if they were unsure. The feet moved on. I heard the water turn on. Then off. I heard the door close. The person left without a word.

After the door clicked shut, a voice spoke.

"We don't have a lot of time, Reece, so listen." The Commander's voice came from the out-of-order stall. "I want you to go back to Mercy General and see if anyone survived. Take Beck. They're not going to let us leave here so you'll have to sneak out."

"What about Faith?" I asked.

"We can't move Eva. I'll stay here with Faith."

I didn't respond. The Commander took that for consent. That or he didn't need consent. He continued, "Tomorrow morning, I'll create a distraction so you can sneak away. That gives you the rest of the day to come up with a way out."

"What's the distraction? How will I know when?"

"I'll figure that out. You'll know. Just be ready."

"OK," I said.

"They have a stockpile of burner phones here. I'm—" The Commander cut himself off suddenly.

Fortunately, he heard it before I did. Someone else had entered the bathroom.

"Are you OK in here?" Someone was keeping tabs on me.

"Yeah," I said, "just an upset stomach. Breakfast didn't sit well." I flushed the toilet for emphasis.

"You've been in here a while."

"That stuff they call food is awful, and I have a weak stomach." The man didn't leave. "I'll be out in a few minutes."

He didn't answer, but after a moment the door clicked closed again.

The Commander picked up where he had left off. "I'll steal one for you. The Nephs have tried to destroy all the burner cell phones because they're harder to track, but somehow these people have gotten their hands on some. I'll get it to you before you leave. I'll call you at noon the day after tomorrow. Try to keep the call as short as possible. Under a minute. Then destroy the phone and move fast. And don't leave the battery in the phone unless you're using it. The Nephilim could discover it, and if they do they'll power it on remotely to listen and track you."

"OK," I said.

"Be careful, Reece."

"I will. Take care of Faith." I wanted to add "for me," but I didn't. Instead I added, "and Eva."

"And you take care of Beck."

I nodded but realized he couldn't see me.

"See you soon."

I flushed the toilet and exited the restroom. I glanced in the Commander's stall on the way by. It was empty. I didn't know how, but he continued to be one step ahead.

28

A hand tapped me on the shoulder. Gently. It was dark. My eyes were closed, but I wasn't asleep. I shifted on my cot so I could see who it was. Faith. I smiled for no reason. Or maybe she was the reason.

"Hey, Nick," she whispered.

I loved the sound of my name on her lips.

"The Commander sent this for you." I felt her soft hands feel for mine in the darkness. She found them and placed a cell phone in my hand. She wrapped my fingers around it. Her hand stayed over mine. I could hear her breathing. She wanted to say more.

"Do you think anyone is left at the hospital?"

"I don't know," I said. "But I'll find out."

"I hope so."

"Me too."

More breathing.

"Did you find a way out of this place?" she asked.

"Not exactly. But the back bus lot looks like it'll be our best chance to get through the fence. There's no direct line of sight because of the buses, so it should give us time to find a way out."

"I don't trust these people," Faith whispered.

"Me either," I said.

"But they're doing what they think they need to do to survive."

"We are too," I said.

"Yes, we are too."

Her hand was still over mine.

"So you make sure you survive," she said.

"OK."

"And come back."

More soft breathing in the darkness.

"I have a question for you, Doc."

"Yes?"

"Why don't I dream anymore? I can remember dreaming before the coma."

There was silence while she thought for a moment.

"I don't know," she said.

"I have another question for you, and I want you to promise me an honest answer."

"I won't lie to you."

"Promise?"

"Yes."

"What happened to all the other coma patients at Mercy, the ones from the files? How did they die?"

"Are you sure you want to know?" she asked.

"Yes."

"We were desperate. We did what we had to do to survive. To find a cure." Her voice was soft. "We did what we had to do . . . " Her voice trailed off.

"You experimented on them?"

"Yes."

"On me too?"

"Yes."

"And they died?"

"Yes, but not from the experiments. They all started flat-lining in the weeks before you woke up until you were the last one. We thought you would soon as well."

"No one else survived?"

"Only you."

"And Beck and Eva," I said.

"Yes. And possibly Asher Geere."

"Do you think surviving gave us special blood?"

"Or maybe you survived because you already had special blood."

"Why the four of us? Why me?" I asked.

"Why King David? Why anyone at all?" She reached up and felt for her necklace; my hand went with hers.

"A higher power?"

She didn't respond for a moment, then she said, "Evil has never been limitless. The world has always been given great men and women with the power to fight back."

I didn't know how to respond to that so I didn't. But I liked the thought.

We were both silent.

An idea popped into my head. I did it before I could rethink it. I kissed her. She didn't kiss me back at first. Then she did. Her lips were softer than her skin. They fit mine just right.

I felt her soft breathing. I inhaled. Breathing her in. The kiss felt like it lasted forever. But it was still too quick. I had never felt anything like it before.

She left too soon. But I remembered the kiss all night. I knew I wouldn't forget for a while.

29

The Commander's distraction turned out to be simple. He pulled the fire alarm.

Chaos ensued. Which was strange after how organized they claimed to be. Beck and I dodged people as we made our way to the exit. We had been anxiously waiting to make our move, so we reached the main hallway quickly. We rounded the corner, and I stopped short. Saul stood at the main door. His focus was outside, so he didn't notice us. I pulled Beck back behind the corner. We headed to an emergency exit. I didn't want to be the only ones seen on camera using the emergency exit, so I called loudly, "This way," and a panicked group followed.

A little red light flashed above the door. The exit also had an alarm. The bar across the door gave easily and a second alarm sounded. I ignored it.

Outside I paused long enough for the group to scatter before I led Beck toward the bus lot in back. The alarm suddenly cut off. I heard the thump-thump of helicopter blades in the distance. Beck scrambled underneath a bus. I followed. The sound got closer. I snuck a peek. A black helicopter passed. Not over us, but not very far away either. We laid still. It turned around. It was hard to tell if it was circling us or if it just happened to pass over. I scanned the schoolyard from my low vantage point. I couldn't spot a single person. Their organizational skills had finally paid off. Everything was silent except for the drone of the chopper rotors. The sound slowly faded. The helicopter disappeared the way it had come and didn't return.

Beck tugged my arm. I turned my head. She pointed.

Blue.

The dog crouched under a bus midway down the row. He was looking our way. We crawled bus to bus until we reached him. I patted his head. His tail wagged. It was good to see him. He darted away. Apparently, he didn't feel the same way. He went two buses further and turned. I realized he and I had been through this before. Beck and I followed him.

The dog led us to the last row of buses and paused. Then he darted to a maintenance structure. He stopped at the door just long enough to nudge it open with his nose and disappear inside.

There was no cover between where we were and the structure. Anyone watching from the windows would see us. And we would be trapped if we went into the maintenance shed.

Beck leaned toward my ear. "That's the wrong way. We have to get over the fence." She motioned behind us.

I scanned the area. "Strange, there don't seem to be any cameras pointed at this side of the yard."

"That won't matter if someone sees us from the window."

"We have to take that chance," I said.

I scanned the building. The windows were empty. I made a break for the shed. Beck followed. I respected that.

The building was dim inside. It was just light enough to make out general shapes. Blue stood in the corner waiting for us. He wagged his tail once, then skirted out of sight around some boxes. Again, we followed.

When I saw where he had led us I wanted to hug him, but he didn't seem the type of dog for hugs so I didn't. Someone had dug a tunnel. I assumed it ran out under the fence. That's how Blue had gotten inside. The tunnel was dark but dry. The dirt walls were packed hard. We followed the dog as best we could in the darkness. He stayed close to us as we felt our way along, as if he could sense our eyes were less useful than his. The darkness was probably best so I couldn't see how small the tunnel was. I tried not to think about it. I could feel Blue's tail brush against my leg every so often. I didn't know if his purpose was to calm me, but it did.

Eventually, my eyes spotted a little light ahead. I felt a slight incline as we walked. Blue stopped. The tunnel ended at a set of steps. I mounted them quickly. The stairs ended in a crawl space. I could see shafts of light between the slats of wood floor above us. I found an opening and crawled out. Everything looked familiar. We were in the church across the street from the school. The tunnel ended underneath the platform. It was a well-hidden tunnel since we hadn't found it in our earlier search of the building. I reached down to scratch Blue behind the ears.

"Good boy," I whispered. Then I started toward the front of the church with Beck and Blue following.

We had just reached the back of the sanctuary when Blue heard a noise. He darted behind a pew. I followed him. Beck followed me. We lay quietly and waited.

Saul appeared from the direction of the tunnel. He was alone. At first, I thought he was looking for us, but he moved quickly and didn't stop to check his surroundings. He hurried straight through the sanctuary. His knife was strapped in its usual spot, accompanied by a gun tucked into his waistband. He exited without a glance around. I waited a split second to make sure he was alone, then darted after him. I made it to the door in time to see him disappear around another building. He was walking purposefully. Unafraid.

And he seemed to be headed in the direction the helicopter had taken.

30

Our SUV was parked where we left it. It still worked. I let Blue in and slid behind the wheel. Beck hopped into the passenger side. The hospital was less than an hour away, and the ride there was uneventful.

I parked the vehicle a half mile away, and we continued on foot. The hospital looked the same. As usual there were Anakim wandering around, except now they were inside the fence. Or what was left of it. Most of the fence hung in a twisted mess. We circled the hospital at a good distance. The delivery bay door I had left from was still open. I could see at least ten of the infected inside.

We made our way to the edge of the woods outside the fence. I tried to keep us downwind to be safe. I used a pair of binoculars from the truck to watch. I counted several dozen Anakim outside. Occasionally, I saw one or two walk past a window inside. I spotted someone I recognized, and my heart sank—Dorris, the cafeteria lady. I refocused the lenses and looked again. Then I lowered the binoculars. I couldn't make out the orange eyes from this distance, but I knew she would have them.

I took a deep breath to steel myself.

I brought the binoculars up. Sometimes I could make out a face; most times I couldn't. But I never spotted someone who moved normally. I lowered the glasses again. Beck asked if she could watch for a while. I appreciated it. I handed them to her.

Blue was antsy. He sniffed the air repeatedly. Searching for a scent he didn't hate. He didn't find one. But he didn't growl. Beck and I sat under a tree and watched the hospital. Blue wandered off, his nose working overtime. I let him go. Not that I could stop him. I knew he'd be back.

Beck and I did what we did best—took turns watching. We stayed at it for several hours. I never saw Steven. And neither of us spotted anything that looked hopeful. I was taking a turn watching when I heard a voice say my name.

The voice was so close I jumped. So did Beck.

I turned and there stood Hector. He was close enough to touch. But I didn't try for fear he would vanish into thin air. As usual he moved like a ghost. He was dressed the same as I had seen him in the warehouse. Like a black ops commando, except now he was covered in mud. A pistol grip shotgun much like the Commander's was slung over his shoulder.

"Hector," I said. "Good to see you."

"Glad you made it out, Reece. Is the Commander alive?"

I nodded. "So is Faith. This is Beck Hastings."

They shook hands.

"When the Commander missed a couple pickups, I came to check on him and found this mess. How did you escape?" Hector asked.

I quickly filled him in, hitting only the highlights. He was silent as I talked.

When I finished, he said, "I found five survivors. They're hiding in the woods. I go hunting each day for food. Then I come back by here to check for others, but . . . " He shook his head.

"Can you take us to them?"

"Follow me."

Hector made his way through the woods noiselessly. Beck and I followed less so. I didn't worry about Blue. He had a nose like a bloodhound, so he would find us when he wanted to. The ground was well traveled so we didn't have to fight our way through the brush. I saw the speakers that once sounded the decoy scream. They remained silent as we passed.

Hector led us deeper into the woods. He stayed several steps ahead of us. Like a scout. I could tell when we were getting close because the ground was well worn. Suddenly, Hector froze. We came up behind him and stopped.

"What's wrong?" Beck whispered.

"Too many voices," Hector whispered back. "My group is always quiet. Something isn't right."

I listened. He was right. I heard several voices. Far more than five. They sounded excited.

We crept closer, careful to stay hidden in the trees. The camp was small. There were two camping tents and a slightly larger tent built out of tarps tied between trees. Ashes from a campfire dusted the small clearing. Somewhere between fifteen and twenty people were spread around the camp. One of the animated voices was Van's. I was glad he was alive. I hoped he stayed that way. But at the moment, he was pinned between two filthy guys, one holding each arm. A third walked up and punched him in the stomach. The wind must have gotten knocked out of Van because he quieted instantly.

Xavier stood by one of the tents clutching his computer. A guy twice his size held him. I recognized another one of the captives, but didn't know his name. Rachel, the girl who had come to the hospital with Pete, sat with an overfed Asian guarding her. A muscular man without a shirt stood in the middle of the clearing, towering over Lucy, the nurse who had offered me the wheelchair. She knelt in the dirt at his feet.

Hector whispered, "This is trouble. These gangs are wanderers who rape, kill, and steal to survive."

Two dirty females appeared from the tents with a few items in hand. The main guy leaned over Lucy and said something. Several of the group cheered. Van found his breath again and objected to whatever was said. He earned two more punches for his trouble. Every member of the group was armed, mostly with bats and knifes, but a few had guns.

The shirtless leader said something else. Then he reached down and grabbed Lucy by the arm. Van protested and tried to jerk free but was held fast. One of the men with a bat walked over and slugged him in the chest. Van went limp.

Lucy tried to fight, but she was no match for the man's strength. He dragged her toward the bigger tent.

"Uh oh," Hector whispered. I motioned toward the shotgun slung over his shoulder. "No use. It's empty. I'm out of ammo. I used the last of my shells hunting this morning."

I reached out and grabbed it off his shoulder anyway. He started to protest, but I was already moving.

31

I made my way around the camp, staying out of sight. Shirtless guy threw open the flap to the tent and dragged Lucy inside. She was screaming. Another guy stood outside the tent. As guard. Or next in line.

No one spotted me. I exited the trees, being careful to keep the tent between the gang and me. I could hear them still searching the camp.

I slid up beside the tent and came up behind the guard. My heart was pumping. My mind was focused. But the gun was empty. If they caught me, I was dead. I grabbed the gun by the barrel and swung it like a bat as hard as I could. Bull's-eye. I connected with the back of the guard's head. Wood against bone. I heard the crack, but I was already moving again. He went down in a heap, and I didn't slow to see if it was permanent.

I entered the tent before anyone had a chance to react. Shirtless guy was standing with his back to me. Lucy was on the ground in front of him shaking. He was saying something that sounded like a threat but I didn't wait to hear what it was. I probably had only seconds before a knife or bullet found me. I reached out with my left hand and grabbed a handful of his long hair. It was matted and dirty. I felt bugs. I pulled hard. His head followed his hair. His body followed that. As he was leaning backward, I shoved the shotgun barrel into the small of his back. I backpedaled. We came out of the tent together. My left hand kept him off balance as I spun him by the hair to face his gang. My right hand kept the shotgun digging into his back.

It all happened in the space of a breath. His people were just starting to react as we exited the tent. Guns and knives came up. I spoke quickly, before anyone could continue their thought.

"Nobody move or you'll be painted with your leader's blood. Whoever moves first gets to paint next." My voice came out deeper than normal. More believable. Nobody moved.

"Set your weapons on the ground and leave."

No one did. They were calling my bluff.

Shirtless guy found his voice. I felt him take a breath to say something. I had to cut the head off the snake. Just as he spoke I jerked his head back sharply. Whatever he meant to say came out like he was choking on his tongue rather than speaking.

"Leave. Now," I growled. "You don't want to die for this scum."

A guy dropped his gun. Then another. Two knifes were dropped. People backed away, turned, and left.

"Don't come back here again," I said. "If you do you die, then he dies. In three days, I'll release your leader. Whether you still want a loser like him to tell you what to do is up to you."

The rest turned to go. Some didn't drop their weapons. I didn't push my luck. I let them go. Leaderless, they scattered into the trees.

32

The phone rang at exactly noon the next day. I knew it would. We had spent the night in camp. We kept watch with their guns. No one came back to avenge their leader. He remained tied to a tree. And gagged.

I pressed the accept button.

"Reece. Listen quickly and don't ask questions. I don't have a lot of time." The Commander's voice was more hurried than I had ever heard it. "I just heard on the wire of a guy the Anakim are afraid of. He's in a prison facility to the east. Some type of gathering is planned there. I only have general directions to the area." He gave them to me. "It might be Asher Geere. I need you to go get him and convince him to come back here with you. And it sounds like you should hurry."

I had a lot of questions. But I trusted the Commander so I didn't ask any of them.

"OK," I said.

"What's the situation there?"

"Five survivors from Mercy are all we've been able to find. Van made it. So did Xavier. Of the hospital staff only Lucy and Luke made it out. And Rachel, the new girl. And Hector says to tell you hello."

"Hector's there?" I could hear the smile in his voice.

"He's the reason those five made it this long."

"I'm sure he is." The Commander's voice turned back to steel. "Tell him to prepare the torches. He'll know what it means. Thanks, Reece, I have to go. Good luck. I'll see you soon."

"Commander?"

"Yes?"

"Is Faith OK?"

"She is."

The line went dead. I powered the phone off. Removed the battery. I thought about destroying it. I knew I should. Instead, I put the battery back in and dropped the phone in my pocket. Hector saw me do it.

"I have to go," I said.

"I know."

"I'll come back for you guys."

"You can come back for them." He motioned to the group. "I'm better on my own."

"I thought you might say that," I said. "But you'll stay with them until I return."

"Yes."

I nodded thanks.

"The Commander said to tell you to prepare the torches."

"The villagers are finally ready?" Then he added without waiting for a response. "It'll be a pleasure."

Beck had been watching us. She walked over.

"I'll come with you," she said.

"I thought you might."

"Be careful with that thing." Hector motioned toward my pocket. "It's a live wire. They'll track it."

"I know," I said, "but I have to lead them away from here."

"Just don't let them trap you."

"I won't," I said.

I lied.

33

Blue waited for us by the SUV. For some reason, I got the feeling he had eaten. I was jealous. We got back on the road and headed east. The further inland we drove the more Anakim we saw in the streets. I gave them a wide berth with the truck and they left us alone. Beck spotted a helicopter once. I pulled over until it passed. It didn't appear to notice us. We kept driving.

When we arrived at the prison, the situation was not what I expected. There looked to be no attempt from the humans to hide. In fact, the opposite was true. Several vehicles passed us with humans inside. Each pulled to the gate and waited. I pulled to the side and watched. A car pulled through the first gate and waited for it to shut. Afterward, someone came to the window and spoke to the driver. Then a second gate opened and let the car into the facility. The next vehicle in line repeated the process.

Anakim roamed around the outer fence. The system worked. I didn't see any infected inside. And whoever was in charge apparently wasn't afraid of the Nephilim showing up.

"Well," I said.

"Yeah," Beck responded.

"I have to try."

"You'll be trapped inside."

"You don't have to come with me."

"I'm coming."

I put the vehicle in gear and pulled into line.

The cars moved forward slowly. Every time we pulled forward, I felt the impulse to get out of line. I ignored it. Blue gave a small growl of disapproval from the back. I ignored him too.

The van in front of us pulled through the second gate. It closed behind them. Then it was our turn. The first gate slid open like the throat of a monster. I pulled forward. It slid shut behind us. No going back now. A man knocked on my window. I rolled it down. He examined us. More Beck than me. Then he glanced in the back of the truck. He had the air of a bouncer at a club. One more close examination of Beck. Then back to me.

"Welcome to The Running Games," he said.

The second gate opened.

We entered the monster.

34

I parked the SUV where I couldn't be blocked in and left the keys in the ignition. Blue stayed in the truck. Under protest. But I couldn't wait for him if we had to leave quickly. I tucked one of the gang's guns in my waistband and pulled my shirttail down to cover it.

We followed the people pouring into the main cellblock. Everyone was anxious. There was lots of chatter.

Beck tapped my arm and pointed to the rooftop. "You see that?"

I didn't.

"Just over the rooftop. Is that a helicopter blade?"

I looked again. I saw what she was talking about. It could have been the rotor of a parked helicopter. Or maybe not. It was hard to tell.

We entered the building and passed through a series of security doors. They all stood wide open, which made me feel a little better. Until I realized that getting into a prison is rarely the difficult part. The line of people went single file. I saw why. We were passing through the cellblock. On either side were cells. Hands reached between the bars toward the visitors.

The chatter died instantly. But other louder noises replaced it. Inhuman sounds. Snarls and growls. I felt Beck slow. I kept walking. She did too. When we were even with the first cell, I looked inside. Orange eyes. A female. She strained at the bars, trying to reach us. But we were out of reach. She strained harder.

Her teeth were locked around the bar, grinding, as she tried to chew through the metal.

We kept moving. The next cell contained a man. He also had orange eyes. He was tall with long arms. Everyone squeezed a little tighter to stay out of his reach, but that didn't stop him from trying. Relentlessly.

The next cell held a woman trying to rip the bars from the wall. They didn't budge. Her orange eyes were frantic. She screamed at us. It was ear piercing and heartbreaking at the same time.

The next cell held a man so skinny I thought he might be able to slip through the bars. He thought he might too. His eyes burned with anger that he couldn't.

Each cell we passed was the same. Orange eyes. Hatred and hunger.

The line kept moving. People kept pushing us forward. The occupants of the last three cells were different. No orange eyes. The first was lean, like a runner. He stood in the corner of the cell and watched us warily as we went by. The next occupant was shirtless and all muscle. He sat on the edge of the bed. He smiled a big smile as we passed. The crowd kept pushing. The man in the last cell was sleeping. Or at least had his eyes closed and paid no attention to the parade going by his cell.

We pushed forward until we were outside. The yard. If you could call concrete a yard. People lined the tops of the walls, watching as if they were in the Colosseum. We joined them. Beck stayed close. The games were about to start.

At the four corners of the yard stood watchtowers. Four people manned each. Three of them had rifles. The fourth man in each tower wore sunglasses and watched. Probably the bosses. Their movements were slow and precise. That worried me.

I wondered what good the rifles would do if the Anakim got out of hand. Then I realized. The rifles weren't pointed toward the yard. They were pointed toward the humans. I also realized there were more humans here than I had seen in one place since before my coma.

I leaned over to the guy next to me.

"What's going on here?"

"You've never been to the games before?"

"First time," I said. "What's going on?"

"People trying to win a pass. People running for their freedom."

"A pass from who?"

He looked at me like I was an idiot.

"How come so many people are here?" I asked.

"Word is there's a man who's immune to the Anakim who is fighting today."

Asher.

"Isn't everyone afraid the Nephilim will find out about the games?" I asked.

"Find out?" He shook his head. "Don't you get it? These games are sanctioned."

I tried to ask more, but the guy waved me away. The games were starting.

35

A ripple of excitement ran through the crowd. A voice came over the PA system. "Let's get these games started! Are you all ready for the show?"

The crowd cheered.

"Folks, that weak cheer won't inspire our contestants. I'm not even sure our Catchers could hear you. Are you all even ready?"

The crowd cheered again, much louder this time. When the cheers did die down, I could hear the sound of Anakim screaming like trapped animals.

"That's more like it," the announcer bellowed. "Here's our first matchup of the afternoon."

A man in handcuffs was escorted from the cellblock tunnel. It was the skinny runner. He looked nervous. He probably still wasn't nervous enough. The guards took the handcuffs off. They left the yard. The runner stayed frozen in place.

The announcers voice sounded again, as if it was a boxing match. "In this corner, weighing one hundred and thirty-five pounds, Richard!"

There were a few scattered claps from the crowd.

"And his opponent today is . . . " The crowd waited in anticipation. "The undefeated . . . Yellow Jacket!"

The crowd cheered. I didn't.

Everyone got quiet. People turned their attention to the tunnel. I watched the runner. He saw it first and took off running. He was fast.

But he was way too slow.

It was over in seconds. Yellow Jacket tore into him like a hungry dog. The crowd gasped. Beck clutched my arm. She muttered something that was either a profanity or a prayer. Yellow Jacket finished with Richard and rushed toward the spectators. He clawed at the wall, trying to climb. People instinctively drew back from the edge. The wall was too tall and too flat to scale, but that didn't dissuade the Nak. He kept trying. Someone leaned over and spat on him. He went into a frenzy. Jumping and reaching. But it was to no avail.

I turned to the guy on the other side of me. He smelled like alcohol. "How can anyone win?"

He pointed to a large electronic clock on the wall. It looked like a basketball shot clock. It said 0:26 in big red letters.

"If the human can last thirty seconds they win."

The runner had lasted four.

"How do they get the Nak to stop after the clock expires?" I asked.

He paused for a moment like he hadn't thought of that. "I dunno. I don't think anyone has ever lasted long enough to find out. But I'm sure they have a way."

He had more faith than I did.

Yellow Jacket still leaped to reach the audience. Eventually, the crowd got quiet. Yellow Jacket paused. He tilted his head like he heard something. He turned and dashed back into the tunnel.

"How do they get them to go back into their cells?" I asked.

"You don't want to know," the guy responded.

"How?"

"They reward them."

"Reward them with what?" Then I heard the scream.

He was right. I didn't want to know.

The announcer wasted no time. "Our next matchup . . . " It was the big guy. They led him out in handcuffs. He was so big they had to use two sets linked together. They took them off, and he smiled at the crowd. A big smile. The guards exited, and he didn't wait. While the announcer was telling everyone his name was Oscar, the big guy was already moving to the corner of the yard, toward the concrete and metal gym equipment. He lumbered. Fast for a big guy but not a run. He made it to the equipment.

"His opponent today is making his first appearance at the games. In his Catcher debut . . . it's Gunslinger!"

The lean Nak with long arms exited the tunnel. The clock started. 0:29.

At first the Nak didn't see Oscar. The crowd booed. The clock hit 0:25.

Oscar picked up a weight lifting bar as if it were weightless. Gunslinger heard it above the crowd. He turned and started for Oscar. It took him less than two seconds to cover the ground. Oscar took that time to move behind a piece of equipment. Gunslinger plowed through the steel machine like it was made of toothpicks. But he stumbled, and Oscar sidestepped him and swung the bar at his head. It missed and the crowd groaned. The clock was at 0:18.

Gunslinger righted himself. Oscar moved so that another piece of equipment was between them. Gunslinger didn't hesitate. Same thing. Same result. A stumble. A miss. 0:12.

Oscar moved behind another piece. He was running out of equipment. Gunslinger charged again. Oscar waited longer to move. Maybe he was tired. He was too slow. Gunslinger stumbled but grabbed Oscar's foot with his long arm. Oscar tried to pull away. His strength was no match for the Nak. Oscar swung the bar like his life depended on it. It connected with the base of the Nak's skull. His grip loosened and Oscar tore his foot free. 0:06 showed on the clock. The Nak was stunned. Oscar turned and ran. Gunslinger shook the blow off quickly. He was back up. 0:03. The crowd cheered. I held my breath. 0:02. Time slowed down. Gunslinger reached for Oscar. 0:01. It was over. One way or the other. Oscar fell. Or dove.

Gunslinger fell too. 0:00.

Neither moved. Everyone looked around confused. Beck pointed. A gunman in one of the towers was reloading his rifle. I looked back at Gunslinger. A tranquilizer dart was stuck in his neck.

Oscar pushed the Nak off him and stood up. A huge smile for the crowd. They cheered. I joined them.

The announcer's voice sounded above the din of the crowd. "A false start has been declared."

The crowd noise died instantly. A female voice booed. Others joined in.

"The match is declared a tie. Oscar and Gunslinger will have a rematch."

The crowd booed louder. Another gunman took aim. A dart hit Oscar in the shoulder. He went down with the smile still on his face.

36

The crowd didn't like the outcome of the match, and they let it be known. The booing continued while the guards carried a sleeping Oscar and Gunslinger back to their cells. A man threw a beer bottle onto the yard. It broke on the concrete. A gunman turned and shot him. Not with a tranquilizer dart. The man's body tumbled over the wall, quieting the crowd.

The announcer's voice came on and refocused them. "And now, our main event of the evening."

The guards brought out the man we had seen sleeping in the last prison cell. His face was impassive. His shoulders were squared and his head level. He ignored the crowd. His chains were removed. He didn't flinch. He didn't turn away from the tunnel.

"I think I recognize that guy," Beck said.

"From the flight?" I asked.

"Weighing a lean two hundred pounds, it's the man you have all been waiting to see . . . Asher!"

He gave no response to his name. The crowd was quiet, waiting for the real show.

"And his opponent . . . always a fan favorite . . . the one and only Red Rock!"

There still wasn't a reaction from Asher. He could have still been napping for all the emotion he showed.

It happened fast. Red Rock exploded from the tunnel. Asher didn't attempt to run away. He didn't even move. The

Nak closed the distance quickly. He didn't seem to be afraid of the human. The Nak growled. Asher growled back. Then the unexpected happened; he lunged at the Nak.

Red Rock flinched. Then backpedaled. The crowd cheered. Asher lunged at him again, trying to grab the Nak. Red Rock spun away. The clock said 0:25 but the match was over. Or maybe not. Another Nak came out of the tunnel. Asher's back was turned. The Nak came fast. When it was almost on top of him, Asher spun. This Nak ran away too. Asher bellowed at both of them.

A dozen more Naks poured from the tunnel. Someone was emptying the cells. I didn't know if Asher could handle that many. Then I saw something I knew he couldn't handle. The four watchers with sunglasses were on the move. They were descending the stairs from the watchtowers. I knew it instantly from the way they moved. They were Nephilim. And they were here for Asher.

The dozens of Anakim closed in. So did the four Nephs.

"Go get the truck," I said to Beck.

Then I jumped over the wall.

It was a long drop, and I landed hard. I tucked and rolled on the concrete but came up running. More Anakim filled the yard. At least thirty. I ran toward Asher. Several Anakim were in my path. I didn't slow. At first, I thought they wouldn't move. Then they did. The wall of bodies parted. I heard the crowd gasp. Someone yelled, "There are two of them!"

Chaos reigned.

The Nephilim were still coming. But they were having trouble getting through the crowd of people. A couple humans fell off the wall in the fray. The Anakim were not kind to them. I made my way to Asher and grabbed his arm.

"Let's get out of here!" I yelled. He didn't hesitate.

We sprinted toward the cellblock. The Anakim made way for us. The cell doors were all open. A few Anakim still roamed the halls. We ran down the corridor. The cells were all empty except one. Oscar lay on the floor where he had been dumped. He was still out cold. We were almost free of the building when Asher stopped. An Anakim had seen Oscar too. She was just entering his cell. Asher sprinted back and chased the Anakim away.

"C'mon!" I yelled. "We have to go. They're coming!"

"I can't leave him," Asher yelled back.

"There's no time. He's unconscious and the Nephs are coming!"

Asher didn't reply. He grabbed the blanket from the bed. Threw it on the floor and tried to roll Oscar onto it. He was too heavy.

"Help me."

I did. Against my better judgment.

We got him on the blanket. It took both of us to drag him. I kept glancing behind us, waiting for the Nephilim to appear. We exited the building before they did. A human guard tried to stop us at the front door. I pulled the gun from my waistband and shot him in the leg. He went down, and we kept going.

Beck had the SUV at the door ready to go. Asher and I wrestled Oscar inside. I heard an engine turn over. Asher jumped in. I looked up. The blades Beck had spotted earlier were slowly spinning. That's why the Nephilim hadn't caught us yet. They were going for the helicopter. I knew it would only take a minute to get the engine up to speed. We had to move fast.

"Get in," Beck said.

I checked the chopper again. No time to open the gates. We weren't going to make it.

"Go. Get the group from the hospital and get everyone back to the school. The Commander will know what to do."

"No!" Beck yelled. "Get in. We can make it."

I shook my head. "We won't. I'll open the gates for you. There's only one helicopter. The Nephs will follow me. You go the other direction."

I slammed the door on her protests. But not fast enough, Blue slid out before it closed. There wasn't time to put him back in. Stupid dog.

I ran to a prisoner transport bus parked by the building. Blue was at my heels. The door was unlocked. We got in. It was built like a tank with reinforced windows and a steel cage. That would come in handy. I hoped the keys were in the ignition. They weren't. I tossed a nightstick off the seat and checked the cushions. They weren't there either. The visor. Bingo. Precious seconds wasted. I could faintly hear the thump-thump of the helicopter rotors working up to speed.

I inserted the key. Said a little prayer. It turned over.

"Buckle up," I said. I wasn't sure if it was to Blue or myself. Neither of us did.

I pushed the pedal to the floor. The diesel engine groaned to life, and the bus lurched forward. I had about fifty yards to get up to speed. It was going to take every one of them. I shifted gears. The bus complained, but obliged.

The bus hit the gate going thirty miles per hour. I kept the pedal down. I heard the sound of steel bending. The gate gave way. One more to go. The second gate offered even less resistance.

I glanced in the rearview mirror. The helicopter was just taking off. It was a military helicopter with guns mounted on the side. Not good. I turned left. Beck was right behind me. She turned right. A single honk good-bye and she was gone. I saw a few humans had made it to their cars and were following our lead. That was good.

I shifted gears again. I needed to create enough of a chase that the truck could get away. Then I needed to ditch the bus. If I lasted that long.

37

I was right. The helicopter followed me, not Beck and company. Which was good for them. And very bad for me.

I pushed the bus to its limit—sixty miles per hour. The chopper kept up easily. I figured I had two choices. Head back west toward the city, or go northeast toward the mountains. I chose the latter. The further I could lead them from Beck the better. The Nephilim were probably calling for backup. But with four Nephs in the helicopter, they had to be spread thin. I guessed the closest reinforcements would take at least a few minutes to arrive. Unless they had already split up and all four hadn't gotten in the chopper, which was a possibility, but one I couldn't worry about.

I kept the gas pedal to the floor. I had to lose the chopper.

The helicopter windows were black. I could only see vague outlines inside. The chopper seemed content to hover above me as we sped along. They knew I had to stop sometime, and they were betting they could outlast me. I looked at my fuel gauge. They were probably right. I had to change the odds somehow.

The road split and the chopper shot out in front of me and dropped low. The blades were even with the bus. It appeared the Anakim weren't the only ones who liked to play chicken. The helicopter's fifty-caliber guns spat bullets that dug into the pavement to my right. I spun the wheel left and kept the pedal down.

I hadn't noticed the road inclining, but I could hear the engine struggle. I saw a sign that read ELEVATION, TWO THOUSAND

FEET. I looked at the gauges. We had slowed ten miles per hour. I didn't relax the gas pedal. The helicopter resumed its hover position above me. My hands hurt from gripping the wheel. Blue sat quietly beside me. If he was as anxious as I was, he sure wasn't showing it. I felt a bead of sweat run down my spine.

The road cut through a hill pass. It was too narrow for the chopper blades, and the helicopter had to climb a couple hundred feet to avoid crashing into the rocks. It stayed just above and in front of the bus. As soon as the road widened, it came back down. I drove on. It flew on.

The road inclined more. Another sign. ELEVATION, FOUR THOUSAND FEET. The bus slowed another five miles per hour. The fuel gauge continued to drop quickly. I pushed on. I couldn't stop. And there was nowhere to turn. A fifty-foot rock wall rose on the left side, and on my right, a guardrail kept drivers from a thousand-foot drop.

The thump-thump of the rotors grew fainter. I looked up as the chopper disappeared around the bend in front of us. The road was still too narrow to turn around. I kept going. The bus rounded the bend. The road split. Again, the helicopter hovered over the road to the right. The guns spat bullets, forcing me to the left. I realized they weren't playing chicken. They were directing me where they wanted me to go.

I had no choice. I went left. Further up the mountain. The helicopter resumed its hover above us.

"What now?" I said out loud.

I glanced at Blue. He had no answer for me.

I continued driving. Toward what? I was sure I didn't want to know. The bus was really struggling with the altitude now. It was built like a tank—too heavy. The realization finally hit me. There was no way to lose the chopper. And there was no way I could fight multiple Nephilim.

The road leveled off slightly. I spotted another split in the road ahead. About a mile ahead. The helicopter lifted and disappeared around another bend. An idea popped into my head. It was stupid. I checked with Blue, but he didn't have a better one. I grabbed the wheel tighter.

We were almost to the bend. I looked around the floor for the discarded nightstick. I spotted it behind the seat. I leaned toward it but couldn't quite reach it without taking my foot off the gas. I couldn't let off. I needed all the speed I could get. I stretched as far as I could reach. My fingertips grazed the stick, but I couldn't grasp it. The bus started to slow. I pressed the pedal back to the floor.

Time was almost up.

I felt something bump my arm. I turned to see Blue with the nightstick in his mouth. I grabbed it from him and jammed it between the gas pedal and the seat. I pulled the lever to open the door. I reached down and grabbed the dangling seatbelt. I looped one end around the door lever and held onto the other. I took the cell phone from my pocket and dialed a random number. Then I tossed it on the seat. I scooped Blue up in my arms. He looked unsure of the plan. I was too.

I yanked the steering wheel and jumped.

We hit the ground hard. At some point the belt was jerked from my hand. I hoped I had held onto it long enough to pull the door closed behind us. I needed the Nephs to think we were still in the bus. At some point, I also let go of Blue. We both hit the ground rolling. I heard him yelp. I probably would have yelped, too, but the wind was knocked out of me. I heard metal on metal.

I finally stopped rolling and lay on my back trying to breathe. It was harder than I remembered. I pulled myself together enough to check on the bus. The guardrail was gone. As was the bus. I could hear it crashing off rocks and trees below. I heard the helicopter go over the side after it.

Blue licked my face. I knew we had to get moving. I figured we probably had ten minutes to clear the area before they found a spot to land and check the wreckage to find out we weren't there. That wasn't a lot of time.

Blue was limping slightly. Favoring one leg. Probably just trying to get sympathy from me. I didn't have time for it. My pants were torn and my leg was skinned but nothing was broken. Both of us moved quickly despite our injuries. We both knew getting off the mountain was life or death.

Fortunately, we happened upon a vehicle quickly. A Jeep was parked in a shed at the first cabin we found. The fuel tank was bone dry, but after a quick search I discovered a full gas can under a tarp. The Jeep was old. Rack and pinion steering old. It also had no doors. But it ran.

I was wrong. The helicopter only took seven minutes to clear the wreckage. By that time, we were already on our way. I pulled over out of sight when I spotted the chopper in my rearview mirror. I saw it dip down again to land, possibly dropping off some of the crew to search on foot. They liked to stay in pairs so that meant two in the helicopter and two on the ground, which also meant all four Nephs had followed me and not Beck and crew.

I spun rocks under my tires as soon as the helicopter dipped. Then pulled over and hid and pulled back on the road each time the chopper came in and out of view. They flew ever-widening concentric circles, looking for us. Obviously, they figured we were on foot or in hiding. We had gotten lucky with the Jeep. I watched the sky and remained tense, always expecting to see their backup arrive.

At least going downhill in the Jeep was faster than uphill in the bus. Blue enjoyed the ride more than I did. He was more relaxed. His head hung outside the Jeep with his black-spotted tongue flapping in the wind. At the bottom of the mountain, I pointed the Jeep west toward the school. I continually listened for the thump-thump of helicopter blades. None came. Maybe I should have hung my tongue in the wind too, and enjoyed the freedom while I could. Because when I got back to the school everything had changed.

38

I hid the Jeep around the corner from the school. It might come in handy if I needed it later. I didn't use the tunnel. I walked in through the main gate. Blue refused to come inside the fence. He didn't like enclosed spaces. I knew the feeling.

The motion sensors must have spotted me immediately because Saul and the Commander met me at the door.

"Welcome back," Saul said. He didn't ask where I had gone. I guessed the Commander had filled him in. Which meant they now trusted each other.

I nodded. "Beck make it back safely?" I asked.

"Yes," the Commander answered. "She brought Van and the hospital crew. Good job with Asher. She told us about the prison."

"Did Faith test his blood?"

"Yes, it was a match. Eva is back on her feet already."

"That was fast."

"You made it back just in time. And everyone is anxious to see you. C'mon, we were just meeting in the library."

I followed. Saul didn't.

I entered the library behind the Commander and found a seat beside Faith. She was toying with her necklace. She dropped it and gave me a smile. I felt like a plant being watered. I returned the favor. Beside her sat Beck and Eva, who looked a little weak but alive. Asher sat at a study table beside Oscar, who had his standard ear-to-ear smile in place. Always happy to be alive. Beside him were the rescued hospital staff and Rachel. All sat except Van, who leaned against a bookcase. He nodded at me when I entered. Xavier was alone at another desk, head buried in his computer. He was chewing on his lip. Together there were twelve of us.

After greetings all around, everyone looked to the Commander. "The people you see around you can be trusted. Most here have risked their life or had their life saved by another person in this room." Most everyone glanced around. The Commander continued, "Despair and fear are easy. Trust and faith are hard. But fear never gives you anything in return. Trust and faith do. Remember that. We are no longer content to survive. We are going to fight." His voice filled the library. Even Xavier looked up from his monitor.

"The Nephilim have used the Anakim to terrorize us and to protect themselves. They've used the fear of infection to guard themselves. But now we have a weapon of our own, and we're going to fight back. We are now a part of the network of uninfected people. We'll all work together to take down the Nephilim." The Commander scanned the room. "If anyone here wants to leave, if anyone here is content to hide and survive, then feel free to leave now. But realize, if you are afraid, as we all are, you can run from your fear, but you cannot outrun it." No one moved. "Together then, we will fight. Doctor."

Faith stood and made her way beside the Commander. "There's still a lot we do not know about the virus. We don't know why in some people's bodies the virus restricts blood flow to the brain and turns them to Anakim while in others it increases blood flow to the brain. Creating Nephilim with higher-than-normal-functioning brains. While still other bodies can't handle it at all and die at the moment of infection. We also don't know if there is a cure. But we now have one example of a human recovering—Eva."

"And what is this weapon we have?" Oscar asked.

"You afraid big guy?" Asher asked.

"No, I got my weapons right here." He flexed his arm and smiled. "I was just worried about the rest of ya'll."

Faith cut in. "Our new weapon is blood. More specifically it is blood found in four people: Nick, Asher, Eva, and Beck. All four of them have the same blood markers that make the Anakim afraid, and if their blood is not immune, then at least it's resistant to the virus. Eva recovered after being bitten."

"What markers?" Lucy, the nurse, asked.

"Elevated T cells for one. Other cell mutations I have not seen before."

"Will it really help us fight the Anakim?" Lucy said. "And what about the Nephilim?"

Van spoke up. "It helped me."

All heads turned toward him. "That's how I was able to escape the hospital. I found this in the doctor's lab." He held up a vial of blood. It had numbers on it. 1437. My blood.

"That's how you got us out of the hospital?" Luke asked.

"Yes," Van said. "The blood also works outside of the body. But I think it loses its power the longer it's unrefrigerated. This blood worked well at first, but the longer I kept it in my pocket, the less powerful it seemed to get."

"That makes sense," Faith said. "Without refrigeration, the cells die, causing the blood to lose its potency."

"So the Anakim are afraid of the blood, but we don't know if the blood has any effect on the Nephilim?" Luke asked.

Faith turned to me. I couldn't tell them that the opposite was true. During every exposure, I had been terrified in the presence of the Nephilim. Fortunately, I never got the chance to answer. The library door banged open and Saul entered the room.

"You should come see this," he said. "We've finally caught one."

39

The Commander and Saul agreed to let me talk to him first, probably as an experiment. I walked into the gymnasium. The faint but familiar buzz filled my ears. I checked the double doors. They were closed.

He sat chained to the post where I had once been chained. But they had used more chains on him than they had used on me. He watched as I walked over. His black eyes followed me closely. He didn't speak. I got the idea he thought he was in complete control despite the chains.

Ten steps away, I stopped. The same fear that overcame me in the hospital hallway was back. Terror descended on me like a curtain. Complete, mindless panic filled me. I wanted to turn. To run. To hide from those black eyes. I couldn't remember why I was here. What I was doing. Small drops of cold sweat beaded my arms.

He blinked. I looked down, as if searching for something. I took a breath. Then another. I looked up. He watched me. No smile. No fear. No emotion. Just watching me. Like he was reading a book. I set my jaw and stepped forward.

He didn't get up. Somehow, I knew he wanted me to sit down. I resisted the urge. He didn't speak. I didn't either. I wanted him to speak first. I waited. He did too.

We stayed locked in a silent power struggle.

I took the opportunity to examine him. I did it without taking my eyes off his. He wore black mixed with shades of gray.

His hair was sandy brown. It looked clean. He had nice skin, also clean, with a healthy glow.

He blinked again. Then he finally spoke. "Not what you expected?"

I couldn't tell if it was a question or a statement. He spoke again. "You expected a monster. A demon. Instead, what you see before you is a man." A pause. Then more quietly, "But also more than a man." Another pause. He was in no rush. "Much more."

"You are a Nephilim?"

A subtle nod. One that might not have happened.

"My name is Coal, like charcoal."

I didn't respond. The fear still lurked in the back of my mind. I shoved it away.

"Again, not what you expected. You didn't expect us to have names and personalities. All you know about us is what you've been told by other humans who are scared, like you." He glanced over my shoulder, then back. "Yet you are not quite like them, are you?"

How could he know that?

"What are you?" I asked

"I am the future. I used to be merely a man. Now I am a Nephilim. We are the race of the future."

"The future?"

"Yes, I am what man has been trying to become for three thousand years. Smarter. Stronger. A new breed of superhuman."

"But you came from the past," I said.

"We are from the past and the future. We are what you could be. What you should be." His voice dropped to a whisper. "What you can be."

I realized I was sitting. I couldn't remember when that happened.

"And Arba?"

"He is transcendental. The new standard. The king of a new empire."

"Why do you want to kill all humans?"

"We don't want to kill the humans. We want to make them like us. Gods on earth. It is true, some humans have blood that is weak and they will die in the process. But they would have died anyway, eventually."

"And the Anakim?"

"A mutation of our perfect genes. A lower life form that is useful to us for now. But once we have converted all humans, we will eliminate the Anakim as well. They have no hope of an elevated state. Only our perfect race will remain."

I said nothing.

"You can join us," he said. His tongue grazed the side of his lip as he spoke. Then disappeared.

"What do the Nephilim want?"

"A new world order. We are building an empire. We offer the opportunity for humans to become gods. And we've been looking for you."

"Me? How did you know about me?"

"Because a coin always has two sides. We always knew you were out there somewhere, or you would be. You are the other side of the coin. It was only a matter of time."

I realized something. "That's what the prison games are about. You're using the fights to find us, like you use the Anakim to flush us out. That's why they said the fight was sanctioned, because they are allowed by Nephilim to find us."

"Sec? There is hope for you." He smiled. "There are limits to our resources, but not our intellect. There aren't enough of us to search everywhere. Why spread ourselves thin and expend our resources when humans will do the job for us?" He paused.

"And now, here you are. Join us. You can leave this place with me. I bring an invitation from Arba himself to join us in the new Babylon."

"New Babylon?"

"The capital city of the new empire—the center of the new world. What used to be called Washington, DC. Join us. Come with me. I can save you."

I didn't feel the fear anymore. At some point, it had disappeared. A strange calm took its place. My mind was clearer than it had ever been. Or maybe it was in a deeper fog. I didn't know which.

"Save me from what?"

A smirk tugged at his mouth. He didn't answer. I had heard enough.

I stood up. It was a sudden movement, but it didn't take the Nephilim by surprise. Neither was he surprised when I drew the pistol from my waistband. He watched. Almost disinterested.

I chambered a round.

He looked at the gun with something that could have been disdain.

I pointed it at him.

He didn't blink.

I pulled the trigger.

Someone grabbed my arm as I fired. The bullet sailed high. Arms pulled me backward. The Commander and Saul.

"What are you doing?" I growled.

They pulled me out of the room. I shook them off.

"Not yet," the Commander said.

"We need to get more information from him," Saul said.

I glared at him.

He spun that long knife of his. "Then I swear I'll personally cut his vampire head off."

40

I woke unusually early the next morning to the sound of a helicopter passing over. I hated that sound. I listened. It faded away and didn't come back. I couldn't go back to sleep so I retrieved coffee from the cafeteria. I sipped it as I watched the empty street outside.

Only it didn't stay empty. Anakim gathered outside the fence. Only one at first—a lone girl. She wandered aimlessly. Then two more arrived. They were obviously Naks, but none of them had orange eyes. Then I spotted several more. By the time my coffee mug was half empty, there were dozens wandering around outside the gates. Strange. There had never been any outside the school before.

Occasionally, one would wander off, but their number never lessened. It kept growing. I finished my coffee and decided to check on Blue. Maybe take him some food. I knew he could scavenge something to eat on his own, but with all the Anakim, it wouldn't hurt to check.

I went to the cafeteria and found some mystery meat in need of rescue. I filled my pockets. Next, I had to find an exit that didn't have someone watching it. The door by the back, where the buses were parked, was clear. And someone had done me a favor. The little red light wasn't blinking. It was disarmed already. I exited and headed for the maintenance shed.

The door was already open and the tunnel illuminated. Light bulbs I hadn't seen last time were strung down its length.

I briefly considered going back and exiting through the main gate. The Anakim might be easier to deal with than the confined space of the tunnel. Instead, I took a deep breath and hurried through. I emerged and did a quick sweep of the church. Blue wasn't there. I made my way to the bell tower to scan the area. I still didn't see Blue.

I kept looking. I knew he would be sneaking around some-where. Probably being extra careful because of the Anakim. I kept looking. No dog. But I did notice something else. Four blocks away were parked several black motorcycles. I couldn't tell how many there were. I counted seven, but that was only what I could see between the buildings, so there were probably more. I watched for movement.

Eventually, I spotted a black figure moving between two buildings. He walked quickly but not frantically. He disappeared.

I spotted another Neph two blocks over from the first. She also moved quickly, but also without appearing to rush. They were headed toward the church. That wasn't good. I had to get moving.

I darted back into the tunnel and rushed through without thinking about how close the ceiling was to my head. I needed to find Faith first. Then warn everyone. The Nephilim were coming.

When I emerged from the shed, I saw it was too late for a warning. The school was on fire.

The flames were already crawling up the sides of the build-ing. I ran inside to find Faith. People were just starting to wake up, slowly realizing something was wrong. I made it easier by pulling the fire alarm. Everyone still moved slowly, probably thinking it was a false alarm again. Then someone screamed and everyone moved faster.

I checked the cafeteria first since it was closest. Faith wasn't there. Next, I checked the nurse's office, where they had stationed her. It was empty. I headed toward Faith's room. I ran into Beck on the way.

"Get everyone out front," I yelled as I rushed past. "Find the Commander and tell everyone to meet in front of the school!"

"We should use the tunnel," she called after me.

"No. Tell everyone to go to the front gate," I yelled over my shoulder.

Faith wasn't in her room either. Her bedding was in disarray. She had exited quickly. That was good. Maybe she was already out front. Flames licked the walls. No more time. I headed for the exit.

The front of the building was already going up in flames. I exited the back. It looked like I was one of the last people out. I didn't spot any of our group. The remnant streamed toward the maintenance shed.

"Stop!" They didn't. I kept trying. A few people turned.

"No! Stop!" I sprinted toward them, waving my arms. "Don't use the tunnel!"

Someone yelled, "The Anakim are out front."

They continued running for the shed.

"I can save you from the Anakim."

Most of the people had already entered the shed.

"No, don't use the tunnel. Trust me, I can save you."

The last few people stopped.

"Trust me," I pleaded. "Don't use the tunnel. Nephs are waiting. Come with me, I can save you."

A couple people nodded. The others entered the shed, headed toward the enemy.

I made my way to the front of the school with the two stragglers I had saved. Or hoped to save.

I heard my name. The Commander. He waved me over to the gymnasium. It wasn't on fire yet. I looked inside. Coal was

288   The Nephilim Virus

gone. The chains that once held him were lying loosely around the post. The cuffs were locked but empty. There was no blood. No sign of a struggle. He was just gone.

The Commander cursed. "Let's get out of here."

"We have to go through the front gate," I said. "Nephilim are waiting at the end of the escape tunnel."

"I knew something wasn't right with a fire and the Anakim at the same time," he said. "The Nephs set a trap for us."

"I told Beck to get everyone out front. We'll have to take our chances with the Naks."

We turned to leave but something caught my eye. There was a sliver of silver on the ground. I bent down to check it out. Faith's necklace lay on the concrete. The chain was broken. I didn't know what it meant, but it couldn't be good. I grabbed it and ran.

The Commander was already moving. I was right behind him. The school continued to burn. We rounded the corner. Everyone was there, huddled out of sight. The Anakim at the fence looked anxious. High strung but not enraged. They hadn't spotted the humans yet.

Then that changed. They saw us. A noise akin to a wolf pack calling each other sounded over the roar of the fire. They tore at the fence bars. The bars were thick, but they didn't stand a chance. They bent like copper wire.

Asher was the first to move. He put himself between the group and the Anakim. Beck joined him. The people huddled together in a tight knot. Eva joined me. The four of us made a ring around the group and walked together toward the oncoming Anakim. I checked Eva. She looked hesitant but kept pace. I scanned the rest of the group. The realization hit me like a hammer. Faith wasn't in the group.

Everything came together for me. The broken necklace. The exit being disarmed. The tunnel light already illuminated.

Someone had taken Faith. Coal? But how had he gotten free from his restraints?

I turned toward the tunnel. My back was to the tightly packed group.

I heard the Commander yell my name, but I didn't care. I had to find Faith. He yelled again.

The group stopped, waiting for me.

"I have to find Faith," I yelled.

"The group needs you, Reece." His voice was even.

"They took her!"

"We'll go after her. But the group needs you. We can't get out without you. There's too many of them."

I looked over his shoulder. The Naks were almost on us. Orange eyes and rage. I scanned the humans. Stark fear in their eyes.

"Save this group, Reece. Then we'll go after Faith."

I looked at the Commander. I found no fear, only steely determination. He wasn't lying.

"They want war. We'll give them war," he said.

I knew what I had to do. I moved back into the circle between Eva and Beck and across from Asher. The uninfected humans stayed in a tight bunch in the middle. The Anakim arrived like a tidal wave. But a tidal wave that broke on the rock of the four of us. They parted as we moved through. There was anger in their eyes at having to give ground. And there was something else. Something that had transferred to them.

Fear.

Book III
Arba

Part I

Faith
Twelve Hours Earlier

1

"Dr. Richards. Dr. Richards."

Nick was calling my name. His voice came through the haze. It was friendly but insistent.

"Dr. Richards, Nick needs your help." The voice changed. It wasn't Nick's voice. My eyes fluttered open, still heavy with sleep.

"Doctor, you need to come with me. Nick Reece is in danger. He needs your help." It was Saul. He was crouched beside my cot.

I sat up and rubbed the sleep from my eyes. "What's going on?"

"Nick's in trouble. He needs you."

My senses sharpened. "What's going on? Where is he?"

"He's in the gymnasium. Come with me. I'll take you to him." He stood, but didn't move away from my cot.

I heard a helicopter in the distance outside.

My instincts told me something wasn't right. Maybe it was the way Saul towered over me. Or the way his hand hovered over his knife. But if Nick was in trouble, I had to help him, so I stood and followed Saul.

As we moved through the main building, Saul stayed close. Too close. He violated my personal space. I felt his hand hovering over my lower back to guide me in case I slowed. I didn't slow. We made it to the emergency exit and stopped. It was armed with an alarm. Saul coded a few numbers in the box next to the door. The little red light stopped blinking. We exited and headed toward the gymnasium.

The gym was dark. Only a little of the early morning light spilled through the high windows. Again, something didn't feel right. Saul guided me in and closed the door behind us. He flipped a switch, and the big overhead lights clicked and flickered and slowly started to glow. The light grew as the incandescent bulbs charged. It took a minute, but finally I was able to make out the shape of someone. Coal. I didn't see Nick anywhere.

Saul handed something to the Neph. A key.

"Where's Nick?" I asked. "What are you doing?"

The Nephilim undid his handcuffs as Saul walked over to me. I backed up a step. I saw Coal carefully re-latch the cuffs and place them on the ground. As if he had melted out of them.

I turned to run, but I was too slow. Saul grabbed me. I jerked away but felt something catch on my neck. It felt like I was being choked with a wire. I felt a sharp pain and then I was free and moving toward the door again.

Saul grabbed at my arm with his free hand. I aimed a kick between his legs. He twisted so my blow glanced off his thigh. He slapped me with the back of his knife hand, and I stumbled backward. I tasted blood. He grabbed and lifted me so that my feet were off the ground. I kicked my legs, trying to connect with anything solid. I found only air. He brought his knife hand around to cover my mouth. Or cut my throat.

I twisted hard, and his grip loosened enough that I slid down. My feet found solid ground. I stomped on his foot with my heel. It was a move Steven had taught me. It worked. Saul grunted and let go. I ran for the door.

Suddenly, Coal was in front of me. I hadn't seen him move. I tried to stop but stumbled right into him. He grabbed my arms. He was surprisingly gentle. But firm.

Saul rushed up and extended his knife to my throat. I saw murder in his brown eyes.

Like the Nephilim's grip, Coal's voice was gentle but firm. "Enough. That won't be necessary."

Saul didn't argue. He lowered the knife and stepped back.

Coal leaned forward toward my neck. He inhaled deeply. My own breath caught in my throat.

"You'll come with us," he said in a whisper. It wasn't a question.

I nodded, though I wasn't sure why.

He slowly reached his hand toward my neck. I stood frozen. My mind screamed for my legs to run, but my body didn't obey. I wanted to cry out, but I couldn't breathe. His finger felt cold as it grazed the soft skin of my neck. I felt vulnerable. Helpless. Naked. I thought of Nick. I wished he were with me.

He drew his hand back. Blood from my neck dripped from his finger.

"You are bleeding, my dear," he said.

Again, I nodded. Again, I was unsure why.

He licked the blood off his finger without expression. His black eyes stared unblinking into mine. We stood that way for a moment.

Then they led me outside, one on either side of me. There was no one else awake yet. There were no lookouts as far as I could see. Maybe Saul had given them the morning off. Neither of my captors spoke. I didn't beg. Or cry. I knew it would do no good, and I was too strong for that. We entered the maintenance shed. Neither bothered to close the door behind us. I hoped Nick would see it open later. I hoped he and the Commander would find me in time.

Saul attached a cable to a large car battery and moments later a tunnel lit up. We went through and emerged in the church across the street. Coal shivered as we passed the altar. He remained expressionless but moved quickly to exit the church.

We walked several blocks, passing a dozen or more Anakim wandering the streets, but they paid us no attention. Now it was Saul who shivered with discomfort. About a half mile from the school, we entered a building. It was empty and had been heavily vandalized. Gang markings painted the walls. Trash littered the hallways. We headed straight to the roof.

My pulse raced in fear when we exited the stairwell onto the roof. A helicopter. Two people sat inside. As soon as they saw us, they started the engine. The blades started to turn slowly. Then faster. Saul and Coal led me forward. I resisted, but it was no use.

Coal got in first. Saul pushed me in beside the Nephilim and then climbed in after me so I was forced to sit between them in the back seat. The two black-clad men in the front turned at the same time. Both had black eyes. One handed Coal a headset. They turned forward without offering Saul one. The traitor didn't look pleased about the oversight but didn't argue.

The rotors continued to speed up, preparing for takeoff.

"Where are you taking me?" I asked Coal above the thump of the blades.

"Patience, doctor, you will find out soon enough," he said. "I invited your friend Nick but he declined."

The blades were up to speed and the helicopter took off.

"He'll come for me," I said as the ground fell away.

"Yes, dear, he will. We are planning on it."

I reached up to rub my necklace. It wasn't there.

2

We landed about an hour later somewhere in the desert. We switched to a larger helicopter, also painted black. It was a military helicopter. Again, I was forced to sit between Coal and Saul. Our first pilots stayed with the old aircraft. But the new pilots looked so similar that if I hadn't seen the switch, I wouldn't have noticed. We flew for what seemed like forever. We landed long enough to refuel the aircraft, and then we flew forever again. When we landed the next time, we transferred back to another civilian helicopter. Another all-black model. Again, the pilots looked the same to me.

We flew on. This aircraft had windows, like a tour helicopter, so I could see out. We flew over a city. As we dropped lower, I recognized where we were. I had been here once for a medical conference. Washington, DC, only it looked different somehow.

We flew over the Potomac. The streets were packed with people. More people than I had ever seen before. They stood in the streets and on lawns and even on the tops of buildings. We dropped lower to land. The people I saw were Anakim. Thousands of them. Hundreds of thousands of them. They were everywhere. My pulse pounded.

We touched down on a grassy area in front of the White House, inside the fence, but still filled with Anakim. Coal helped me from the helicopter, holding my arm. Saul followed close. The infected ignored us.

A female Nephilim met us at the White House door. Coal left us with her. I followed her into the building. I had no

298 The Nephilim Virus

choice. Saul watched uneasily as Coal left, and then he followed us inside. He appeared to have no other choice either.

The Nephilim introduced herself as Brandi. Brandi led us to an empty room, probably an office, and left us alone. The room was large and had a bathroom attached. There was only one exit.

I immediately put as much space between Saul and myself as possible. I went to the window at the far wall. He was upset and didn't even notice me. He obviously hadn't counted on being treated like a prisoner. Treated with the same level of disrespect as me. But there wasn't anything he could do about it either. He held his big hunting knife in his hand and spun it slowly. I understood. I wished I hadn't lost my necklace.

We waited. I didn't talk to Saul. I knew I should use his new fear to gain his loyalty and get him to help me. But I sensed it was too soon. I needed to let him stew a little more. Plus, he still had the knife so I would need to be careful. I looked out the window. Anakim wandered as far as I could see. Occasionally, a Nephilim would leave or arrive. The Anakim never seemed to notice.

Brandi brought us food on a room service cart. Saul tried talking to her. She left without responding or even appearing to hear his complaints. I ate. Saul did not. It was very good.

We went back to waiting. I moved from the window to the couch. I laid down to rest but didn't close my eyes. Saul continued pacing the room. At one point, he tried the door and found it was locked.

He was getting antsier. I decided it was time to talk him down.

"How did they get to you?"

He looked over, like he had forgotten I was there. He didn't respond. I let the question hang.

"They were going to win, eventually." I waited, and he continued. "There was no use resisting anymore."

"What's in it for you?"

"They promised to forget about me. To let me disappear."

"You know they won't let you do that. They won't let any humans live."

"They will," he said, but he didn't sound confident. "We have a deal."

I didn't respond. I watched him, letting the silence work on his doubts.

"We made a deal," he said, "and I've kept my part and so will they."

I tucked that away to use later.

"How did they contact you to make this deal?"

I knew he would tell me to validate his making the deal. I didn't have to wait long.

"I ran into Coal on one of my recon missions. He was very close to the school, so they would have found us soon anyway. I had to do something. After that we met together many times. Whenever he needed to talk with me, a helicopter would fly over the school so I would know he was in town for a meeting. We had an arranged place. The helicopter was my idea. It was our signal, but it also worked to give my people a reason to hide every once in a while." He said it proudly.

"And?"

"And Coal kept the Anakim from the school as part of the deal. Why do you think the Anakim were never around the school? That's how it started, with me giving him useless information in exchange for our safety. The deal was necessary for our survival."

"But he continually asked for more."

"Yes." His voice grew louder. I had to be very careful. "So, I had to make a new deal."

"And once you found Nick, you had something to trade, right?"

"I had to." He wasn't yelling, but his voice was tight. "They were going to win anyway."

I felt it was time to push him a little. "But now you've lost your bargaining chip."

He didn't speak. I could see the vein in his neck bulge.

"Now they have both of us locked in here," I said quietly. "You're just as much of a prisoner as I am."

He stopped spinning the knife. "We have a deal. They'll let me go."

"They're treating you the same as me."

"I told you, they'll let me go."

"No, they won't"

"They will," he shouted.

"You know they won't."

I had pushed too hard. I knew it when I said it.

He took a step toward me. "I still have one card to play," he said with clenched teeth.

He took another step.

The opening door saved me. Coal entered.

Saul glared at him and spoke first. "We had a deal."

Coal answered slowly, using measured words. "Yes, we have a deal."

"I want to leave. Now," Saul said.

"You will be allowed to leave when we're finished with you and when we say you can go. Not before."

Saul took a step toward Coal. Coal didn't move.

"I kept my part of the bargain. Now I'm leaving."

Coal didn't speak, but his no resounded in the room.

Saul raised his knife and extended it at shoulder level. The tip almost touched Coal's neck.

That was a mistake.

It happened fast. Coal moved so quickly I barely saw it. All in one quick motion he hit Saul in the inside elbow of his outstretched arm, bending it inward. Then Coal stepped forward and used his weight to push the knife toward Saul. The knife that was still in Saul's fist buried itself into his own chest. Coal and Saul stood locked in what could have been a hug. Saul's eyes had widened as if he couldn't believe what had happened.

They stayed frozen that way for a moment, Coal staring into Saul's wide eyes. Then Coal stepped back. Saul crumpled to the floor with his own knife buried in his heart, his own hand still on the handle.

Coal turned to me. "I'm sorry you had to see that."

Then he left.

3

Two men came in and removed Saul's body without speaking. Then I was alone again. I stayed that way for an entire day. Alone, except for Brandi dropping off a meal every four hours during the day. I ate to keep my strength up.

While I waited for something to happen, I thought about Nick. And about the Commander. And about Steven. But mostly about Nick. I closed my eyes and replayed his kiss over and over again. Felt his warm lips. I wondered when I would see him again. If I would see him again. As time wore on, I imagined never seeing the Commander again. I imagined never kissing Nick again. I imagined never finding a cure for Steven. And I cried. Silent tears. I took a nap and woke feeling a little better.

After a while, I got mad. I yelled at the walls, shouting for my freedom. Cursing all the Nephilim I knew by name, and some I didn't. I pounded my closed fist on the door. I tried to kick it open. I tried to break the window before I realized it had to be unbreakable glass. I pounded on the walls.

Nothing I did garnered a response. Eventually, my loneliness and anger boiled into a calm resolve. I decided that even though I might be helpless to the Nephilim's will, I would not die powerless. I would not be used to advance their cause. This thought steeled me as I waited another twelve hours.

I sat on the couch when the door opened. The doorway was large, probably nine feet tall, and the man who entered still barely cleared without ducking. He was a giant. I spotted his hand on the door handle. Six fingers. It was the man from the security video. Arba.

He closed the door behind him but stood by the doorway to let me examine him. He was tall, but proportioned correctly. Unlike some people whose height out-performs their width, his arms, legs, and torso all matched each other in a perfect way. He was overly muscular, but not grotesque. He had the long solid musculature more reminiscent of a lion than a rhino. Unlike in the video, his clothing was now modern and fit him perfectly. His skin was evenly bronzed. His eyes were black, piercing, and deep. They met mine without blinking. I could feel primal power and confidence emanating from his presence.

He remained motionless as I examined him before he spoke. He was not at all self-conscious or unsure of himself.

When he did speak, his voice was deep and even. "Hello, Dr. Richards. It's nice to finally meet you. Welcome to New Babylon."

I opened my mouth to respond, but nothing came out. I closed it quickly. I reached for my necklace before I remembered it wasn't there. I really missed it.

"Don't be afraid," he said. "I'm not here to harm you. In fact, quite the opposite. I'd like to help you get what you want, and in return, I believe you can help me."

I found my voice. "I'm not helping you."

"Dr. Richards," his words chided. "I expected more from a woman of your intelligence."

The first wave of shock was gone. I decided not to be afraid anymore.

"I know what you're doing. You're playing on the psychology of me needing to be needed. Let's not play games. You don't need me."

"Dr. Richards . . . Faith. May I call you Faith?"

I didn't respond.

"Faith, have you heard of Lewis Terman?"

I had but I didn't respond. He continued as if he hadn't noticed. "Lewis Terman was a professor of psychology. In 1921, he made it his life's work to scour the world and find children with the highest IQs. These children he branded "termites." His theory was that this group of geniuses would be the next evolution of man—that with their intelligence they would rise to the top of human history."

I stared at him blankly.

"His theory was never validated because he overlooked one essential aspect of human evolution. He was only looking at one half of the picture. Had his subjects been physically superior as well, then maybe his dream would have been realized. But you, Faith, have standing in front of you the realization of that dream. I am the new Lewis Terman, the father of the new group of elite. I found you and now I am offering you the opportunity to join me, to realize your own dreams."

"You don't know me," I said. "You don't know my dreams."

"You are correct, Faith. I don't know you, but I know about you. You graduated high school two years early and made remarkable grades even as you took all AP classes. You received your undergraduate degree in two years. From there, you went on to grad school and continued into medical school, where you became the youngest female hematologist in the State of California.

"But that wasn't enough for you. While practicing medicine, you went back to school and earned a degree in psychology. And while you have never practiced in the field, you passed the California Board of Psychology exam and could legally practice if you so desired.

"Your parents are both dead, but you have a younger brother named Steven Allen Richards whom you practically raised and whom you love very much. You weigh a hundred and twenty-one pounds, and when you were in medical school, you dyed your hair brown because you thought it made you look smarter. Now you don't dye your hair anymore, but you sometimes wear glasses you don't need because you are aware of how pretty you are and feel the glasses help you to be taken more seriously."

He ended his litany without blinking. "So while I may not know you, Dr. Faith Richards, I know everything there is to know about you. I know you are transfixed with blood and the human brain. And I will give you the opportunity to discover things you could never otherwise discover about them. You are smart, Doctor incredibly smart, but what I am offering you is the next level of consciousness. Join me. Help us and I will give you everything you have ever wanted."

I couldn't look into his black eyes anymore. It was making it too hard to think. I broke eye contact and looked out the window. Anakim wandered the grounds aimlessly. Mindless. I thought of Steven. I thought of what I did to him, and what I owed him.

I looked back at Arba. His face was calm. Reassuring. He didn't seem like the monster I had imagined him to be. He almost seemed like he wanted to help people. Maybe his way was different than the way I would choose, but maybe I could help him find a better way. I wrestled with that thought for a moment.

"What would you want me to do?" I asked.

"Come with me," he said. "I'll show you."

4

Arba led me through the once-hallowed halls of the White House. But all semblance of American history and culture was gone. There were no portraits of former presidents on the walls; no decorations or artifacts remained. The house felt empty despite the abundance of Nephilim running around. It was no longer full of life. Now it was dead. Undecorated. Utilitarian.

The hallways and rooms were busy with Nephilim going about their tasks. No one paid any attention to us. They moved about the offices of the West Wing as I imagined people must have before the Nephilim took over. Arba towered over me as we walked, and I had to take two steps for every one of his. We made our way to a balcony that overlooked the rear lawn.

"You see those buses?" Arba pointed toward the back gate, where four large prison transport buses pulled in. I watched as they slowly wound their way up the drive. The first bus stopped at the back of the East Wing. It was filled with people, shuffling around inside the bus, anxious to get out. They looked and moved like uninfected humans.

"Those people have been waiting for weeks for their chance to come here. Do you know why?"

I shook my head.

"They want to achieve a higher consciousness. They come for the chance to become a Nephilim. Do you know what their odds are of gaining this higher consciousness? Only one in a hundred. Out of all four of those buses filled with people, the odds are only one human among them will become a Nephilim. I want your help to change that."

"My help?" I said.

"I want you to develop a cure. Every day thousands of humans come here willingly to be bitten by a Nephilim on the chance that they, too, will become Nephilim."

I looked back at the people who were now exiting the bus under the watchful eye of the Nephilim. I was horrified. Coming to be intentionally infected? It was so contrary to my thinking for the last three years. The Nephilim were the enemy. Arba was the enemy. The virus was the enemy. Who would try to get infected on purpose?

Arba continued. "I want you to examine the blood of humans and the blood of Nephilim. I want you to create an antidote for humanity so any human who chooses to join us is able. I want you to make me an army. I want you to use my blood to make everyone Nephilim."

I shook my head. "Why would I do that?"

"In curing them, you will have the opportunity to cure yourself. You, too, can be Nephilim. You can live hundreds of years. You can be worshiped. You can be a god."

"Why would you need me? I'm smart, but I'm smart enough to know there are smarter people than I am. Your Nephilim could do the experiments. Why do you need me?"

"Like you said, Doctor, you're smart. You tell me."

I thought for a second. What would I know that the Nephilim wouldn't? It came to me. "You need me because you think the key lies in the blood only I have knowledge of—Nick Reece's blood."

"Yes."

"You want me to bring Nick Reece here," I said.

"You are already bringing him, Faith. He will come here whether you help us or not. In fact, he is on his way here now."

My heart skipped a beat. Nick was coming for me.

"You want me to find out why his blood is resistant to the Anak virus. And then find a way to use his blood and your blood to create a Nephilim vaccine that can make anyone a Nephilim."

"Very good, Doctor. That is correct. And you were correct about one more thing. I don't need you. We are smarter than you, and we will figure it out eventually with or without your help. But I believe in grace. And I am inviting you to join us."

"Why? Why would I do that? The virus hurts people. It doesn't save people. It kills them."

"That's why I want you. I want you to create the strain that doesn't kill. I want you to save those people." He nodded toward the buses.

I stood frozen, suddenly unsure of what was right.

"Let me show you something else," he said. "I believe you will find the reason more than convincing enough."

5

We descended by elevator to the lower level, the basement, and stopped at a reinforced door. Arba punched a code into a keypad. He didn't try to hide the code: 1437. We walked inside.

It was a lab, a very familiar lab. It was, in fact, a replica of my lab at Mercy General, except this one was bigger, newer, and had better equipment. I looked around. All my records had been brought here from Mercy—folder after folder filled with my handwriting. There was a walk-in refrigerator with the blood samples from the hospital. I looked. Only one was missing—1437—Nick's sample. I turned to Arba.

"I want you to meet someone," he said.

A woman stood up from where she had been examining a sample.

"This is Dr. Mercury Malek."

She stood and offered her hand. The name sounded made up. I said so.

She laughed an easy laugh. She was thin. Her clean, white lab coat contrasted the black hair that fell over her shoulders. Her eyes were deep brown and, thankfully, not black or orange. She seemed vaguely familiar, but I couldn't place her.

"You two have some things to talk about. I'll wait outside." Arba left.

"Come." Mercury motioned me to the lab desk where she had been working. "Take a look at this. I could use your expertise."

312 The Nephilim Virus

She had an unusual walk, as if one leg might be a half-inch shorter than the other. I followed her cautiously. She pretended not to notice my reservation.

I looked through the microscope at a blood sample on a slide. It was marked "Patient A." Mercury added another drop of blood. The first blood reacted to the new drop. The cells went crazy, mixing together and frantically bumping into each other. As I watched, they multiplied rapidly, then settled down into a calm order. But they had coagulated into thick goo.

"What was that?" I asked.

"Nephilim blood. No matter how many times I add it to that patient's sample of blood, it always manifests itself as the Anak virus."

"Nephilim blood?" I had never gotten to examine it before. "Why would you add their blood? Isn't the virus transferred through their saliva?"

She smiled. "I'm sorry. I forgot there's so much you don't know yet. The Nephilim bite their own tongue before they bite someone else. Their power is only transferred through the blood. That is why they prefer the neck, or carotid artery. It makes for the fastest transfer of their blood to the patient."

"Patient? You mean victim."

Anger quickly flashed in her eyes, then it passed. "Arba's blood holds the key to unlocking immortality if only I could find out why some blood manifests as the Anak virus."

Mercury squared her shoulders and looked me right in the eye. I realized where I'd seen her before—on the security video from George Washington University. She was the woman with dark hair who had a conversation with Arba. It clicked.

"You are Patient A. The blood that reacts by turning into Anak is yours," I said. "You've made a deal with Arba."

"It's more than a deal. He's mine and soon I will be his. Forever. But I need your help, and in return, you will get what you want."

"What's that?"

"Arba will let Nick live."

I froze. My blood felt cold.

"Why does Arba want Nick so badly?"

"We know the Anak virus has no effect on Mr. Reece, and we know the Anakim are not afraid of him. Do you think Arba will stand by with that type of danger to his power roaming around, especially when Nick's blood could be the last key to Arba's ultimate power? You see, Faith, Nick Reece is in great danger. His blood will be used with or without your help . . . or his consent. He would be much safer here under your care."

I didn't respond.

"Nick is coming, Dr. Richards, and we will be prepared. If you work with us, you can watch out for his safety while we use his blood. If you don't . . . well, there's no telling what will happen to him."

She let the threat hang in the air.

"We'll take our chances," I said.

Arba reentered the room at just that moment. "Then you need to see one last thing."

Arba led me to a room on the lower floor. A Nephilim stood guarding the door, but at Arba's nod, he disappeared down the hall. Arba turned the knob, and we stepped inside.

At first, I thought the room was empty. It was void of furniture. But then I realized someone, or something, huddled in the corner. He knelt with his face away from us, rocking back and forth like a child. It sounded like he was mumbling to himself. I looked at Arba with a question in my eyes, but his attention focused on the creature.

Finally, the man in the corner sensed we were there. He turned and I saw who it was—Steven. Our eyes met. I searched for recognition in his expression. I found none. His eyes slowly turned orange, and he growled. I locked my gaze on him, begging him with my eyes. Pleading for him to recognize me. I thought I saw a flicker of something, recognition maybe. Then it was gone. If it had been there at all. It had probably only been my strong desire to see that reaction.

Steven growled again. He watched me with his orange eyes. But he didn't move to attack me. I tried to step forward, but Arba stopped me.

"No," he said in a low voice. "You can't. He's not ready."

I hardly heard Arba.

"Steven," I called softly.

My voice agitated him. He glanced back and forth from me to Arba as if searching for permission. He inched forward, then back. He bounced from one foot to the other, anxious and angry.

I felt tears well up. I didn't resist them. I whispered Steven's name again. Again and again and again.

Arba made no move to quiet me, but he stayed between Steven and me.

Eventually, Arba said, "You can save him. Work with me, and I'll let you come up with a cure for Steven as well . . . for all the Anakim. It's the only way to save him."

I wanted to save Steven. I needed to save him. I had to. Maybe working with the Nephilim was the only way. I almost agreed, but I couldn't. I was torn.

"Come." Arba reached down and took my hand.

I let him lead me out of the room. My legs had turned to jelly. I loved Steven so much. We weren't just brother and sister; he had saved my life. And I had done the opposite to him.

6

It had happened during the first six months of the outbreak, when we didn't know enough about the virus. No one did. The first sign of trouble was when all communication went down as people scrambled to locate loved ones and friends. Looking back, this was the smartest thing the Nephilim could have done. People had become so dependent on technology to communicate, we were helpless without it. Families, businesses, and government agencies were cut off from each other and from all information about what was happening. Survival became just a matter of dumb luck.

The virus spread like wildfire. The only saving grace was the virus hadn't had yet mutated into its most virulent state. What we figured out later were the Anakim were slowly building their recovery time and immunity to our weapons. People soon went to ground and hid wherever they could. Again, surviving was mostly luck.

People banded together in large groups, and no one realized this was the worst thing they could do. Often groups of uninfected humans fled to rural areas and congregated. It took too long to figure out that hiding in cities with tall buildings, power plants, and electrical grids gave them a better chance of avoiding the Nephilim's satellite and heat-sensor searches. We didn't even know they were looking.

Like I said, dumb luck mostly. At the time, everyone was hunkered down and waiting for the government to fix the problem. What we didn't know was that the government didn't exist anymore, and it couldn't have helped us if it had survived.

When the power went out, Steven's first thought was me. Somehow, he made the overland trip from his home in Colorado to mine in California. Things happened so fast in those first few months that if you weren't one of the first people to rush the stores for food, water, and other survival supplies, you were just as likely to die from starvation as you were from the Anakim. Fortunately, Steven had been one of the first to react. He brought food with him, along with his collection of hunting rifles that most likely helped him procure the supplies.

The beginning of the end was the day I left the house while Steven was napping. I have often asked myself why I decided to take a walk. Up until that day, Steven and I rarely went out at all and never alone. I tell myself it was for noble reasons, like finding someone to help, but the truth is I think I just had cabin fever. That's why I decided to walk instead of drive. Big mistake.

To be fair, we had not seen any Anakim in our area yet, and no one knew how the virus spread, so I didn't know how bad my decisions were going to turn out. I walked for close to a mile before I came across the Anakim. He was the first one I had seen up close. He was bent over another human midway across a bridge. Again, I lie to myself by saying I thought I could help the victim, but the truth is I knew she was probably dead and I went closer simply to satisfy my own curiosity. I should have run before the Anakim noticed me, but I didn't. Instead, I started walking across the bridge.

It was a sad irony that the only thing that saved me was someone else losing their life. It was my neighbor whose dying screams woke Steven from his nap. He immediately set out in his truck to find me. Obviously, the Anakim had discovered our area was a new food source. I'm still not sure how I walked a mile before I came across one. I'm also not sure how Steven happened to take the same road I'd walked, nor how he found me in time. But he did.

The Anakim grabbed my leg, and that's when I finally tried to run, but it was too late. I toppled forward toward the concrete and put my arm out to break my fall, but instead, the fall broke my arm. Steven fired his 12-gauge and the spread of pellets caught the Anakim in the shoulder, cutting his arm completely off and spinning him sideways and over the railing. We heard him land in the water below and assumed he was dead. I know now he wasn't, but Steven didn't wait to find out. He pulled me into his truck and that's when I made my biggest mistake. I ran back and grabbed the Anakim's severed arm. I don't have to lie to myself on this one point. I did it to save people's lives. But I ended up ending Steven's instead.

We drove to the nearest semi-operational hospital we could find to get me fixed up. It was called Mercy General. A military man everyone called the Commander was in charge of the facility. A nurse reset my broken arm and put it in a cast and sling. I immediately asked to use their lab equipment to drain and test the blood from the Anakim's severed arm. They agreed, and Steven and I never went back home.

After draining, analyzing, and testing the Anakim blood, I set out to develop an antidote. First, I had to identify and separate the virus strain. I did so, but after a year, I was still unable to develop anything that resembled a cure or slowed the progression of the disease. During that year, the future of the human race got exponentially bleaker. Information trickled into the hospital through various sources, and we realized just how dangerous our real opponent was. The Nephilim. But as much as we managed to learn in those early days, there was still so much unknown about the super-intelligent creatures.

I continued working on developing a cure, but eventually I realized it wasn't going to work and tried another idea. Instead of an antidote to cure people, I would use the Anakim's blood to create an antivirus so that no one else could be infected. It seemed like a good idea at the time.

I spent the next six months working on my antivirus. I narrowed the choices down to two: the first was to create a live, attenuated vaccine. This meant taking a live but weakened version of the Anak virus to use as the vaccine. The second choice was to create an inactivated vaccine. This required inactivating or killing the virus to create a less powerful vaccine. I figured that although the second choice would take longer to build up immunity in the body, it was the safer choice. What I didn't realize was that in the end it didn't really matter.

I created the inactivated vaccine and tried to test it as best I could. But eventually, the only choice was a human trial. Steven volunteered. I resisted at first, but there were no other volunteers. Steven was the only person who trusted me implicitly.

What I never realized in all my testing was that the Anak virus could not be killed. It could lay dormant and look inactive, but it would always recover and turn out to be stronger than it had been before inactivation. I figured that out too late.

The first time I injected Steven was the hardest. He didn't flinch as I pressed the needle into his skin. I looked into his green eyes, and I saw recognition and trust. I didn't realize it would be the last time I would ever see that look, or any look of humanity in his eyes at all.

I gave him his next injection a week later. But it was too late by that time. His eyes were already clouded and turning orange. I knew then I had gambled with my brother's life and was only trying to salvage any part of Steven that I could. It was hopeless, and we both knew it, or at least I did. I don't think he knew anything anymore.

I had killed my brother.

7

All I ever wanted to do was save people's lives. That's why I became a doctor. It's why I studied psychology. That's why I injected Steven, and when my experiment failed, that's why I started using coma patients as subjects. And that's why I decided to help Arba and Mercury find a way to save the human race.

I knew that if I had the chance to fix the virus so that it didn't kill any more humans, either totally or in the way I had killed Steven, then I had to take it. I wasn't sure if I could succeed, but if there was even a small possibility to undo what I had done to Steven, then I had to try. And I had to do it before Nick arrived because there was no telling what Arba would do to him if I failed.

I worked all day, through the night, and into the next day. Mercury never left my side. She watched my every move and made detailed notes on everything I tried. She made a great assistant and knew as much as I did about blood. She also knew more than I did about chromosomes and genomes and helped open my eyes to a different approach to solving our mutual riddle. What most people don't understand about medicine is that it is as much an art as it is a science. Two well-educated doctors can look at the same thing and reach two different conclusions.

I had been able to examine lots of blood over the past three years, including Nick's and Anakim blood, but I had never gotten a chance to examine Nephilim blood. Now I got to work with not only Nephilim blood but also patient zero—Arba. The first thing I did was to spin the blood to separate the red from the white cells. Arba's had the same ratio of red to white blood cells as the Anakim blood. Next, I broke it down and did a thorough analysis of the blood. I focused mainly on the white blood cells since they're the ones that carry the DNA.

On the second day, I found a gene mutation common to all the Nephilim. It was a mutation of the gene csf3r found in the white blood cells of every Nephilim we tested. Next, we had to find out if the mutation was already present in their blood and therefore caused the virus to respond by turning people, or if the virus was the catalyst for the mutation. To do this, we had to find a human with the same mutation of csf3r. We pulled people from the willing volunteers until we found one with the gene mutation. We injected a sample of Arba's blood into him and waited.

We didn't have to wait long. He turned. Another Nephilim now roamed the earth. Mercury sent for more humans to do further testing. We went through every busload without finding another human with a mutation in csf3r, so Arba sent out a hunting party to find more humans. These came back less willing to be test subjects.

It was my third day working with the Nephilim when they brought the first prisoner into my lab, bound and gagged. The Nephilim left the new patient with us. He was strapped to a hospital bed. He reminded me of the coma patients I had experimented on. I blinked the thought away and got to work. He pulled against the restraints as he watched me insert a needle into a vile and withdraw a portion of Arba's blood. He tried to speak, but his mouth was firmly gagged. All I heard was a muffled groan. I pushed the plunger slightly to remove an excess air bubble. We didn't need our patient dying accidently. His brown eyes pleaded with me to let him go. He knew I wasn't a Nephilim.

My hand shook, and I glanced at Mercury to see if she noticed.

"Do you want me to do it?" she said.

We had both been awake for three days straight, and I was exhausted. Mercury looked calm and rested. I wiped my arm across my eyes and shook my head. The prisoner was still pleading with me, and for a second I saw Nick strapped to the bed. He was pleading with me not to inject him.

I blinked and Nick was gone. In his place was Steven. He was lying on the bed, wordlessly waiting on me to inject him. Waiting on me to kill him. Watching me with orange eyes. I looked away. When I looked back our prisoner was still strapped to the bed, still trying to speak through the gag.

I reached an unsteady hand toward him while Mercury watched closely. He froze. His eyes were as big as saucers, watching the needle close in on his neck. My hand bumped the side rail of the bed, and the syringe crashed to the floor and broke. Arba's blood stained the tile. It was thick and gooey.

"What have you done?" Mercury said. "That blood is precious. That is the blood of a god."

"I'm sorry," I said. "I'll get another vial of Arba's blood."

I started to move toward the back of the lab where we kept Arba's blood separate from the rest of the samples. Mercury held out her hand to stop me. I waited with my heart pounding in my chest.

"I'll get it," she said.

While she was gone, I quickly filled a syringe with uninfected blood. The prisoner quieted as he watched me. I slid it up the sleeve of my lab coat as Mercury walked up behind me. She handed me a new syringe filled with Arba's blood. Our eyes met as she handed it off. She didn't smile.

I uncapped the syringe and placed the needle against the prisoner's neck. He had stopped struggling or trying to speak. I rubbed my hand over his sweaty forehead. "It's OK. In the end, you will be happy about what I'm about to do. This will hurt a lot." I hoped he understood what I was telling him.

He did. He bucked against the restraints and started yelling into the gag. I nodded at Mercury, and she came over to hold his head down. I used the distraction to drop the syringe filled with Arba's blood into my pocket and slide the alternate out of my sleeve into my hand. Mercury didn't see the switch.

I inserted the needle into his neck and emptied the syringe. The patient flailed for another few seconds and then stopped. His eyes opened wide, and I saw a terror that couldn't be faked. Purple spots appeared on his skin. He closed his eyes and didn't move.

I knew it took incredible willpower for the prisoner to stay still. Giving him the incorrect blood type would make him feel like he was doomed. His insides would be boiling. But he would live. Or at least the blood wouldn't kill him. The Nephilim might if I didn't stop them.

I pulled the syringe of Arba's blood from my pocket and slid the cap off. Mercury was bent over the patient, about to pull his eyelids open to check their color, when I stuck the needle in her neck.

She froze.

"This is Arba's blood, and I don't have to tell you that if I press this plunger down, you'll either be dead in seconds or a mindless animal forever. So do exactly as I say. Do you understand?" My hand was no longer shaking.

"Yes," Mercury said.

"Stand up slowly."

She did. I grabbed a roll of medical tape and used it to secure the needle to Mercury's neck. I needed my other hand free, and I didn't need her pulling free of the syringe.

Our test subject opened his eyes. He wordlessly squirmed, asking me to loosen him from his restraints. I reached my free hand down and released the strap on his left wrist.

"Don't follow me," I said.

He nodded and pulled the gag from his mouth. I motioned for him to remain silent.

"Thank you," he whispered.

He reached to undo the rest of his restraints while I guided Mercury from the room. The hallway outside was empty. I stopped and considered my plan. But I really didn't have one. I wanted to trade Mercury to Arba for my freedom, but that's as far as I had thought ahead. I didn't even know if that would work. Would Arba sacrifice Mercury without batting an eye? All I knew was I couldn't inject an unwilling human. Not anymore. Not after Nick had awakened from his coma.

Mercury sensed my hesitation. "It's not too late. We can go back in there and continue our work. I will forgive and forget and no one has to know. Right now, you still have a choice. But if you continue down this path, you will find that Arba is not as forgiving as I am. You will die. As will Nick Reece after Arba drains every drop of his—"

I pressed the syringe, and she quieted instantly. One more push and Arba's blood would rush into her blood stream. Whatever happened after that would be extremely painful. And irreversible.

"Tell me how to get to the buses that drop off people."

She thought for a moment. "Down the hall and through the double doors is a service elevator. You can take that up. Then you can get out through the service entrance in the back."

"Take me."

Mercury led me down the hallway without hesitation. I held the syringe tight with my right hand and used my left hand on the other side of her neck to make sure she didn't pull away. We passed through the double doors, and I saw Mercury hadn't lied. There was a large freight elevator.

"The security card is in my left pocket," she said.

"Scan it."

She complied and the elevator started its ascent. Moments later, the elevator doors opened and I guided Mercury outside.

"Which way now?"

Mercury never got a chance to answer. A large hand clamped down over mine, covering the syringe so I couldn't press it. The hand had six fingers. Another hand grabbed my shoulder in a vise-like grip. I twisted, but the grip was too strong. He pried my hand free of the syringe and without a word guided me through the White House. I didn't cry out because I knew it was useless. I had failed and this was the end.

Arba pulled me to the door overlooking the front lawn. A Nephilim opened the door for him and he stood for a moment framed in the doorway, but he held me at arm's length out of sight behind the door. Then he pulled me forward, and I saw thousands of infected humans rushing the White House lawn. My breath caught. He was going to feed me to the Anakim. I tried to pull back, but Arba held me tight. That's when I spotted him. Nick. He was running toward us.

I told my legs to run. To go to him. But Arba held me back. His six-fingered hand gripped my shoulder. I looked up at him. Then back at Nick.

Before I could react, Arba leaned over and bit my neck. I felt his teeth break my skin. I felt his soft tongue flick against the wound. I willed it not to happen. But I was powerless. It was too late.

I screamed.

8

I felt my blood turn cold. It felt like ice water sliding through my body, pushing all the warmth away. My body went limp. I tried to resist the power of gravity, but I couldn't. I fell. It felt like I was falling forever. Then I was floating. Swimming through the air. Or maybe I was being carried. Everything was foggy. I was having trouble making sense of anything. I tried to remember who I was. I couldn't. I remembered a couple names: Steven. Nick. I was pretty sure they weren't mine. But they could have been. Was I named Steven? I couldn't remember. I knew the names were important, but I couldn't remember why, or how.

I continued floating. Both my mind and body. As soon as my mind settled on something, it dissipated. I felt like I should be able to piece together answers out of the jumble in my head. But I couldn't. Then even the questions were gone. Everything was lost in the fog.

When I awoke, I had landed. I was no longer floating. Or at least my body wasn't. My mind was. I laid on something solid. A floor maybe. Or the ceiling. My mind still had trouble sorting through facts. I think they were called facts. But the word didn't sound right. Where was I? Who was I? I couldn't remember. Everything was foggy. I was hungry. I knew that. Very hungry. I looked around for something to eat. I saw something in the yard. An animal of some sort.

Lots of others saw it as well, and they ran toward the food. I did too. I was hungry, and I couldn't let them get to it first.

My legs moved faster than I had ever felt them move. My hunger drove me. It was all I could think about. All I wanted. My mind only focused on hunting and eating. I smelled blood, pure blood. The smell drew me forward. My hunger made me angry. I would be fed. I was angry at my hunger. I was angry because of my hunger. I was hungry for my anger.

I stopped. We all stopped. Something was wrong. Something smelled wrong. Our food smelled wrong. Impure. It was standing only a few feet away from us, making animal noises. I wanted to eat it, but the smell of its blood nauseated me. It scared me. I pulled back. All of us did. None of us wanted to eat It. I was still hungry. I hated it.

It looked at me. It made noises at me. Taunting me. Baiting me. It wanted to destroy me. It wanted to destroy my hatred for it. I stared back. It blinked. Something wasn't right. I felt something inside that didn't feel right. Not anger or hatred or hunger. Something else, something unfamiliar. I pushed that feeling back down. The thing in front of me was saying something. I growled. I wanted to leave, to go find other food. But I couldn't.

The thing made faces at me. It made noises. It was trying to get me. My anger returned. And my fear. I was afraid of this thing. Of what it wanted to do to me. The fear seemed unfamiliar to me. Like it didn't belong. I didn't like the fear. Or the thing making animal noises at me. Why me? Why was it focused on me? It was surrounded by lots of us, but it was focused on me.

I looked into its eyes. I saw something there I had never seen before. I felt something new. But it wasn't new. I think I felt it before . . . a long time ago. A lifetime ago. The fog in my mind almost cleared. I saw it for a second like sunshine through the clouds. Love. I felt love. For a split second, I felt love. I wanted to dive into it. I wanted to bathe in it like water. I wanted to run forward and let the love envelop me. I wanted to. And I almost did.

But I didn't. The moment passed.

The hunger returned.

The anger returned.

The fear returned.

Book III
Arba

Part II
Nick

1

Asher led the group as far away from the burning school as we could go on foot. We ended up in an abandoned auto shop. The smell of oil and machines still hung in the air after three years of stagnation. The Anakim didn't follow. But Blue did. The Commander posted Luke as a lookout to watch for any Nephs who may have seen us escape the trap.

The rest of us met in the back room to discuss a plan. Minus the lookout and Xavier, who ran around looking for something to power his computer, there were eleven of us crammed into the small room. And one dog.

I spoke first. "The longer we wait the further away Coal gets with Faith. I'm going after them."

"I'll go with you," Oscar said. "I have some scores to settle."

"If they were going to kill her, they would have done it here," the Commander said. "That means they want her alive. So we have time to come up with a plan instead of rushing in headlong."

"I'm going. I'm not waiting for everyone else to be ready." My words rushed out, sharper than I intended.

"Poor Dr. Richards. I would hate to be her right now," Rachel said. No one acknowledged her.

"They won't kill her so there are only two reasons they would have taken her," the Commander continued. "The first is for her medical knowledge of blood. But given their intelligence, it's unlikely they would need her unless it had to do with the special blood of you four. Their second motive would be to bait you, Reece, which is another reason we should be prepared when we go after her."

I stopped arguing.

"So, what's the plan?" Asher asked.

"The Nephilim have always hidden behind the Anakim. They've used them as weapons and shields and hunters to keep us in fear. But now we have four people with blood the Anakim are afraid of. For the first time we can get to the Nephilim. We need transportation to get to Washington, DC, and the proper weapons for when we do."

Heads nodded.

"Van, what are our options for transportation?"

"Whatever you can find, Commander. If it drives, flies, or floats, I can pilot it."

"Transportation will be the easy part," Asher said, "but there are too few of us. We'll need an army to take on the Nephs."

"We have these. " Oscar flexed his biceps with a smile. "My right army and my left army."

Everyone smiled, even the Commander.

"I'm sure those will come in handy," Asher said, "but we might need more."

Xavier made his way into the room carrying his computer and a bundle of electrical cords. He found an outlet and plugged several into the wall.

The Commander saw him. "X, get on the wire and put the word out. Tell everyone who will listen to be ready for instructions. We're about to storm the castle."

"You got it," Xavier said.

"Can you do it in transit?"

Xavier punched a couple buttons, unplugged a couple cords, shuffled them around, then re-plugged them into a black box. "Give me three minutes and I can."

"Good, you're with me," the Commander said. "Reece, you come too. The rest of you hold down the fort until we get back. Van, I saw a passenger van outside. How long will it take you to gut the inside? We'll need some space."

"Five minutes."

"Get to it."

Van left, and Oscar went with him.

Beck spoke up. "I'd like to go with you."

The Commander didn't respond immediately.

"For safety," she said. "That way you'll have me as well as Nick to protect you and Xavier if we get separated or run into Anakim. One for each of you."

The Commander nodded. "Let's move out." He strode out the door.

"Where are we going?" I asked.

"To get the weapons we'll need."

"What weapons?"

"I knew this day would eventually come."

I should have guessed. Always prepared.

"Everyone stay here until we get back," the Commander said. "And stay inside. Asher, Eva, you two watch over everyone."

They nodded.

We hurried to one of the maintenance bays to see how Van was coming with the vehicle. When we arrived, he was wrestling with the passenger seats, trying to remove the bolts securing them to the floor. Oscar watched with a smile. Then he tapped Van on the shoulder. "Let me try."

Van shrugged and offered Oscar the wrench. He waved it away. Oscar bear-hugged one of the passenger seats. He twisted left, then right. The bolts snapped. Oscar turned and tossed the seat away. A single bead of sweat ran down his face. He smiled at us, then turned and repeated the feat on the others, leaving only the two front seats. Maybe he was an army of one.

We piled in and left to find some weapons worthy of killing monsters. I hoped the Commander had a better plan in mind than five smooth stones.

2

Beck drove and the Commander directed her from the passenger side of the van. The rest of us sat behind them on the floor. We headed north, passing Hector's warehouse. It looked quiet, but as we drove by, I saw that two semi-trucks in the loading bay were black. Burned. We didn't stop.

Several miles up the coast, the Commander directed Beck to pull onto a side road. We followed it to a chain-link fence. A deserted factory stood behind the fence. The Commander got out, cut a rusty padlock, and opened the gate. We pulled around to the side. A sign over the loading bay read CALIFORNIA METAL WORKS. Two white SUVs sat on either side of the door. They were in good condition, but I bet they were rigged to burn.

The doors were chained and padlocked shut. The Commander used the bolt cutters again. Inside, it was dark and smelled of oil. The Commander closed the door behind us and waited. Just as our eyes adjusted to the dark, a light came on. Hector appeared in front of us, using the light in our adjusting eyes to look as if he had appeared from nowhere.

Everyone exchanged greetings.

"Ready for the torches?" Hector asked.

"Yes," the Commander said.

Hector motioned to a pile of duffel bags on the floor next to him. "Packed and ready for shipment." He reached into one and pulled a weapon out—a shotgun, modified with a pistol grip and short barrel. He tossed it to the Commander, who looked it over.

"Nice work," the Commander said. "Ammunition?"

Hector motioned to five large cardboard boxes. "This is all I could make in time." He pulled a shell out of his pocket and tossed it to the Commander.

"It'll be enough."

"What is it?" I asked.

The Commander held it up so I could see it. It looked like a normal shotgun shell to me.

"The pellets inside are made from silver instead of lead or steel," the Commander said.

"I found a coin collector who once had the largest collection of real silver coins in the world. Now he has the largest collection of silver bullets," Hector said with a smile.

"Why silver?" I asked.

The Commander looked at Xavier.

"Traditionally in folklore, vampires are allergic to certain things: garlic, holy water, silver crosses." Xavier pulled out the silver crucifix around his neck. "The reality is that Nephilim aren't allergic to anything that we know of, but they do have a dislike for some things. We don't know why, but water for example. They don't like to be around water. It doesn't hurt them as far as we know, but they just don't seem to like it. That's why they avoid rain and large bodies of water."

"And silver?" I asked.

"I'm getting to that, dude." Xavier pushed up his glasses. "We think the Nephilim have a harder time recovering if their blood comes in contact with silver. We think it might slow down their recovery process."

"How do you know?"

"We don't. So far, it's only a theory. Faith's theory."

"So, we shoot them with silver bullets," I said.

"Exactly."

"Isn't that a little cliché?"

"Clichés are clichés for a reason, dude. There's always a grain of truth hidden in folklore and tradition. Besides, do you have a better idea?"

"I guess it's better than a slingshot."

"I made a little something else as well," Hector said. He undid the latches on a trunk and opened it. It was filled with knives and blades of every size and shape. The Commander reached in and plucked one out. A machete.

"I coated all the blades with silver. Just a little something extra to help with the head thing if you get the chance."

"You mean like David did?" I asked.

"Precisely."

The Commander nodded his approval and stuck the blade in his belt. "Let's load this stuff up."

When we finished, the Commander turned to Hector. "Thank you, my friend."

Hector nodded solemnly. They had an understanding. The Commander didn't ask him to come. Hector didn't volunteer.

They shook hands. Like men who knew it would be their last opportunity to do so.

We drove away.

The Commander was quiet for a few miles before he spoke. "X, did you put the word out on the wire?"

"Yes sir."

"Good. Any response?"

"Lots of chatter. Some groups are for it, some against it, but no one really thinks it's doable to take down these dudes."

"So, will we get any help?"

"Hard to tell. Everyone's hesitant to say too much. Afraid it's a trap. But I'll keep working."

The van got quiet again. Outside, the sun started its descent. It reminded me of something.

"I've been meaning to ask you, Commander," I said. "Why do you like to travel at noon?"

"Do you remember the story of David and Goliath?"

It seemed like a lifetime ago since X had read it to me.

"According to the story, Goliath came out to yell his taunts in the morning and evening."

Xavier quoted from memory. "1 Samuel 17:6, "For forty days the Philistine came out every morning and evening and stood before the Israelite army."[7]

"But when David defeated him, it was midday," said the Commander. "Like the silver thing, I'm not sure why the Nephs don't like high noon, but if it worked for David, it's good enough for me."

3

Our next step was to secure a means of transportation to Washington, DC. Which was why I was standing in an empty parking lot in Memphis, Tennessee, with a cell phone in my hand. Our whole crew had taken a bus from California across the country, driving through the night and stopping for nothing but fuel. It took twenty-five hours, and the drive was surprisingly uneventful. We got lucky. We saw very few Anakim and not a single Nephilim.

I wasn't fond of this last part of the Commander's plan, but no one had offered a better one. The truth is, the Commander had probably come up with the quickest and safest way to gain access to the Nephilim headquarters. The plan was sound, except for the next step—the step that involved using me as Neph bait.

So, I waited. Alone. Blue wanted to come, but I left him locked in the bus. I knew he wouldn't be fond of the plan either.

I put the battery in the cell phone, dialed the number Xavier had given me, and waited as it rang. A machine picked up. "You have reached the office of the White House. Please leave a detailed message, and your call will be returned. Your call will be recorded and monitored for security reasons. Thank you."

I took a deep breath. Xavier had told me to leave a message that lasted at least thirty seconds, just to make sure.

"This is Nick Reece, the human you've been searching for, the human the Anakim are afraid of." I paused. "You have something I want, something I need. I don't want to live like this anymore. I'd like to meet. To parlay." I paused again. That had to be thirty seconds long. "Come and get me."

I waited a few more seconds to be sure, then hung up the phone. I left the battery in.

Then I waited. It was evening, and there was a slight chill in the air. I held a jacket loosely in my right hand but didn't put it on. I wished I could. I also wished I had brought a chair. Xavier had estimated it might take as long as ten minutes, depending on how close the Nephilim were to my current location. He also promised the cell phone would be easy to track so it might be sooner. He hadn't lied.

The thump-thump of helicopter rotors arrived five minutes later. It sounded like a big chopper. That was good. Except for the fact that it might be holding a lot of Nephs. It took another three minutes for the bird to land in front of me. Three minutes I spent wishing someone had come up with another plan. I dropped the cell phone from my left hand. I no longer needed it. I gripped my jacket a little tighter.

The chopper was as big as the sound advertised. Military grade. All black. Perfect.

The blades powered down but didn't stop spinning. I hoped that would help. The door opened, and a Neph stepped out. I waited for more to jump out, but none did.

The Nephilim walked toward me. He moved like he wasn't even moving. As if moving took no effort. Giving the illusion he was in one place, then suddenly another. I waited until he was two steps away, close enough I could hear him above the sound of the aircraft if I had wanted. I didn't.

I raised my arm. The jacket slid away with the movement. I let it go. It didn't matter now if the Neph saw I held a shotgun or not. I pulled the trigger. The Nephilim reacted fast, but not fast enough to dodge the spread of pellets. Thank God for shotguns.

They hit him in the chest like a punch. The blast tore through clothes, skin, and bone. He flew backward and landed with a thud. Xavier once told me he had heard rumors of Nephilim shooting themselves to build up their immunity, but I didn't wait to see how quickly he recovered. I was already running.

I heard two shots and prayed Van and the Commander's aim was good. I kept running. Better safe than sorry. Oscar and Asher ran past me with machetes. By the time I stopped and turned, the Neph had been separated from his head.

4

Eight humans and a dog prepared for the flight from Memphis to DC. The hospital staff and the two school survivors decided it wasn't their fight. They wished us luck when we left them with the bus. We were going to need it.

The Commander passed out final instructions as Van prepped the chopper. Asher and Oscar were giving Beck and Eva a crash course on how to fire the guns. Asher was a good teacher and good with a gun. Very good. I wondered if finding him in a prison wasn't such a rare thing. Blue watched dubiously from his post by the helicopter door, apparently unwilling to be tricked into being left again.

"What's the plan, Commander?" I asked at a break in the action. "I know we're flying to DC or New Babylon, or whatever they want to call it, to kill Arba."

"And cut off his head," Xavier added.

"And cut off his head," I continued, "but how exactly do we accomplish that with only eight of us?"

Blue barked. He probably objected to me counting only eight.

"The Nephilim have a weakness they're working to remedy every day. Now that we're prepared, we need to strike while we still have the opportunity."

"What weakness?" Eva asked.

"Numbers."

Eva looked at him questioningly. We all did.

"Xavier, how many Anakim are there in these United States of America?"

Xavier shoved his glasses up his nose and answered without looking up. "Millions."

"And how many Nephilim are there?"

"Best guess, only about a hundred thousand."

"That number grows every day as they turn more humans," the Commander said.

"Only a hundred thousand?" Oscar said. "Why didn't you say so? This should be a cake walk."

"That's still a whole lot more than eight," Asher said to the Commander. "How are we going to fight a hundred thousand Nephilim?"

"A technique as old as Sun Tzu: divide and conquer."

"How so?"

"The hundred thousand are already spread thinly across the country. We spread them even more thinly. Xavier has been on the wire since yesterday telling anyone who will listen that we're going after Arba. Telling them that tomorrow at 10 a.m. Eastern time we need them to create havoc however they can: cut power lines, attack Nephilim, steal supplies, anything anyone can think of that will divide the Nephilim's attention and distract them from DC. How are we looking on that, X?"

"OK. The idea seems to be gaining some support. I'm still working on it."

"Good. Focus especially on anyone in the area directly outside the capital. We need the Nephs close to DC dispersed before we get there."

"Aren't you afraid the Nephilim might crack the wire code and set up a trap?" Beck asked.

"There's nothing we can do about that. They'll crack it eventually, so now is our best chance. You just keep that thing handy." The Commander pointed toward the gun she held, the one she had been practicing with. She nodded. A natural.

"By my math, that still leaves us half a plan short," I said. "What about conquer?"

"That'll be up to the eight of us," the Commander said.

"Nine if you count the dog." I didn't need him mad at me.

"Those numbers ain't gonna be fair," Oscar said. Everyone looked at him. "For them, I mean."

5

The helicopter we had commandeered, a UH-60 Blackhawk, could make the trip from Memphis to DC in three hours. But that was if we flew at a higher altitude and took the most direct line of flight, which would have been easy for the Nephilim to spot. Instead, we made the trip in five. Van kept the helicopter below radar level, which drained our fuel. Fortunately, the chopper was outfitted for ferry, which increased its distance capability.

We came in low over the city. I could smell fear mixed with excitement in the chopper. As the rotors thumped toward the White House, Xavier pulled up a live satellite image of the grounds. The Commander outlined a plan of attack and passed out orders. Surprisingly, there were only a few Anakim wandering the grounds, and even more surpisingly, the video didn't show a single Nephilim. Maybe they were all inside? Or had Coal baited me into a trap with the DC information? We had no way to see what was going on inside the structure, so once we got there, we would be flying blind.

The Commander had assigned two of the special four to cover the grounds and two of us to go inside. The same ratio would go for the humans. He chose Beck and I to go inside with himself and Oscar. He knew I would have gone in regardless, so he saved me from having to disobey his orders.

The city looked silent as we buzzed over it. I had been to DC many times before and never seen it this quiet. Maybe the Commander's plan to draw the enemy away had worked. I could see the White House in the distance. The roads were jammed with vehicles, especially semi-trailers and armored trucks. I guessed that all of them had probably been there since the outbreak. Or maybe the Nephs put them there to make ground access difficult. I tightened my grip on the shotgun.

Van brought the chopper in fast; this was all going to happen very quickly. I took one last look at our ragtag army. Oscar caught my eye. His body swayed with the motion of the aircraft. He smiled his big smile. A vial of my blood hung on a chain around his neck. Each of the humans had one— Van's idea. I hoped it made them feel better, because it didn't me. I checked to make sure my knife was tucked into my belt. I thought about Faith. And how stupid this plan was.

"You should stay in the chopper," I whispered to Blue.

I glanced out the window. We were seconds from touching down. The sky was empty except for us.

"Something isn't right," I said.

"What?" Beck said.

"Something isn't right," I said louder.

The Commander responded through my headset. "Talk to me, Reece."

"This is wrong. It's been too easy to get here."

"We've been lucky," Beck said.

"Exactly," I said, "we've been too lucky. The Nephilim are too smart for us to be this lucky. Think about it. Have you ever seen a Neph working alone? They almost always travel in pairs, but we only had to kill one to steal this helicopter. And he walked into our trap pretty easily."

"Go on," the Commander said.

"And think about the bus ride. We covered two thousand miles and didn't see a single Nephilim. Even going from Mercy to Eva's hospital I saw at least a couple motorcycle sentries. It's too unlikely that we wouldn't see any this whole trip. And look around outside. No helicopters in the air. We're about to touch down at their home base and there isn't a single Nephilim guarding the airspace. It's too easy."

"You may be right, Reece, but this could be our only chance," the Commander said. "We—"

But he didn't get a chance to finish his thought because at that moment the helicopter rotors stopped spinning.

"They've cut our power somehow," Van said over his headset. "Everyone hang on. This will be a rough landing."

Seconds later the chopper banged down on the White House lawn. We had arrived—still in one piece, thanks to Van.

6

We scrambled off the helicopter onto the lawn. At first it looked as if it was going to be easy. By my quick count, there were only a dozen Anakim on the grounds. Nothing we couldn't handle. I still didn't spot any Nephilim, which was strange. If this was their headquarters, then the place should be teeming with them.

Maybe the Commander's plan to draw them away had worked, and it wasn't the trap I thought it was. But I doubted it. There was something else at the periphery of my mind I knew we were missing. Something important. But I pushed the thought away and focused on finding Faith.

I ran beside the Commander as we made a beeline for the White House entrance. Beck and Oscar followed closely. Four of the Anakim spotted us and moved to cut us off. I didn't break stride. They would realize who I was soon enough. We kept running. They got close enough to smell me and gave up pursuit, turning instead toward the remainder of our group.

We were halfway to the White House door when it opened. A figure appeared in the doorway. He was huge. The six-fingered man from the security video. Arba. He watched as we approached. He looked calm. Undisturbed. The opposite of how I felt. My legs churned as I raced toward the showdown. I started to outdistance the other three.

Another figure appeared beside the giant. She was much shorter. I would recognize her anywhere. Faith. She was alive. And unharmed. I ran even faster. Then time slowed down. I'm sure it happened all at once, but in my mind it happened slowly. Frame by frame. I saw recognition in Faith's green eyes as she spotted me. A smile curved her lips. She shifted her weight to move toward me. But she didn't move. Arba's large hand on her shoulder held her in place.

Faith's eyes left mine. She looked at the monster and reached up to fight against his grip. He was too strong. She turned back to me. Her eyes were wide. All green and white. I was still fifteen yards away. Helpless. Arba leaned toward Faith. I screamed. So did she. He bit her. Blood ran down the soft skin of her neck. She froze for a moment. Then blinked. Her green eyes pleaded with me. She blinked again. Her eyes were no longer green. My legs stopped working. Suddenly, I couldn't run anymore. My limbs turned to jelly, and I fell to my knees. Orange hate filled her eyes. Arba pushed her away.

The doorway around them filled with bodies, but I hardly noticed. Anakim poured from the entrance. Hundreds of orange eyes. I lost sight of Faith. The Anakim kept coming, flowing around Arba like water around a rock. Faith got caught in the flow. Something hit me from behind, and I fell headlong onto the concrete drive. Instinctively, I put my hands out to break my fall. I felt my palms burn as they scraped across the pavement. All I could think about was Faith.

Rough hands pulled me to my feet. The Commander. He yelled something, but his words didn't register. I frantically tried to spot Faith in the madness. The Commander grabbed my shoulders and yelled again. I still didn't hear what he said. He slapped me across the face. It brought me around enough to focus.

I turned. Anakim were fighting each other to get out of the now-open doors of the vehicles in the streets. There were thousands of them. The streets and lawn were filled with them. They were coming out of buildings, vehicles, and sewers. An army of Naks.

I spotted the rest of our team. Six of them were bunched together. Hundreds, maybe thousands, of Anakim were almost on them. Asher, Beck, and Eva stood tall. The first lines of Anakim to arrive tried to turn back but were forced forward by the crowd. I lost sight of the group. I wondered where Blue was. I hadn't seen him since we got off the chopper.

My time was up. The Anakim were all over me. The Commander yelled, and his gun fired repeatedly. I threw Anakim off me. Orange eyes were everywhere I looked. They were a mob. I spun, looking for the Commander. For a second I spotted him between two Anakim. They were all over him. I rushed toward him. Yelling. Throwing the Anakim aside who were too slow to react to their fear of me. I reached the Commander as he fell to the ground underneath two large Anakim. I grabbed one by the neck and yelled in his face. His orange eyes widened in terror. I threw him off and he stumbled away with my bloody handprint on his neck. The other only took a moment to join him.

I spun in a circle around the Commander. I screamed hatred of my own. The Anakim pulled back, but only a few steps. They stood outside my protective bubble, glaring hatred at us. The Commander stood up, bleeding but alive. He held a hunting knife in one hand; he picked up his fallen gun with the other. Blood dripped down my fingertips onto the concrete.

"Faith!" I yelled.

No response.

Then I saw her. She stood at the edge of the ring of infected humans. Her neck was still bleeding from where Arba had bitten her. Her once beautiful green eyes stared back at me. Hateful. Angry. Scared. Cold. Orange. Her mouth opened and closed, but no words came out. Her skin was pale.

I yelled her name again. She didn't recognize it. Or me.

Tears burned my eyes. I stepped forward. She pulled back. The other Anakim moved with her. I forgot about everyone else but her. Arba, the Commander, the others, Blue. All I could see was Faith. I pleaded with her to recognize me. She didn't. I held my hand out, reaching for her. I heard words coming from my mouth, but I had no idea what I was saying. Everything in me pleaded for her to reach out for me. To come to me. To recognize me.

Nothing. Her orange eyes drilled me with hatred and fear.

I held out my other hand, pleading. Tears ran down my face. There was nothing but her. And she was gone. She was one of them. She couldn't recognize me. Her once-beautiful mind couldn't process the simplest thought. She was lost in her own body. She was no longer human. It was hopeless. She was afraid of me. She hated me.

I shook my head. I was unwilling to accept reality. Ignoring the truth in front of my eyes, I whispered her name. My eyes pleaded with her to hear me. To feel my heart. I refused to hate her back. I no longer spoke with my mouth; I spoke with my soul. I stepped forward slowly, arms outstretched, refusing to let her go. Every fiber of my being pleaded with her.

The Anakim retreated a step as a group. Except one. Faith. She stood frozen before me. Caught between them and me. I stared into her eyes. Into her soul. I realized at that moment that I loved her. And I saw the Faith I loved in there somewhere. I looked past the fear in her eyes. I looked past the hate. And I saw the green eyes that had cried over Steven. I saw the mind that had searched day and night for a cure to save the human race. I saw the doctor who had believed in me. It was only a flash. But I saw it.

I took another small step forward. My bloody fingers were almost touching her. Her body swayed, stuck somewhere between staying and leaving. Between love and fear. I stayed frozen. Pleading. I could feel her soul wrestling with itself. I needed her to choose me. To take that last small step forward. I willed her to step into my arms. She almost did. But she didn't. She pulled back. Fear covered her face. And anger. She raised her foot to step back in line with the other Anakim.

Time stood still. There was nothing but us. I heard nothing, saw nothing, and felt nothing but the two of us. Everything else was nothing.

"Faith . . . I can save you," I whispered. Or at least I think I did. It might have only been in my head. But she heard me.

Recognition flickered in her eyes.

She stepped forward.

7

I cupped Faith's face in my hands. My blood stained her skin. It ran down her neck. I stared into her eyes. They still looked unsure and afraid. She reached up and grabbed my wrists with her hands, and her fingernails dug into the soft skin on the inside of my arm. She began to struggle against me. I held her face tight. My eyes poured feeling into hers. I saw her struggling inside. Trying to see through the fog. Trying to come to the light. But still afraid of it—afraid of me. She continued to struggle, as much with herself as with me. Somewhere deep inside, her soul fought for freedom, for clarity.

Blood from my wrists ran down my hands onto her face. It ran down her face onto her neck. It mixed with the blood from the bite on her neck. My blood with hers. She fought against it. Then she accepted it. I could see it in her eyes first. The orange slowly started to fade, replaced by deep pools of green. Her grip on my wrists loosened. Her hands fell free as the fog in her eyes cleared. I wrapped my arms around her and held her tight. She felt soft, fragile, and broken. I held her wordlessly.

I felt her energy return. She wrapped her arms around me, clinging to me. Then Faith Richards said my name. It sounded wonderful.

"Nick. I'm glad you're here," she said.

"Me too." It was all I could think to say.

I'm not sure how long the moment lasted, but it could have been a lifetime.

Then for the first time in a while I realized we weren't alone. I looked around the circle of Anakim faces that ringed us. Thousands of angry, orange eyes stared back. Something had changed. Again. I knew it, and I could feel that they knew it. Somehow through the fog of disease that enveloped their minds something clicked. Hope maybe.

I turned to the Anakim closest to me. It was a thin female with long hair. I held my hands out, my fingers still dripping blood. I held my breath and waited. She looked back and forth between Faith and me. Unsure. I saw the hate in her eyes start to lessen. She stepped forward and held out her own hands.

I quickly drew the knife from my belt and extended it toward her. She looked unsure but didn't run. I made a small cut on her neck, and then placed my bloody hand on it. She screamed in pain and grabbed her neck. She fell to the ground fighting the pain. After a moment, she was still. I waited.

She opened her eyes—a deep beautiful brown. We smiled at each other.

"Thank you," she whispered when she found her voice. "Thank you, thank you, thank you."

I nodded and turned to the next Anakim. There was a lot of work to do.

The Commander and Faith stayed close as I made my way through the crowd of infected souls. I healed as I went, giving my blood to anyone who would accept it. Some were more cautious than others, but eventually everyone came forward. Each person healed became an advocate for me. No longer afraid, they went and brought other infected humans to me.

Eva, Beck, and Asher saw what was happening and they began to heal others. Using their blood to save Anakim. Eventually, someone realized cured blood could be used to cure. After that, the antivirus spread like fire. Infected Anakim who poured into the city to fight left healed and left to heal others.

The whole time Faith held onto my arm like I was a life preserver in a storm.

Maybe I was.

8

I felt weak from blood loss. When the wounds on my hands had clotted over, I had reopened them with my knife in order to save more Anakim. But now I stood weakly on the lawn, unable to give any more. Most of the infected had been healed anyway and left to heal others. I took a breath and tried to regain my strength. I knew we still weren't out of the woods. I knew there was one last thing for me to do. I had to kill Arba once and for all.

I scanned the lawn. Everything was quiet, too quiet. Eerily quiet. There were still a few stray Anakim wandering around. I spotted Van and Oscar covered in blood, but it was hard to tell whose. Beck and Eva walked toward the few souls who were still infected. Xavier peeked out from the helicopter where he had stayed hidden the whole time. Everyone appeared to be OK. But something didn't seem right.

Then I figured it out. Where were the Nephilim?

The Commander must have sensed my thoughts because he walked up beside me. "I don't like how this feels. This was a trap. There's no way using the Anakim to overwhelm us was their only play. Arba is too smart for that. We need to regroup."

"You're right. Even if they didn't know my blood could heal the infected, they do know the Anakim aren't afraid of the four of us. They have another plan. I'd bet on it."

I scanned the sky—still clear and blue, but empty. The sun was just descending from its apex. No sounds of airplanes or vehicles filled the air. No noises of a busy city.

"Commander!" Xavier's voice cut the silence. "You need to see this."

We bolted for the chopper. I was still a little weak, and the Commander beat me there. Xavier pointed at his computer screen when I ran up. I couldn't tell what I was seeing at first. The screen was black with a rotating green line and flashing dots. There were hundreds of dots. I realized it was radar.

"Aircraft," Xavier said, pointing at the dots.

"Coming here?" I asked.

He nodded, repositioning his glasses with his finger.

I held my breath and listened. I thought I could hear them in the distance.

"That's not all." Xavier's fingers flew over the laptop keyboard. Another screen showing a bank of traffic cam videos. The picture was black-and-white and grainy, but it was clear enough to see what Xavier was worried about. Nephilim. Thousands of them. Marching down the streets. All armed. Military tanks rolled along behind them. "It was a trap within a trap," Xavier said. "The Anakim were only here to distract us from the real attack. They're coming, Commander, all of them."

"Van!" the Commander yelled. "Can you get this thing back in the air?"

"I think so. Xavier blocked the signal that brought us down. Give me a minute." Van flipped switches on the control panel.

"You have three, and then I want us airborne. What's the max capacity on this bird?"

"Ten people. Maybe eleven."

"X, how far away are those Nephs?"

"It'll be tight."

"We don't have another choice. Load up."

The chopper blades started their slow spin. I gave Faith a hand up. She didn't let go of my hand. Beck and Eva hopped in next. The space was filling fast.

Faith realized I wasn't getting on. "What are you doing?"

"I'm not going."

"You have to come," she said forcefully.

I shook my head. "I have to finish this. This could be our only chance. Arba is inside."

"Then I'm staying too." She tried to get off the chopper, but I pushed her back. The blades were now spinning fast.

"Time to go!" Van yelled.

"I'm staying," Faith said.

"No. You have to go. Find Steven. You've been cured. You *are* the cure. Find your brother and cure him. I need to finish this and then I'll come find you. I have to stay."

She wrestled with her thoughts for a moment. "You better come find me, Nick Reece."

"I promise." I stepped back, but she didn't let go of my hand.

"Wheels up!" Van yelled over the sound of the blades.

Faith gave my hand one last squeeze and then let go. I stooped and backed up as the chopper eased into the air. She was gone.

Faith realized I wasn't getting on. "What are you doing?"

"I'm not going."

"You have to come," she said forcefully.

I shook my head. "I have to finish this. This could be our only chance Arba is inside."

"Then I'm staying too." She tried to get off the chopper, but I pushed her back. The blades were now spinning fast.

"Time to go!" Van yelled.

"I'm staying," Faith said.

"No. You have to go. Find Steven. You've been cured. You are the cure. Find your brother and cure him. I need to finish this and then I'll come find you. I have to stay."

She wrestled with her thoughts for a moment. "You better come find me, Nick Rosse."

"Wheels up!" Van yelled over the sound of the blades.

Faith gave my hand one last squeeze and then let go. I stooped and backed up as the chopper eased into the air. She was gone.

9

As I expected, the Commander didn't leave on the chopper either. He stood with our pile of weapons at his feet.

"I thought you might need some help," he said.

Oscar and Asher stood beside him.

"I never told ya'll this, but I'm afraid of flying." Oscar smiled. "Besides, I'd take up too much space on that bird anyway."

Asher shrugged. "Couldn't let this big oaf stay by himself. He's scared of being alone."

"That's sweet," the Commander growled. "If you ladies are done flirting, let's move inside."

We each grabbed our weapons and ran toward the White House. We entered together via the north portico. Three Nephilim met us in the entryway. Guns sounded simultaneously. All three were dead before I could bring my shotgun up. Asher was fast, faster than I had ever seen. He had a gun in each hand and had used both. I couldn't be sure, but he may have killed two of the Nephs. The Commander quickly moved to cut off one of their heads. Asher and Oscar followed suit with the other two, and soon three headless bodies poured blood onto the carpet.

"Wow." I nodded toward Asher's weapons. "Remind me not to give you a reason to point those in my direction."

Asher shrugged. "Maybe one day I'll share the reason I was in prison. If we make it through this alive."

"We have to find Arba and kill him before all the Nephilim get here," the Commander said as he chambered another round.

"It's our only chance. They'll be crawling all over this place in less than five minutes. We need to split up to cover every room. Asher, you search the ground floor. Oscar, you take the second."

I cut in. "I'll take the West Wing."

The Commander looked at me for a moment but didn't argue. "I'll take the East Wing, and Reece will take the West. Call for backup when you spot Arba." He tossed each of us a walkie-talkie. "Good luck."

We split up.

I entered the West Wing via the Palm Room. When we flew in on the chopper, Xavier had pulled up a map of the White House, and I had memorized it as best I could. I figured Arba would run operations out of the Oval Office.

After quickly searching the Palm Room, I entered the press rooms. They were empty. But the press briefing room was filled with weapons of all kinds, from swords to rocket launchers to things I didn't recognize. I had my knife, pistol, and shotgun loaded with Hector's special ammunition, so I kept moving. I imagined the sight of helicopters and tanks arriving outside the building. I moved faster.

I could feel my strength had returned after giving away my blood. My body had recovered quickly. Maybe I was building my own immunity to injuries. Was that possible? I looked down at my palms. They were covered in dried blood, but they didn't hurt anymore. No time to ponder what that might mean, so I kept moving.

I entered the corridor that led to the Oval Office. At the far end, two Nephs with their backs turned to me were talking. Both held handguns and had swords strapped to their backs. I would have to sneak by them and enter through the secretary's office. I quickly opened the door to the cabinet room. The Nephilim must have heard me because they turned.

I stood frozen for a split second with my shotgun in one hand and a partially open door in the other. I had two choices: dive through the door or raise my shotgun and get off the first shot. I chose the latter. They were just bringing their guns around when I pulled the trigger on my shotgun. It kicked hard against my palm, but I chambered another round and pulled the trigger again. Not aiming, just firing. Hoping the shotgun would do its work. It did.

The Nephilim were smart though. As they brought their guns to bear, they dove for opposite walls to make smaller targets. But they didn't count on my shotgun. The two shots sprayed the hallway with silver lead. I chambered and fired two more rounds as the Nephilim got peppered with the first two. I counted shots in my head. Four. I had eight left before I had to reload.

The second round of shots knocked the Nephs back but didn't knock them over. They had both fired just as my shots hit them so their bullets went high. I needed to get closer for the shotgun to have maximum effect. I ran forward and fired at the Neph on the left. The blast hit him in the shoulder and spun him sideways. He dropped his gun. His right arm hung useless at his side.

I turned the shotgun toward the other Nephilim. I saw his finger whiten on the trigger. I didn't have time to dive, so I let my legs go soft and fell straight down. It wasn't graceful, but it was effective. I felt the bullets split the air over my head. I fired as I fell. The blast hit the Neph in the chest. He jerked backward. I pumped the lever and fired again. It went high over his head. Five shots left.

The first Nephilim had reclaimed his gun with his left hand. I fired at him, but he dove and rolled. I fired again, and the spray peppered his back but didn't take him down. Two more Nephs appeared in the hallway behind them, responding to the shots. I fired, and they ducked back behind the wall. Plaster rained down. I rose to a knee and fired blindly down the hallway, then dove and rolled toward the cabinet room door. I felt a bullet burn through my leg. I heard it thump into the wall behind me and knew it had passed all the way through. I kept rolling and tried to remember how many shots I had left. Two? One?

I didn't feel any pain, only adrenaline. My body found the wall as bullets cut the drywall above me. They got lost somewhere in the steel reinforced wall. It was hard to see with drywall dust in the air. And my ears rang, I thought I saw another Nephilim join the fight, but I wasn't sure. I fired in their general direction.

I crawled toward the partially open doorway of the cabinet room. I was almost there when I started moving backward. Someone pulled my leg. I looked over my shoulder; it was the Nephilim from the right. He had snuck up in the chaos and grabbed me. I rolled onto my back and cocked the shotgun in one motion. The other Neph stopped firing. Eerie silence filled the vacuum it left. I pulled the shotgun trigger.

Nothing happened. It was empty.

There wasn't time to reload. The Nephilim pulled me down the hallway toward the others. I couldn't reach the handgun stuck in the back of my waistband. I tried to jerk my leg loose. No luck. His grip was too tight. I swung the shotgun at him like a baseball bat, trying to loosen his grip. Bad idea. He caught the gun with his free hand, jerked it from my grip, and flung it down the hallway.

Another Neph arrived and grabbed my arms. I unsuccessfully tried to pull away from him. It hit me suddenly why they had stopped firing. They wanted me alive. They were going to bite me. They were going to turn me. I struggled even more frantically. It was no use. The Nephilim at my head leaned over me. His mouth was a foot from my neck. But that was as close as he got.

I heard a roar that could have belonged to a lion—Oscar. He grabbed the Neph and slammed him into the wall, then head butted him in the face so hard the Nephilim's body sagged. Oscar held him like a rag doll. The other Nephs raised their weapons and fired, but Oscar held his ground using the groggy vampire as a body shield. Most of the bullets thudded into the dazed captive, but a few found their way into Oscar. The Nephilim was big but still didn't cover half of Oscar's bulky body. Trickles of blood ran from several spots on Oscar's torso and legs.

The big man responded the way a rhino would respond to a bee sting. He roared at the Nephilim. Then threw the Neph he held into the one still holding my foot. They both tumbled to the ground. My leg was free.

Oscar looked straight into my eyes.

"Go, Reece. Now we're even." Then he smiled that huge smile of his and rushed the Nephilim like a charging bear. They opened fire, but he hit them like a bowling ball. Somehow, he was still strong enough to grab one and snap his neck.

Bullets tore into his body, but he stood like an oak tree. One Nephilim drew his sword and cut him at his legs. I crawled toward the door as Oscar fell to one knee, still fighting, his huge arms still grappling. When I entered the cabinet room, he still roared. I got to my feet and ran into the secretary's office. When I slammed the door behind me, I could no longer hear his roar.

From there I opened the door to the most famous room in the world—the Oval Office.

10

Arba stood motionless in front of what used to be the most powerful man in the world's desk. I guessed it still was. His back was turned to me, looking out the window. Over his shoulder I could see the advance of the Nephilim outside—thousands of them. I could also see spontaneous black storm clouds moving in fast, bringing rain.

Arba turned and looked at me for the first time. I felt the weight of his presence. I thought I might melt under his gaze. Breathing deeply, I steeled myself. I could feel the terror that always accompanied my meeting a Nephilim rising in my soul. I tried to fight it. I reached for my walkie-talkie, but it was gone. Lost in the scuffle outside. I felt panic rise. I fought it down. I refused to give in to it. My mind started to freeze, but I didn't let it. I had to finish this. I took another deep breath. I clenched my jaw and thought of Faith. And about what Arba had done to her. I squared my shoulders and took one more deep breath and squared my shoulders. I was ready.

Two guards stood against the wall on either side of the desk. Dressed like commandos, they were well-armed. Each held an assault rifle loosely at his side and had a sword strapped to his back, as well as a handgun on his belt. Neither moved or spoke . . . or blinked.

"Leave us." Arba's voice left no room for argument. One of the Nephilim tried anyway.

"But—"

"I SAID LEAVE US!" Arba roared. "I AM A GOD. YOU THINK I CANNOT HANDLE ONE MAN?"

They hustled out of the door behind me.

Arba motioned me forward into the Oval Office. I obliged. Up close he looked even taller than I thought. He towered over me. My hand clutched my machete; I wished it were a shotgun. I felt the handgun pressing into my lower back, and it made me feel a little better. But not much.

As far as I could tell, Arba wasn't armed. Only about eight feet of carpet stood between the monster and me. I figured I should act sooner rather than later. In one motion, I tossed my knife from my right hand to my left and at the same time reached behind my back to draw my gun with my now-free right hand. Arba was already moving as I brought the gun up and fired. He was fast, and I rushed the shot. The bullet missed his torso and tore through his arm, splattering blood into the air. He kept moving, unfazed.

I brought the gun closer to center mass and fired once more. But again, Arba moved too fast. His closed fist crashed down on my arm. A lightning bolt of pain shot through my brain, and the bullet went low, burying itself into his thigh. Again, he didn't seem to notice. The gun flew from my grip and landed with a thud on the carpet. I reached for it, but the giant slammed me into the wall. Hard. Every bone in my body jarred from the blow. Arba was strong. Incredibly strong.

I remembered the knife. I swung it into his side. I felt the blow land, but we were so close I didn't have enough leverage for a fatal strike. I drew the knife back. Blood on the blade. It was encouraging.

I swung the knife again, but Arba blocked it with his free forearm. He picked me up like a ragdoll and flung me across the room. I slammed across the back of a couch and then somersaulted across the floor. But I didn't drop the knife. I switched it to my dominant hand as Arba made his way toward me. I crouched low and tried to prepare myself for his attack. But preparation was futile.

He grabbed my neck and held me off the ground with only one hand. I choked, gasping for air as his six fingers tightened on my windpipe. The room started to go black. I kicked, but my feet only found air. I remembered the knife gripped in my hand and swung it at his neck. He batted it away with his free hand. I saw spots. I knew it was over. But Arba wasn't quite finished with me. He tossed me across the office. My back and head slammed against the desk.

Dazed, I shook my head to clear the cobwebs. I tried to feel my legs, but I wasn't sure they were still attached to my body. I tried unsuccessfully to stand. And to fill my lungs. Both were harder than they should have been. I realized I no longer had the knife in my hand. I looked around for it. Then I spotted it . . . in Arba's hand.

He advanced toward me, knife hanging loosely at his side, like it was of no consequence. Like I was of no consequence. Like I didn't warrant the effort. Using the desk, I pulled myself to my feet. He stood before me, his eyes filled with hate. He raised a hand and slapped me across the face. I felt my jaw pop, and pain shot through my nose. I felt blood running down my chin.

Arba slapped me again. I tried to fight back, running on adrenaline. I punched him in the stomach. I put everything I had behind it. I rained punches until my knuckles started to bleed.

Arba laughed. He slapped me again. I almost passed out, but fought the darkness at the edges of my vision. Arba grabbed a fistful of my shirt, lifted me off my feet, and slammed me against the wall with his forearm. I hung there between heaven and earth, my feet flailing.

Arba leaned his face close to mine. I stared into his soulless, black eyes. I felt the tip of the knife dig into my stomach. It just pierced the skin.

"Your blood isn't special," he said. "My blood is special. I am a god."

The knife slid deeper into my body.

"I will spill your blood as a sacrifice to me."

He shoved the knife deeper, piercing my body. Blood poured from my stomach. We both looked down. My blood stained the knife and his hand. I watched my life drain away. It was over.

Then, out of nowhere, something hit Arba from behind. All I saw were fangs and fur.

Blue.

I had forgotten about him. I had no idea how he had survived or where he had been. His teeth tore into Arba's exposed neck. Suddenly, free from Arba's grip, I slid down the wall and crumpled on the floor. Arba turned and rammed the knife into Blue's side. The dog let out a cry of pain. Arba flung him to the other side of the room.

I looked down. My gun lay on the floor by my hand. I seemed to be outside my own body, watching as I picked it up. My hand shook, but I focused all my will to steady it. I fixed the sights on Arba's head. He turned and looked at me.

I pulled the trigger.

The shot rang true. It found its mark in Arba's skull. He toppled over like a felled oak. I matched his path of motion with the gun and pulled the trigger again. He hit the floor and remained motionless.

I dropped the gun. I didn't have the strength to hold it anymore. I couldn't move. My time was short. But I knew I wasn't finished. I knew I had to do one more thing. I had to do what

David had failed to do. I had to do what Solomon had failed to do. I had to cut off Arba's head.

I mustered all my strength and crawled over to him, trailing my blood behind me. I took hold of the knife. It felt heavy. I took a deep breath and raised it. I brought it down as hard as I could on Arba's neck. I separated his head from his body.

I dropped the knife and crawled to Blue. His fur was stained with blood. His. Mine. Arba's. He tried to raise his head but couldn't. I rolled, half sat against the wall, and pulled his head onto my lap.

"Stupid dog. I told you to stay in the chopper." Blood gurgled from my mouth.

Blue let out a little whine.

"I know. I feel the same way," I said. "But we did it."

He thumped his tail once and then lay still. "We did it, Blue." I patted his head. "We did it."

I felt my blood, my life, soaking into the thick Oval Office rug. I was dying. But I knew it was OK. I thought of Faith. I knew I should find her. Save her one more time. Keep my promise. But I knew I couldn't. So instead, I sat on the rug, bleeding, with thoughts of her face filling my mind. I focused on those thoughts of her until they started to fade. I held onto them as long as I could. I felt my heart struggle to keep pumping. It thumped slowly in my chest. Intermittently.

I reached down to my pocket. My fingers grasped Faith's cross necklace. I wrapped my fingers around it as tightly as I could. I felt the soft silver bite into the skin of my palm. I held onto it like it was life itself. I saw Faith's smile in my mind. I reached out for her as the walls closed in. I could almost touch her.

Everything went black.

David had failed to do. I had to do what Solomon had failed to do. I had to cut off Arba's head.

I mustered all my strength and crawled over to him, trailing my blood behind me. I took hold of the knife. It felt heavy. I took a deep breath and raised it. I brought it down as hard as I could on Arba's neck. I separated his head from his body.

I dropped the knife and crawled to Blue. His fur was stained with blood. His. Mine. Arba's. He tried to raise his head but couldn't. I rolled, half sat against the wall, and pulled his head onto my lap.

"Stupid dog, I told you to stay in the chopper." Blood gurgled from my mouth.

Blue let out a little whine.

"I know. I feel the same way," I said. "But we did it."

He thumped his tail once and then lay still. "We did it, Blue." I patted his head. "We did it."

I felt my blood, my life, soaking into the thick Oval Office rug. I was dying. But I knew it was OK. I thought of Faith. I know I should find her. Save her one more time. Keep my promise. But I knew I couldn't. So instead, I sat on the rug, bleeding, with thoughts of her face filling my mind. I focused on those thoughts of her until they started to fade. I held onto them as long as I could. I felt my heart struggle to keep pumping. It thumped slowly in my chest. Intermittently.

I reached down to my pocket. My fingers grasped Faith's cross necklace. I wrapped my fingers around it as tightly as I could. I felt the soft silver bite into the skin of my palm. I held onto it like it was life itself. I saw Faith's smile in my mind. I reached out for her as the walls closed in. I could almost touch her.

11

The first thing I saw when I woke up was a clock on the wall: 4:37.

I woke up at exactly 4:37 p.m. from the second-longest nap of my life.

Then I saw her face. It was the most beautiful face I had ever seen. Faith Richards' face. She leaned forward and her soft, blonde hair fell over her eyes. She reached up to tuck the lock behind her ear. A familiar cross hung from her neck.

"I'm glad you're here," I croaked.

She smiled. "Me too."

"How long was I out this time?"

"Three months."

"Three months?"

"Three months. You lost a lot of blood."

"What happened?"

"The Commander saved your life. When he found you in the Oval Office, you were almost gone, but he stopped the bleeding as best he could. You may be as resilient as you promised after all. That blood of yours is more special than I thought."

"What about the Nephilim?"

"The Commander took Arba's severed head and walked out onto the front steps and threw it in front of them. The Nephilim revered Arba as a god. They thought he was invincible, but when they saw he was dead, they scattered. Between their headless god, the healed Anakim, and the rain, they didn't put up much of a fight."

I sat up in bed. "Where's the Commander now?"

"Out there. You know the Commander. He organized the humans and has been hunting the Nephilim for the last three months. The Nephilim are afraid of us now that the Anakim are out of the picture. They are mostly dead or in hiding thanks to the Commander and his new army. He stops by every so often to see if you are awake yet."

"Van's with him?"

"And Hector."

"Is Asher OK? How did he take the loss of Oscar?"

A frown flashed across Faith's face. "We don't know Asher disappeared. We never heard from him after the White House fight."

"Is he dead? Did you find his body?"

"We never found his body."

"That's strange."

"Yes, it is."

We both thought about that.

"What about Steven? Did you find him?"

Faith smiled. "Yes, he's cured. And Beck and Eva have organized groups that go out and heal any Anakim who are left. Soon everyone will be healed. There will be no more infection."

"Good, I'm glad Steven is OK." I paused. "As soon as I'm feeling well enough to get out of here, there's one more person I want to make sure gets healed."

"Who?"

"Dorris, the cafeteria lady at the hospital. I'd like her to finally get that cabin in the woods she always wanted."

The tips of her fingers brushed the hair off my forehead. "You are a special human, Nick Reece."

I always liked the sound of my name on her lips. "Am I?"

"You are. And after we take that long walk you promised me I'm going to find out why your blood is so special. But there's someone else you're missing," Faith said. A smile twinkled in her green eyes.

"Who's that?"

"He's been here every day to check on you. Out of everyone, he's been the most anxious for you to wake up," she said. "Besides me, of course."

Faith stood and walked to the door and opened it. "He's waiting in the hall. He'll want to see you."

She closed the door again without anyone entering. I thought it must be a joke. Then sixty pounds of dog landed on top of me. Blue.

He licked my face once. The only time I would ever let him do that, I decided. Then he turned his head to the side as if trying to figure out why I had been ignoring him for three months.

"Stupid dog," I muttered with a smile. He barked once, saying "stupid human" no doubt. Then he plopped down across my legs.

"That's been his usual spot for the last three months," Faith said. She sat back down beside me.

I smiled. She looked beautiful.

"I have an apology to make," I said.

"You do?"

"I stole our last kiss . . . the one in the school."

"You did." She smiled.

"I'm sorry."

"I'm not."

"Can I kiss you again?"

"I don't know," she said. "Can you?"

"I can. May I?"

"You may."

I did.

"You are. And after we take that long walk you promised me I'm going to find out why your blood is so special. But there's someone else you're missing," Faith said. A smile twinkled in her green eyes.

"Who's that?"

"He's been here every day to check on you. Out of everyone, he's been the most anxious for you to wake up," she said. "Besides me, of course."

Faith stood and walked to the door and opened it. "He's waiting in the hall. He'll want to see you."

She closed the door again without anyone entering. I thought it must be a joke. Then sixty pounds of dog landed on top of me. Blue.

He licked my face once. The only time I would ever let him do that, I decided. Then he turned his head to the side as if trying to figure out why I had been ignoring him for three months. "Stupid dog," I muttered with a smile. He barked once, saying "stupid human," no doubt. Then he plopped down across my legs.

"That's been his usual spot for the last three months," Faith said. She sat back down beside me.

I smiled. She looked beautiful.

"I have an apology to make," I said.

"You do?"

"I stole our last kiss . . . the one in the school."

"You did?" She smiled.

"I'm sorry."

"I'm not."

"Can I kiss you again?"

"I don't know," she said. "Can you?"

"I can. May I?"

"You may."

I did.

Without you, the reader, all the books by all the authors in the world would be nothing more than manuscript pages saved on a computer or shoved into a drawer to be read by only friends and family. So, thank you for reading my debut novel. It's important for first-time novelists to do well. If you liked this book, please share it with others and take a few minutes to post an online review. Thank you.

You can find out more about me and keep up with my latest work at www.johntprather.com or follow me on Twitter and Instagram: @JohnTPrather

Without you, the reader, all the books by all the authors in the world would be nothing more than manuscript pages saved on a computer or shoved into a drawer to be read by only friends and family. So, thank you for reading my debut novel. It's important for first-time novelists to do well. If you liked this book, please share it with others and take a few minutes to post an online review. Thank you.

You can find out more about me and keep up with my latest work at www.johntprather.com or follow me on Twitter and Instagram: @JohnTPrather

Endnotes

1. Gen. 6:1–6 (NIV)
2. 1 Sam. 17:2–7 (CEB)
3. 2 Sam. 21:15–22 (NCV)
4. 1 Sam. 17:2–7 (CEB)
5. 1 Sam. 17:8–51 (NIV)
6. 1 Kings 10:13 (NLT)
7. 1 Sam. 17:6 (NCV)

Endnotes

1. Gen. 6:1–6 (NIV)
2. 1 Sam. 17:2–7 (CEB)
3. 2 Sam. 21:15–22 (NCV)
7. 1 Sam. 17:6 (NCV)

Printed in the United States
By Bookmasters

Printed in the United States
By Bookmasters